DEADLY VEIL

A DETECTIVE JANE PHILLIPS NOVEL

OMJ RYAN

INKUBATOR
BOOKS

Published by Inkubator Books
www.inkubatorbooks.com

Copyright © 2023 by OMJ Ryan

OMJ Ryan has asserted his right to be identified as the author of this work.

ISBN (eBook): 978-1-83756-259-6
ISBN (Paperback): 978-1-83756-260-2

1

It was just after 7.30 p.m. on a balmy Saturday evening when Tex led the gang along the pavement towards the salubrious David Lloyd private members leisure club, located approximately five miles south of Manchester city centre in the suburb of Cheadle. Planes coming in to land at the nearby airport roared overhead every few minutes, but aside from the exclusive tennis club and a nearby TGI Fridays steakhouse, the surrounding Cheadle Royal Business Park was all but empty and deafeningly silent.

'This way,' said Tex, pointing to a shortcut through the car park of an adjacent office block. His associates, who like him used code names – in this case Clem and Squeaky – tucked in behind as he guided them into the shadows of the thick trees that surrounded the club.

As per their well-rehearsed plan, they stopped, then ducked down opposite the entrance to the club. In spite of the close summer heat this evening, each of the gang was wearing sunglasses and hooded tops pulled up over their heads to hide their faces.

Satisfied there was no one around, Tex checked his watch: 7.37 p.m. 'We have just under an hour.'

Clem, a bit of a tomboy, with long limbs and wavy auburn hair, swallowed the lump in her throat. 'Are we really doing this?'

Tex let out an involuntary giggle. 'Yeah, we are.'

Squeaky, crouching next to Clem, stared silently towards the entrance to the club. Yet to turn seventeen, he was the baby of the group, but what he lacked in age he more than made up for in sheer brawn: a second-row rugby player of some repute who, at six feet four, towered over almost everyone he encountered.

Wiping away the sweat from his brow, Tex pulled his backpack from his right shoulder, then set it down on the ground between them. After releasing the zipper, he reached inside and pulled out the remote device in readiness for the next stage of the plan, holding it firmly in his hands.

'Are you sure we're doing the right thing?' asked Clem, her voice nothing more than a whisper.

Tex nodded firmly. 'It's the only thing we *can* do.'

Squeaky nodded his approval but again remained silent.

'You each know what to do, right?' Tex asked.

'Yes,' replied Squeaky.

Clem nodded. 'Yeah.'

'Right,' said Tex, standing. 'Let's move out.'

Clem and Squeaky duly followed suit.

Thankfully it seemed that tonight's target was a creature of habit and had parked his car in the same spot that he occupied almost every Saturday evening while playing tennis on the courts inside the large club. Luckily for the gang, his gargantuan SUV was located towards the rear of the parking lot, out of sight of the main door and a good distance from the access gate to the car park. Staying low, they shuffled along in and out of the stationary cars until Tex brought them to a stop next to the imposing black Lexus 4x4.

'Keep your eyes peeled and shout if you see anyone heading this way,' Tex whispered before ducking down on the ground and sliding under the engine block.

To his considerable relief, the underside of the vehicle looked exactly as he'd researched and planned for. 'Piece of cake,' he muttered, removing his sunglasses and lowering his hood as he prepared to attach the device. Lying on his back under the car, the heat of the recently used engine, coupled with the muggy evening air, soon began to take its toll as sweat trickled from his forehead into his eyes, causing them to sting.

He had no idea how much time had passed when Clem dropped to her knees and bent down so her face was level with his. 'What's taking so long?' she asked, her voice brimming with tension.

'It's bloody roasting under here,' he spat back. 'My hands are sweating.'

Clem remained in position but didn't reply.

'I'm going as quickly as I can,' he added.

'There's someone coming,' warned Squeaky from above.

As Clem disappeared back out of view, Tex attempted to quell the rising panic gnawing at his gut as he finally managed to connect the small device to the fuel line despite his slippery fingers struggling for grip.

Clem dropped back down once more. 'They've gone,' she

whispered, 'but it's only a matter of time before someone else appears. Are you nearly done?'

Wiping away the sweat from his eyes, he secured the final cable-tie in place. 'Sorted,' he said, replacing his sunglasses and hood before rolling out from under the car.

Squeaky was standing by with a firm hand to help him to his feet.

As he pulled on his backpack, Tex took a quick look around, then nodded in the direction of the tree line. 'Come on, let's get out of here.'

Once safely under the overhanging trees, they each turned back so they could see the whole of the car park and the entrance to the club, then again crouched down out of sight.

Fishing a small mobile from the backpack, Tex glanced down at his watch. It was 8 p.m. 'Now we wait,' he said.

Thirty minutes later, the man they had come to know as Ross Grayson stepped out of the revolving door at the front of the club. Wearing tennis whites, his cheeks remained flushed from his recent exertions, and he carried a large sports bag over his shoulder, the handle of his racket sticking out through the zip.

'Here he is,' said Squeaky in a low, deep voice.

Tex nodded, licking his dry lips.

As Grayson reached the end of the path, he hung a right towards the Lexus, which was parked about fifty feet away.

'I'm not sure about this,' muttered Clem, from her position crouching next to Tex.

Strolling casually across the car park, Grayson unzipped the side pocket of his sports bag, rummaging inside for a second before pulling out his car keys.

Tex carefully activated the mobile handset in his right

hand, and a second later the tiny screen turned green, indicating it was now ready for use.

As Grayson walked alongside the Lexus, the rear tailgate opened automatically, allowing him to sling his bag into the boot before closing it again and jumping into the driver's seat a second later. After pulling the door to with a clunk, he sat motionless for a moment and appeared to be staring down at his phone.

'What the hell's he doing?' asked Clem, her voice cracking.

Tex didn't respond; his eyes were locked on Grayson.

Suddenly a young couple entered the car park, chatting and laughing, each wearing tight Lycra outfits darkened by sweat.

Squeaky craned his neck to get a better view of them from his position. 'Looks like we've got company.'

'Shit,' exclaimed Clem. 'What do we do now?'

Tex's gaze remained unflinching. 'We execute the plan.'

'But what if those two get hurt?' she spat back. 'We're only supposed to be going after Grayson.'

'Every battle has its civilian casualties,' replied Tex coolly.

'I didn't sign up for this,' she growled in a low voice. 'Legitimate targets only. That was always the deal.'

Tex ignored her as he turned his attention to the keypad on the mobile device.

Evidently Grayson had finished with his phone, tossing it into the passenger seat before starting the engine.

'Looks like he's getting ready to go,' said Squeaky.

All the time the young couple were getting closer and closer to Grayson's Lexus.

Tex dialled the sequence of numbers he'd committed to

memory – 07-75-22-28-989 – then allowed his finger to hover above the green call button.

Grayson's Lexus edged slowly forward, and he waved towards the couple, who in turn waved back as they arrived at their own car now, parked just a few spaces away.

As his adrenaline spiked, Tex took a deep breath, fighting hard to control his racing pulse. It was now or never.

'Do it!' insisted Squeaky.

Slamming his finger down onto the call button, Tex waited for the sequence of numbers to connect. A split second later a thunderous boom sliced through the air as the front of the Lexus exploded into a fireball, bringing the car to a stop as plumes of black, acrid smoke rose up into the air.

The couple in Lycra instinctively bent double in the wake of the blast, holding their position for a few seconds before screaming for help as they rushed to try to help Grayson, who was now slumped against the driver's window inside the burning vehicle.

'Like the Fourth of July,' murmured Tex, unable to take his eyes off the macabre scene unfolding in front of them.

Suddenly hordes of people began swarming out from the main entrance of the club, evidently in total shock as they screamed and shouted for someone – anyone – to call an ambulance and the fire brigade.

As the inferno raged, Squeaky clasped his meaty hand on Tex's shoulder. 'Let's get the hell out of here, man.'

Clem was already on the move as Tex nodded and slung the backpack over his shoulder, then turned and ran head-long deeper into the trees.

2

THREE DAYS LATER

Detective Chief Inspector Jane Phillips was sitting at her desk, working her way through a thick pile of active case files, when her second in command, DI Jones, wandered in carrying a steaming hot mug in each hand.

His slim build and thinning hair head prematurely aged him, and someone could be forgiven for thinking he was well into his fifties, but the reality was he'd just recently turned forty-five.

'Here you go, guv,' he said as he placed an instant black coffee down in front of her. His south London accent remained as strong as ever despite having lived in Manchester for over fifteen years. Taking the seat opposite her desk, he cradled a mug of his favourite peppermint tea in both hands.

Phillips took a sip of her drink as she reclined in her chair. Glancing at the clock on the wall, she realised she'd already been in the office for almost an hour. 'Since when did a 7 a.m. start become the norm?'

'Since Fox decided to cut our recruitment budget,' quipped Jones, crossing his left ankle over his right knee.

Phillips smiled thinly. 'Very true.'

'Anyway,' Jones continued, 'I heard the counter terrorism boys are in town, investigating the car-bomb attack on Saturday evening.'

She placed her mug down on the desk. 'Yeah, apparently so.'

'Nasty business, that.'

'The driver's in a bad way, from what I'm told.'

Jones shuddered. 'That's my worst nightmare, that is: being trapped in a burning car.'

'Me too; it sounded horrific.' She paused. 'You know, I really thought we'd seen the last of car bombs in Manchester after the IRA attack in '96.'

'I remember watching that on TV at the time,' said Jones. 'I was still living in London and working at the Met back then.'

Phillips nodded sombrely. 'It's a miracle nobody was killed, to be honest. The explosion pretty much flattened the bottom of the city centre. The blast was so powerful our windows rattled at home with the aftershock – all the way out in *Didsbury*.'

'Seriously? That's over five miles.'

'I know.'

'Incredible, really.' Jones took another sip of his drink. 'Funnily enough, I actually walked past the infamous post box on Saturday as I was heading into Marks & Spencer with Sarah. Hard to believe the bomb was detonated right next to it and it survived.'

'Yep. Half a ton of semtex and hardly a scratch on it,' Phillips added. 'Victorian engineering at its finest.'

Just then her attention was drawn to her boss, Chief Superintendent Carter, as he filled the doorway. He cut an imposing figure in his pristinely pressed uniform with his chiselled features, broad shoulders and thick salt-and-pepper hair.

'Morning, sir,' said Phillips.

Jones turned to face him too. 'Sir.'

'We've been summoned,' he said as he stepped into the room, his accent giving away his origins in the northeast of England. 'Fox wants to see us both immediately.'

Phillips frowned as she glanced at Jones, then back at Carter. "What about? As far as I'm aware, we've not been on her shit list for at least a week now.'

'Must be a new record.' Jones chuckled.

Carter shrugged. 'Beats me. She left a message with Diane saying she wanted to see us both as soon as we landed.'

Phillips sighed as she pushed back her chair and stood. 'Well, whatever it is, I'm sure it can't be good news.'

Jones flashed a wry grin as he got up from the chair. 'Rather you than me.'

Carter offered a knowing smile, then turned and led them out.

TWO STORIES up on the fifth floor, Phillips and Carter walked side by side as they made their way to Fox's office located at the end of the long, dark corridor. As usual, her assistant, Ms Blair, was seated behind her small desk in the outer office, her expression fixed in what seemed to be a permanent sneer. Phillips had often remarked to Jones just how miserable Blair appeared every time their paths crossed. Mind you, she reasoned, she was sure that spending every minute of every day working with Chief Constable Fox would be enough to leave even the happiest person feeling dispirited.

'She's waiting for you inside,' Blair said bluntly.

Carter nodded and led them in through the open door.

Chief Constable Fox was sitting at her impressive glass desk, dressed as ever in full uniform, her glasses perched on the end of her overly tanned nose. Judging by the grey badger-like stripe running down the centre of her dyed blonde hair, she was well overdue a trip to the hair salon.

In front of her desk and to Fox's left sat a slim man with dark hair and a thin, elongated face.

'Chief Superintendent Carter, DCI Phillips, this is Detective Chief Inspector Flannery from the Counter Terrorism Unit.'

Flannery stood and offered his hand to each of them in turn.

'Please call me Danny.'

Considering his rank, he was casually dressed, wearing a sports jacket over a white shirt and jeans.

After shaking hands, Phillips turned her attention back to Fox, trying hard to hide the puzzled look that threatened to hijack her face.

Fox continued, 'I've asked DCI Flannery to bring you up to speed on Saturday's car-bomb attack outside the David Lloyd club in Cheadle.'

Phillips glanced at Flannery, then back to Fox. 'Begging your pardon, ma'am, but what has a terror attack got to do with Major Crimes?'

Flannery sat forward. 'That's just it, we don't actually believe it was a terror attack.'

'Really?' said Carter. 'How so?'

'Our forensic teams have been over the device that was attached to the underside of the car and caused the explosion, and it's like nothing we've come across in at least forty years. It looks homemade and quite rudimentary. The last time we saw something similar was back in the 1970s and the early days of the IRA bombings on the mainland – before they scaled up their efforts.'

'I'm no expert on Irish politics,' said Phillips, 'but from what I've read recently, there are several new factions over there looking to wage war on England. Could the attack be down to one of them?'

Flannery shook his head. 'MI5 say it's unlikely. According to their intelligence, there's been no chatter from any of the known cells still operating, and tellingly no one has come forward to take credit for it. If it was a new group trying to get noticed, they'd be sure to announce their arrival to the world as soon as possible.'

'What about ISIS? Or one of the other foreign terror groups?' asked Carter.

'We have nothing to indicate it was down to them. Again, intelligence suggests this attack was a complete one-off, especially given the victim's background.'

'So, who is he?' Carter asked.

'Ross Grayson,' replied Flannery. 'Chief financial officer for GBOG Energy.'

'Look, I don't mean to be rude,' Phillips said as she shifted in her seat, 'but what does any of this have to do with us?'

'As there's no obvious link to any terror groups, the investigation has been passed over to the Greater Manchester

Police,' said Flannery, 'and, specifically, the Major Crimes Unit.'

Phillips's face crumpled. 'MCU? But we've got zero experience of dealing with anything like this.'

'Well, now's your chance to rectify that,' Fox shot back.

'With respect, ma'am, I'm sure this is a job better suited to the Serious Crimes guys as opposed to my team.'

Fox shook her head. 'This is an incredibly high-profile investigation, and the world is watching. The victim of a seemingly unprovoked attack is fighting for his life in the burns unit. A family man with a wife and kids. This sort of stuff scares the shit out of the public, and as you'd expect, the media have jumped all over the story. Everybody's talking about it, especially as the anniversary of the Manchester bombing is only two weeks away. It's stirred up a lot of memories for people.'

Phillips shifted in her seat. 'I'm sure it has, ma'am, but—'

'The fact is,' Fox cut her off, 'I've already spoken to the police and crime commissioner this morning and assured her I'm putting my very best team on it, which means it's down to you, Jane.'

Despite the inadvertent compliment, Phillips's heart sank. The team had found a steady rhythm lately and been making real headway through their mountain of open cases. Morale was high, and they were getting the job done. The last thing the guys needed was to be thrust into the limelight on a case they had no idea how to solve. And with the world's media watching, the pressure to get a result would inevitably ramp up as time went on. For once in her more than twenty-year career, Jane was determined to hand the case on to someone else. 'Er, honestly, ma'am. I'm sure DCI Cleverly and the Serious Crimes team would jump at the chance to handle such a high-profile case like this.'

Fox shook her head. 'I've already assigned it to MCU, and I'm not going back on my promise to the PCC. So, it's all yours.'

Phillips opened her mouth to offer one final protest but thought better of it when she caught sight of Carter's stiff glare: it was evident he would prefer that she accept the assignment with good grace. 'Very well, ma'am,' she said finally.

Flannery passed across an A4 manila folder. 'This is everything we have on the victim.'

Phillips took it and quickly began leafing through the contents.

'Grayson's forty-two. Originally from Edinburgh, now lives in Manchester with his wife and two young daughters.' Flannery handed Phillips another file.

Placing the first folder on her knee, she opened the second.

'That file contains eyewitness statements,' Flannery explained. 'Plus stills of CCTV footage from the club itself, as well as all the private cameras we could access from the surrounding area. As you'll see, three individuals with their heads and faces covered can be seen moving around near Grayson's car about forty-five minutes before the explosion, then running away from the scene just after the blast.'

Phillips stared down at the grainy black-and-white stills in the file.

'Sadly, we lost track of them after they entered Brunt-wood Park approximately ten minutes later.' He passed over a pen drive. 'All the live CCTV footage we gathered is on there.'

'It seems you have everything you need,' said Fox, evidently keen to bring the meeting to an end.

Phillips took the hint as she closed the open folder in her hands before scooping the other one up from her lap and placing the pen drive in her pocket.

Flannery gave her his card. 'All my details are on there; if you have any questions, or if I can help in any way, just give me a bell.'

'Thank you.' Phillips slid it into the top folder.

'No doubt you'll want to speak to Grayson's wife, Lynda,' Flannery added. 'Unless anything's changed significantly, you'll find her at the burns unit of Wythenshawe Hospital. Last time I spoke to the doctors, she'd not left his bedside since Saturday night.'

Phillips nodded.

'Right, then,' said Fox. 'If there's nothing else, you'd better get cracking.'

BACK DOWNSTAIRS, Phillips made her way across the office to the bank of four desks that housed the core team of Manchester's Major Crimes Unit.

'How did it go, guv?' asked Jones as she approached.

'Well, there's good news and bad news.'

'Not sure which I want first,' he replied.

'Nothing good ever comes out of a meeting with Mein Fuhrer,' said Bovalino, a copper whose significant height and muscular physique belied his Italian heritage and razor-sharp wit.

'You'd better not let her catch you calling her that.' Entwistle – or Whistler as he was affectionally known –

laughed, the fourth member of the team, whose chiselled mixed-race features and easy-going nature ensured he was rarely without a date on any evening of the week.

'I won't.' Bov grinned. 'Let her catch me, that is.'

Phillips cut back in. 'So the good news is, Fox says we're her number one team.'

'Well, there's a first time for everything,' quipped Jones.

She placed the two folders down in front of her and took a seat at the spare desk. 'The bad news is, it means we're now in charge of investigating the car-bomb attack in Cheadle on Saturday night.'

'Car bomb?' said Bovalino. 'But we don't know the first thing about explosives.'

'My thoughts exactly,' Phillips replied as she opened the files. 'But it seems we're stuck with it, so we'd better learn fast.'

For the next ten minutes she brought them up to speed on the details of her meeting with the chief constable, Carter and Flannery, and explained the importance of getting a result as quickly as possible, something they had all grown accustomed to, given the high-profile nature of many of the cases assigned to Major Crimes in recent years.

She turned to Entwistle. 'I want everything you can find on Grayson. Flannery's pulled together a brief dossier, but we need to dig a lot deeper. Someone tried to blow him up on Saturday night, and I want to know why. Get a warrant for his phone records if need be.'

'Yes, guv,' he said as he made a note in his digital pad. 'What about financials?'

'Leave that for the moment. We need to speak to his wife first.'

'No worries,' he replied.

Phillips turned to Bov next as she handed him the pen drive. 'I want you to go through the CCTV and see if you can find anything that might help us identify the three individuals spotted messing with Grayson's car. Until we know different, they're the prime suspects.'

The big man nodded. 'Will do.'

She looked to Jones now. 'Flannery reckons we'll find Grayson's wife at Wythenshawe Hospital.'

'You want me to drive?' he asked.

'Yeah,' she replied as she stepped up from the chair.

Jones grabbed his keys and matched her.

'I don't need to tell you the clock's well and truly ticking on this one, guys.' Phillips glanced at Entwistle and Bovalino in turn. 'So let's get to it, yeah?'

She turned and headed for the door as a chorus of 'Yes, guvs' filled the air.

3

Wythenshawe Hospital was a sprawling mass of different buildings, which, to the untrained eye, could easily be mistaken for a small town centre, complete with its own tram stop and connections to nearby Manchester airport. Unlike its sister facility, the Manchester Royal Infirmary, situated in the city centre, Wythenshawe was made up entirely of low-level buildings, never more than four storeys high.

After parking the squad car in a space reserved for police vehicles just outside the main entrance, Phillips and Jones made their way to the burns unit located in the A Wards adjacent to the A&E department. Stepping through the doors to the specialist unit, Phillips was struck by how quiet it was but for a few low voices further along the corridor.

Arriving at the burns unit reception desk, she presented her credentials to a nurse who stood gazing into a laptop. According to the name badge on her chest, she was the ward sister, Agata Dabrowska.

'We're looking for Ross Grayson. Can we speak with him?' asked Phillips.

Dabrowska shook her head softly. 'I'm afraid that's not possible; he's been heavily sedated and is on a ventilator. His lungs were badly damaged by the fire.' Her accent was eastern European.

'When is he likely to come round?'

'I honestly don't know,' Dabrowska replied. 'He has burns to thirty percent of his body. We'll know more in the next few days.'

'I see,' said Phillips. 'We were told his wife, Lynda, has been with him since he came in. I don't suppose she's still here, is she?'

Dabrowska nodded. 'In his room. We've tried to get her to go home, but she won't leave him.'

'Are we okay to talk to her in that case?' Phillips asked.

'Sure.' Dabrowska pointed down the corridor. 'Third on the left.'

'Thank you.' Phillips smiled softly.

'Please persuade her to go home,' added Dabrowska. 'She needs to rest.'

'We'll see what we can do,' said Phillips before turning and heading off down the corridor with Jones at her back.

The stench of disinfectant was pervasive and brought back unwanted memories of the dark moments Jane had spent in Intensive Care only last year, watching over her boyfriend, Adam, as he fought to survive a near fatal knife attack. She shuddered at the memory before firmly relegating it to the back of her mind.

A minute later they stepped carefully into Grayson's private room, where, as expected, they found Lynda perched on the edge of a high-back chair close to her husband's bed, a tissue locked in her right hand. Ross Grayson himself was out cold, covered in dressings and surrounded by a protective see-through canopy to help stave off infection.

'Mrs Grayson?' said Phillips in a gentle voice.

Lynda's swollen red eyes shifted slowly towards them but appeared vacant. Her lank blonde hair looked like it had not been washed in some time, her white blouse creased and grubby; hardly surprising given the fact she'd not been home for days.

Phillips opened her ID wallet and held it close enough for Lynda to see. 'I'm DCI Jane Phillips, and this is DI Jones.'

Lynda nodded absentmindedly.

'How is he?' asked Jones.

Lynda turned her gaze back to her husband, her bottom lip trembling. 'They're worried about infection.' Her voice was low, the accent a mixture of Manchester and Scotland. 'The doctor said he's got burns to over a third of his body.'

Phillips nodded. 'We know this is a very difficult time for you, but we really need to ask you a few questions, if that's okay?'

Lynda's brow furrowed. 'I've already spoken to the police. DCI Flaherty, I think he said his name was.'

'Flannery,' said Phillips. 'He was initially in charge of the investigation, but it's been reassigned to my team, the Major Crimes Unit.'

Lynda fell silent as she stared at her stricken husband. 'Will you catch who did this to him?' she said finally.

Phillips glanced at Jones – feeling suddenly out of her depth – then back to Lynda. 'We'll do everything we can to bring them to justice, yes.'

Despite the obvious strain Lynda was under, Phillips needed answers. MCU was already late to the investigation, and if they were to stand any chance of catching Grayson's attackers, there was no time to waste. She glanced at Jones, who pulled out his police notebook, then focused once again on Lynda. 'Has anyone ever made threats to Ross?'

'No, never,' Lynda replied.

'And have you noticed anyone near the house lately? Anyone you've not seen before, perhaps?'

Lynda shook her head. 'Not that I'd noticed.'

'How long has your husband been a member at David Lloyd?' asked Phillips.

'We started going when we first moved down from Edinburgh.'

'When was that?'

Lynda took a moment to think. 'Must be ten years now.'

Jones scribbled in his notebook.

'And how often did he go there?' said Phillips.

'Every Saturday for tennis with his best mate Kevin, and then once the kids came along, every Sunday morning for a swim and some lunch.' Lynda wiped her nose with the tissue, evidently fighting away the tears. 'Because he was away a lot with work, Sunday was his favourite day of the week: it gave him a chance to spend time with his girls.'

Phillips took a moment before continuing, 'You mentioned Kevin. Can you tell us his full name and where we might find him? We'll need to ask him some questions as well.'

Lynda nodded as she reached down and pulled her phone from the handbag resting on the floor next to her feet. 'Kevin Hunt.' She took a few seconds to scan through her contacts before reading out a number.

Jones made a note of it.

Phillips continued, 'Can you tell us a little bit about Ross's work?'

'What do you want to know?'

'DCI Flannery mentioned he's the finance director for GBOG Energy.'

'International finance director,' Lynda corrected.

'And how long has he been doing that?'

Lynda glanced at her husband and then turned her focus back to Phillips. 'He's been with them since we both graduated in 1996. Started out as a business analyst in the Edinburgh office and worked his way up. We moved down to Manchester when he was promoted to finance director for the UK side of the business.'

'Which was when?' Phillips asked.

'In 2013. The year we got married.'

'So, when did he move into the international role?'

'Just last year,' said Lynda. 'Before that, he was head of European financial operations.'

'Sounds like he's a very important person at GBOG,' ventured Phillips.

'He loves his job.' Lynda wiped her nose again with the battered tissue.

Having been in a similar situation herself when Adam had been attacked, Phillips was acutely aware of how much stress Lynda was currently under, and the last thing she wanted was to add to that. Conversely, she still needed to ask a few more questions, which she decided to do as quickly as possible so they could leave her alone. 'Can you tell us a bit more about what he did at GBOG?'

Lynda nodded. 'They have licences to drill oil and gas all over the world. Ross oversees the finance teams for each country.'

'I see,' said Phillips. 'Did he ever talk to you about the company being targeted by any environmentalist groups?'

'Why?' Lynda's eyes suddenly widened. 'Do you think they were behind this?'

'It's our job to look at all possibilities. Maybe the anti-oil activists had something against your husband's line of work, for example.'

'Not that I recall, no.' Lynda's lip trembled again as she turned her gaze back to Ross lying motionless in the bed behind the protective membrane.

Phillips's heart ached for the poor woman. She knew herself, only too well, how terrifying Lynda's current situation was – a week ago she could never have imagined what lay ahead and how much her life would change after receiving the terrifying news that her husband had been the victim of a car-bomb attack.

Phillips had one last question before she could leave them both in peace. 'Is there anyone who can support you and the girls right now?'

'My sister, Florence.' Lynda turned back to face them. 'She came down from Edinburgh as soon as she heard. She's at home with the girls at the moment; plus Kevin has been calling in here every day.'

'That's good to know,' said Phillips. 'Look, I don't want to speak out of turn here, Lynda, but I went through something similar last year, and what I can tell you is that sitting here, waiting for things to change, isn't always the best thing for you or Ross.'

Tears welled in Lynda's eyes.

'It's okay to go home and rest.' Phillips placed a reassuring hand on the woman's shoulder. 'After all, he's going to need you firing on all cylinders when he comes out of this.'

Lynda nodded as a tear streaked down her cheek.

'We'll leave you to it,' said Phillips softly. 'But please look after yourself.'

'I'll try,' Lynda replied without conviction.

Phillips offered a faint smile, then signalled for Jones to lead them out.

As soon as they left the burns unit and entered the main body of the hospital, Phillips dialled Kevin Hunt.

He answered almost immediately, his voice laced with tension. 'Hello?'

'Mr Hunt, I'm DCI Phillips, and I'm investigating the attack on Ross Grayson. Can we meet?'

'Er...sure.' He sounded anything but. 'When were you thinking?'

'Now, ideally,' replied Phillips. 'Is that convenient?'

'Well, I guess so.'

'We'll come to you.'

There was a pause before Hunt finally answered, 'I'm in the office, Spinnaker Court in Salford Quays.'

'What number?'

'Seven. Hunt and Lightly Media on the third floor.'

Phillips glanced at her watch. It was coming up to 4 p.m. 'We'll be there in twenty minutes.' With that, she ended the call.

4

The exterior of Spinnaker Court was quite unremarkable, a redbrick, three-storey building overlooking the water in Salford Quays. The shared reception area on the ground floor was reminiscent of an insurance brokers or some equally generic office space, but the interior of the Hunt and Lightly Media offices, located on the top floor, was very different indeed. It was evident – from the vast array of posters, photographs and artwork that filled the walls around the agency's own reception desk – that Hunt and Lightly specialised in promoting major sports brands around the globe.

After being greeted by a smart but casually dressed receptionist whose name badge suggested he was called Bobbi, they made their way as directed, through the wide open-plan office space filled with large desks and even bigger computer monitors. As they walked side by side to the conference suite at the far end of the building, Phillips noted the breakout area to her left that contained a red baize pool table, a classic American jukebox, and a full-size basketball hoop complete with a transparent backboard. A far cry from MCU's run-down offices in Ashton House.

Kevin Hunt, a tall, heavyset man with a shaved head and black-rimmed glasses, was waiting for them in the doorway of the conference room, holding the door open to what appeared to be the only private space in the entire office. 'DCI Phillips.' He offered his hand as soon as she was within reach. 'I'm Kevin.'

Phillips shook it as Jones moved next to her. 'This is DI Jones. Thanks for seeing us.'

Hunt offered his hand to Jones now. 'Glad to help in any way I can.'

They each took seats at the large conference table in the middle of the room, Phillips and Jones facing Hunt, his back to the window and the water of the quays beyond. He looked tired, his eyes red and puffy, his chin covered in what appeared to be a couple of days' stubble.

'How are you doing?' asked Phillips.

Hunt shook his head. 'Not great. I can't stop thinking about Ross and Lynda and the kids. I mean, what if he dies?'

'He's in the best possible place right now,' replied Phillips. 'Try to stay positive if you can.'

'I can't shake the image of Ross slumped in the burning car when I ran outside.'

Phillips was happy to let Hunt talk.

'I keep finding myself staring out the window,' he continued. 'My business partner, Geraldine, says I should go home, but I'm much better off here. I'm recently separated, and being in an empty house is hard enough, even without all this.'

Phillips could relate. Burying herself in work had been the only way she felt she could deal with Adam's injuries. 'I hope I'm not speaking out of turn here, but what you witnessed is bound to have had an effect on you. It might be worth talking to your doctor about it.'

Hunt said nothing for a moment. 'Yeah, maybe.'

Phillips continued, 'Look, we know this is going to be difficult, but are you up to answering a few questions about what happened on Saturday?'

'If you think it'll help, of course.'

'Thank you.' Phillips sat forward now. 'So, did you actually see the explosion?'

'No, but I heard it. At first, I thought a plane had crashed, and then when I ran outside, I saw Ross's car on fire. I couldn't believe what I was seeing. It was like something out of a war zone.'

'And what happened then?'

'Nothing,' said Hunt sombrely. 'I just froze. It was as if my feet were stuck to the pavement. Maybe if I'd reacted quicker...' His words tailed off.

'You were most likely suffering from shock,' Phillips cut in. 'And the reality is if you had tried to get him out of the car, you'd have been seriously injured too.'

Hunt took a few seconds before responding, 'Is it true it was a terror attack?'

Phillips shook her head. 'The Counter Terrorism Unit's intel suggests not. That's why we've taken over the investigation.'

'I see.' Hunt appeared deep in thought.

Phillips continued, 'How did Ross seem on Saturday?'

'How do you mean?'

'Well, was he distracted at all? Or did he seem nervous or worried? Agitated maybe?'

'No, quite the opposite. He was in a bloody great mood, actually. Couldn't get the smile off his face.'

'Do you know why that was?'

'GBOG had just signed off a deal that would secure drilling rights in Norway for the next ten years. He'd helped broker the agreement with the Norwegian government, and it meant a hefty bonus for him, which he'd already decided was going on a new car for Lynda and a family holiday to Disney.'

Jones scribbled in his notebook.

'That sounds like one hell of a bonus,' Phillips added.

'Yeah, it was. Close to a hundred grand for that deal alone. From what he told me, the Norwegian deal was potentially worth hundreds of billions to GBOG over the next few years, so his bonus was a drop in the ocean in comparison.'

Phillips changed tack now. 'Does Ross have any enemies that you know of? Anyone who might want to hurt him?'

Hunt shook his head vigorously. 'You'd struggle to find anyone with a bad word to say about him, to be honest. He's a rarity in this world, a very successful bloke in business and someone everybody likes in real life. He has every reason to be like the rest of the billy-big-balls guys at David Lloyd with their flash cars and massive houses, but he's the total opposite. Modest, kind and more interested in other people than himself.'

'What about the anti-oil protestors?' said Phillips. 'Did he ever mention having issues with groups like that?'

'He did, actually,' Hunt replied, 'but nothing major, just the odd email now again from the "eco-warriors", as he called them.'

'Did he ever share what the emails said?'

'Not really, but the way he described them, they were

aimed more at the business as opposed to Ross himself. By the sounds of it, his boss had a harder time with that sort of stuff.'

'So he wasn't worried about those kinds of groups?' Jones asked.

'Not at all,' replied Hunt. 'In fact, he had a bit of sympathy for some of them, for fighting for what they believed in. But that's Ross, always trying to see someone else's point of view.'

Jones made a note.

'Did you notice anyone suspicious in or around the club on Saturday?' said Phillips.

'No, but to be honest, I wasn't looking, either.'

'What time did you meet up at the tennis club that night?'

'Same as usual, half six. It was just like every other Saturday. We met in the locker rooms, changed into our tennis whites and then had an hour on the court. Ross beat me, as usual. Then a steam and sauna and a quick drink in the bar before heading home.'

'I see,' Phillips said. 'You mentioned that you were in the club when the explosion happened.'

'That's right.'

'Was that normal?'

'How'd you mean?'

'For Ross to leave before you?' she clarified.

'No. Normally, we'd always walk out together, but I stayed behind to book the court for next Saturday. We normally do it online while we're sitting in the bar, but they were having issues with the booking system.'

Phillips glanced at Jones – who continued making notes – then back at Hunt as she pulled her phone from her pocket. After taking a moment to find what she was looking for, she passed the screen across. 'These three individuals were spotted around Ross's car about thirty minutes before the explosion.'

Hunt pushed his glasses up onto the top of his head, frowning as he scrutinised the image on-screen.

'They were also seen running away after it,' she added. 'Do you recognise any of them?'

'No. Can't say I do.' Hunt passed the phone back across the desk.

'So you didn't see them running from the scene when you ran outside after the explosion?' Jones cut in.

'The only things I saw were Ross and the flames.' Hunt scoffed. 'A pink elephant could've charged past me and it wouldn't have registered at that point.'

Jones flashed a thin smile. 'Understandable in the circumstances.'

Phillips pulled one of her business cards from her inside pocket and slid it across the table. 'I think we have everything we need for now. But if you remember anything that might be of help, no matter how small it may seem, my number's on there.'

Hunt examined the card in his hand before turning his gaze back to Phillips.

'Well, thank you, you've been very helpful.' She pushed back her chair. 'We'll leave you to it.'

Three minutes later they walked across the car park towards the squad car.

Phillips glanced at the clock on her phone: 5.58 p.m. 'I think that's enough for one day.'

'Do you want me to drop you at home?' asked Jones.

'Please, and I'll need a lift in the morning as well.'

'At eight o'clock?' Jones disengaged the central locking.

'Better make it seven.' Phillips pulled open the passenger door. 'We're going to need an early start.'

'I'll call the guys and let them know,' said Jones before opening his own door and dropping down into the driver's seat.

5

It took Jones thirty minutes to navigate the rush hour traffic from Salford Quays to the boho suburb of Chorlton-cum-Hardy, a couple of miles south of the city, that Phillips had called home for the last twenty years. With her own car safely parked up outside Ashton House, Adam's brand-new F-Type Jaguar coupe took centre stage on the wide gravel drive.

'New toy?' asked Jones, pulling the squad car to the kerb in front of the Victorian semi-detached house.

Phillips glanced left at the gleaming red sports car. 'Adam picked it up last week.'

'Very nice.'

'If you say so,' Phillips replied flatly. 'I prefer the classics myself.'

'Like a Mini Cooper?' Jones grinned.

Phillips matched him. 'If it's good enough for Michael Caine and his boys in the *Italian Job*, then it's good enough for me.'

'Speaking of which, what's happening with that? Will your dad be wanting it back soon?'

'Probably.' Phillips sighed. 'Thanks to the epilepsy meds, it's been twelve months since his last fit, so with a bit of luck, he should be back driving fairly soon.'

'You'll miss it, won't you?'

'I really will. I've loved having it this last year: goes like a rocket, easy to park, looks the business. I even feel the British racing green colour suits me. It's the perfect car.'

'Maybe if you ask your dad nicely, he'll let you keep it.'

'Somehow I doubt it.' Phillips reached for the door handle. 'Right, well, thanks for the lift.'

'See you at seven?' asked Jones.

'Yeah, great,' she replied as she stepped out of the car.

A few minutes later, as she opened the front door and stepped inside the house, she was greeted by her cream-and-brown-coloured ragdoll cat, Floss, who snaked around her legs, purring loudly. Bending down and scooping her up in her arms, she wandered through to the kitchen, where she found Adam, still wearing his blue medical scrubs, sitting on a stool next to the large cooking island in the middle of the room, scrolling through his phone.

'Hey.' He looked up. 'How was your day?'

Phillips blew out through her lips. 'Intense and full of surprises.'

Adam raised his eyebrows. 'Sounds interesting.'

'How about you?'

'Long. So long in fact that I have no desire to cook tonight, so I've made an executive decision, and I'm taking you out for dinner. I've booked us a table at San Juan's.'

Phillips smiled. 'You read my mind. I was thinking the exact same thing in the car on the way back.'

Adam slipped off the stool and drew her close, kissing her lightly on the lips. 'I'll just get changed, and we can go.'

Half an hour later, after making the short walk from the house to the village, they found themselves sitting outside their favourite tapas restaurant. Ever since their early days as a couple, dinner at San Juan's had been a regular event whenever their busy schedules would allow them time together at home. The sun was shining, and a warm evening breeze carried wonderful aromas through the air from the nearby kitchen as their regular waiter, Elian, appeared with their ice-cold drinks, a Pinot Grigio for Jane and a Cruzcampo for Adam.

'So how come today was so intense?' asked Adam before taking a gulp of his lager.

Phillips took a mouthful of wine, then set the glass down on the table. When she spoke, her voice was almost a whisper. 'I had a meeting with a guy from the counter terrorism team first thing.'

'Really? What about?'

'The car-bomb attack at David Lloyd's on Saturday.'

Being a senior A&E doctor, Adam had shown a keen interest in the news reports that had followed the explosion over the weekend. 'What does a terror attack have to do with Major Crimes?'

'That's just it, they don't believe it was actually a terror attack. All their intel suggests it was more likely an attempted murder...'

'And is that why they were talking to you?'

'Yeah.' Phillips took another mouthful of wine. 'But the problem is we have zero experience of investigating car-bomb attacks within the team. It feels like the blind leading the blind.'

'So what did Fox think?'

'All for it. She even managed to give me a backhanded compliment. Said she'd told the PCC that she was putting her *best* team on it.'

Adam's eyes widened. 'Wow. High praise indeed coming from her. And what did Carter have to say about it?'

'What could he say? Once Fox has made up her mind, there's no changing it, so we're stuck with another super-high-profile case and no idea how to solve it.'

At that moment the waiter reappeared to take their order. Adam took charge and ordered their favourites, small plates of sizzling gambas pil-pil, spiced chorizo, patatas bravas, as well as Spanish omelette and a small portion of paella.

'Excellent choices,' said Elian, in his Spanish accent, before gathering the menus and heading back inside.

'Anyway, I'm too tired to talk about it,' said Phillips. 'So let's talk about your day.'

Adam chuckled, then took another drink.

'What?' asked Phillips.

He fixed his gaze on her as he placed his glass down on the table. 'I'm thinking of quitting A&E.'

Phillips felt herself do a slight double take. 'Wow. Where's this come from?'

'I'm bored, Jane,' he said, very matter of fact.

'I thought you loved working there.'

Adam's face crumpled. 'I did, but ever since going back after the attack, it's just not been the same.'

'You never said anything.'

'No. In all honesty, I guess I've been trying to work out what was going on with me as opposed to the job. I mean, nothing's changed, the team are great, I'm pretty much my own boss, and the facilities are top-notch. But despite all that, I feel like I'm going backwards. Like life is passing me by.'

Phillips reached across the table and wrapped her hand around his. 'Understandable given what happened to you.'

Adam remained silent.

'Have you given any more thought to the trauma counselling we talked about?'

'I have, yeah, and I know it would do me good, but for whatever reason, something stops me getting it booked in.'

Phillips smiled softly. 'I felt the same after the shooting, but it really did help me get my head in order. I think it could do the same for you.'

Adam flashed a faint smile. 'Yeah, maybe.'

'So what will you do? If you change jobs, I mean.'

'I'm thinking of applying to be a HEMS doctor.'

'The flying doctors?'

'Yeah.' Adam's eyes sparkled now. 'Aintree hospital are looking for four doctors to make up a new chopper team. They are asking for applications in the next three weeks, and I'm thinking about putting my hat in the ring.'

'If it's what you want, then you should totally do it,' said Phillips. 'The change of scene would do you good.'

'That's what I was thinking.'

Phillips smiled. 'Of all people, we know better than most, Adam, that life is too short to wonder what might have been. Go for it and see what happens. If it's meant for you, you'll get it, and if it's not, then we can figure things out together.'

Adam smiled back, his shoulders visibly relaxing now. 'Thanks, Janey. I was worried you'd think I was mad to even consider it.'

She chuckled. 'Not at all. If anyone's mad, it's me. I got

out of the rat race, remember, and for some unknown bloody reason, I went back. Back to the bullshit and police politics.'

Adam drained his almost empty glass. 'You went back because protecting people is part of who you are. Sadly, the politics and the bullshit come with the territory.'

'True,' she replied. 'But I do sometimes still catch myself wondering why I put myself through it every day.'

'It's in your DNA. Pure and simple.'

Just then Elian arrived, his hands full of steaming hot dishes.

'Perfect timing,' said Phillips. 'I'm starving.'

6

Tex closed the blinds, then locked the door before making his way across the room to the desk where his laptop was positioned. After plugging in the headphones with the built-in lip mic, he opened the machine and fired it up. A few minutes passed before the home screen appeared and he was able to access the specific internet browser Charlie had insisted he install when they had first connected earlier in the year. Careful to type in the correct address and series of passwords, he hit return and waited for the encrypted website to load. A few seconds later, he found himself staring at a black screen; the only clue that it was connected to an active link was the tiny cursor flashing in the bottom right-hand corner. Finally, after what seemed like an eternity, the screen burst into life, and the now familiar image of a masked and hooded avatar appeared before him.

'It seems the mission was a success,' said Charlie, his voice mechanically distorted but unmistakably American.

'I saw on the news that Grayson survived,' Tex replied,

trying hard to control the nervous energy coursing through his body, something he'd struggled with since carrying out the attack. 'I thought we wanted him dead?'

'In an ideal world, yes, but the explosion made headlines, which was our primary objective.'

Tex checked over his shoulder to ensure the door remained locked behind him. 'So, when does Terra take the credit for the attack?' he asked impatiently.

'When the time is right,' replied Charlie.

'And when will that be? I mean, what's the point in making all this noise if nobody knows who we are or why we did it?'

Charlie remained silent, the avatar motionless on the screen.

Staring at the hooded figure glaring back at him, Tex felt his panic rising. Had he overstepped the mark? After all, Charlie had made it crystal clear from the start that his word was gospel; anyone questioning the strategy would be considered insubordinate and dealt with accordingly. And while he'd never been explicit in regard to what that actually meant, the implied threat to his and the rest of the gang's safety if they stepped out of line was obvious. 'Look, I'm sorry, I didn't mean to speak out of turn.'

'I'm very pleased to hear it,' said Charlie flatly. 'If Terra is to prevail where so many have failed in the past, then there can only be true faith in the battle plan.'

Tex nodded. 'There're no doubts. None at all.'

Charlie paused before responding, 'I'm glad we understand each other.'

'Completely.'

'You'll be pleased to know the next attack is now in play.'

'Who, where and when?' asked Tex.

'Details will be delivered to you in the usual way in the next twenty-four hours. You'll need to be ready for immediate deployment, so make sure the team is prepped.'

'We will be,' said Tex confidently.

'I do hope so, because the future of our world is in our hands,' replied Charlie. 'I'll be in touch.'

With that, the connection was severed, and Tex once again found himself staring at his own reflection in the blank screen in front of him. After removing his headphones, he closed the laptop and stared in silence at the burner mobile phone sitting on the desk next to it. Picking it up, he keyed in the number he'd spent all morning memorising.

The call connected a few seconds later and was answered almost immediately.

'Hello?'

'Clem, it looks like Slice and Dice is now operational.'

'Where and when?'

'We go live in the next twenty-four hours. Details will be sent soon.'

'Have you told Squeaky?'

'Not yet. He's my next call.'

'Will I see you tonight? I need to talk to you about something.'

'Not tonight. I have some things I need to sort out, but I'll call you later.'

'You promise.'

'Yeah, I promise.'

'I love you.'

'I know you do,' he said, then ended the call.

7

As planned, the team gathered the following morning at 7.30 a.m. in the MCU conference room. Owing to the early start time, Phillips had asked Bovalino to fetch hot sandwiches and drinks from the Ashton House canteen, which were quickly distributed by the big man as everybody prepared to do battle for the day.

Wasting no time, Phillips and Jones spent the first fifteen minutes of the briefing updating Bov and Whistler on the details of their meetings the previous day with Lynda Grayson and Kevin Hunt – the main takeaway being they'd so far found nothing to explain why anyone would want to plant a bomb under Ross Grayson's car.

Entwistle, whose laptop screen was now projected onto the large conference screen fixed to the wall at the end of the room, backed up this fact after doing his own background checks on the man. 'From what I can see, he's as clean as they come.' He opened a previously minimised window. 'And if his Facebook and Instagram accounts are anything to go by, a happily married, doting family man.'

'Yeah, but people lie about living perfect lives all the time on social media,' said Bovalino before taking a bite from his bacon roll.

'True, but those kinds of posts generally look too good to be true.' Entwistle clicked on the photos folder from Grayson's Facebook account and began scrolling through. 'These seem quite genuine.'

Phillips studied each photo as they came and went as she grazed on her own sandwich.

Entwistle continued, 'I'm still waiting on phone records, but I'm expecting those today from his network provider. They've been pretty good in my dealings with them so far, so hopefully I'll have eyes on them early this morning.'

'Good work,' said Phillips before focusing on Bov. 'Any updates on the CCTV around Brentwood Park?'

'I've been through three of the five cameras positioned at the various exits to the park, and so far I've found nothing. I'll start on the remaining two feeds as soon as we're done here.'

Phillips nodded, then turned back to look at the big screen, which was now showing Grayson's Instagram feed. On the face of it, it seemed Whistler's observations were correct, and their victim was a down-to-earth, wholesome family man, but her gut was telling her they were likely missing something – something that would explain why an inoffensive finance director had become the target of an IED attack. She swallowed the last mouthful of her bacon roll and tossed its grease-stained wrapper into the waste bin before facing the team once more. 'When something or someone appears squeaky clean, it usually means we're not looking hard enough, or we're searching in the wrong places. I know we've had the case less than twenty-four hours, but we need to dig deep and find out why anyone would want to blow up Ross Grayson. Sadly, for us, the world is watching, and that means Fox is expecting regular updates. Something – *anything* – you can find will help keep her at arm's length, because the last thing we need now is the chief constable riding shotgun on the investigation.'

'Understood,' said Jones.

Bovalino and Entwistle nodded in unison.

She turned to Jones. 'Can you set up a meeting with Grayson's boss?'

'Sure, I'll sort it now,' he replied.

'Great.' Phillips stood. 'While you're doing that, I'd better get upstairs and brief Carter.'

TWENTY MINUTES LATER, Phillips was sitting opposite Chief Superintendent Carter as she finished updating him on the team's progress so far.

His thick brow was furrowed when he spoke. 'So we're no further forward since yesterday.'

Phillips shook her head. 'No, sir, but it's only been twenty-four hours since the case was dumped in our laps.'

Carter folded his arms as he rested his elbows on the desk in front of him. 'So why does it feel like it's been a week?'

'Probably because Fox is circling on this one.'

'She really is,' replied Carter. 'She must have rung me five times yesterday for updates on the investigation.'

Phillips let out a sardonic chuckle. 'True to form. The slightest sniff of bad press and she's all over it, sticking her nose in, demanding results.'

Carter nodded sagely as he sat back in his chair. He said nothing for a while, and when he did finally speak, his voice was little more than a whisper. 'Can I be candid, Jane?'

'Of course.'

'Since you discovered she hasn't always played with a straight bat, I'm finding it harder than ever to deal with her, questioning everything she's doing or saying. Wondering if she's playing me in some way.'

'It's the same for me, sir.' Phillips felt her shoulders relax; her relief at being able to share her own concerns on the matter was palpable.

Carter pursed his lips and appeared deep in thought. 'I take it you've yet to find any concrete evidence that she *did* actually interfere with the Crowther investigation?'

'No. I'm afraid not, but to be honest, that doesn't surprise me, either. Fox is way too canny to leave a trail. All we have is Entwistle's word on the matter.'

'And you're sure you can trust him? After all, if what he says is true, he was the one who helped her.'

'I trust him,' replied Phillips. 'He's a good copper, and apart from that one time, he's never lied to me. Plus, you and I both know how manipulative Fox can be. Would either of us have stood up to her when we were young DCs like him? I mean, she threatened to end his career if he didn't go along with what she wanted. That would scare even the most battle-hardened coppers in this place.'

'You're probably right,' said Carter.

Phillips continued, warming to her subject, 'If anything, I trust him all the more. He didn't have to confess to what he did, Fox would never have let it slip, so he was essentially in the clear. The fact he came clean to me speaks volumes about the kind of copper he is. He risked his whole career because it was eating away at him.'

Carter nodded, taking on board her perspective. 'But I still can't believe Fox did it.'

'Oh, I can,' replied Phillips. 'If it meant she could get rid of evidence that might indicate she was once a bent copper, I can totally believe she'd do it.'

'Does anyone else in the team know about it?'

'No, sir, but I think it's time to tell Jones.'

'Why's that?' asked Carter.

'I've been giving it a lot of thought, and as much as I originally wanted to protect Whistler from being judged by the other guys in the team, Jones is the beating heart of MCU. The squad is as much his as it is mine. I've kept stuff from him in the past thinking I was doing the right thing, and that bit me on the backside. I don't want to make that same mistake twice.'

'Seems sensible,' Carter agreed.

The room fell silent for a time before Phillips finally spoke again. 'Seriously though, sir. What do we do about Fox? We can't just let her get away with it, surely?'

He shrugged. 'I'm not sure there is much we *can* do, as it stands. Without anything concrete to take to the PCC, it's the word of a young detective constable against the most senior cop on the force. We both know only too well who comes out on top in a situation like that. Especially knowing the lengths to which Fox will go to protect herself.'

Phillips was struggling to hide her frustration. 'What, then? We just carry on as if nothing happened?'

'Until we have evidence to the contrary, I'm afraid that's exactly what we do.'

'It's not right, sir.'

'I know that as well as you do, but it is what it is. Police politics at its finest. I'm sorry, Jane. I wish it were different.' He sat forward again. 'In the meantime, we can still try to root out the bastard who keeps leaking confidential case details to the press. Any updates on that?'

'We've narrowed the list of potential moles down to five people. Two cops from uniform and three from forensics. All five worked on all the cases in question at some point.'

'Do we have names?'

'Yes.' Phillips pulled out her phone, taking a moment to find what she was looking for in her emails before passing it across.

Carter stared down at the screen for a few seconds, then passed it back.

'So what now? How do we go about identifying the bad egg or – God forbid – bad *eggs*?'

Phillips winced. 'That's the tricky part. While we know each of them was involved in each of the cases, as yet we've found nothing to prove any of them shared confidential intel with Townsend.'

'Jesus, what a mess,' muttered Carter, running his fingers through his thick hair.

'I know it's frustrating, sir, but we will find the mole, and we will get Fox in time. I'm certain of that.'

Carter smiled weakly. 'I wish I shared your optimism, Jane. I really do.'

8

Later that morning, Phillips and Jones arrived at the head office of GBOG Energy for their meeting with the company's CEO, Pascal Bouché. According to Entwistle, GBOG had recently relocated forty miles from an industrial unit in Ellesmere Port to a magnificent converted Victorian hospital in the salubrious south Manchester village of Didsbury.

As Jones pulled up in an allocated visitor's space, Phillips gazed out the window at the imposing building surrounded by three acres of land.

'Well, this is rather nice,' she said.

'Wow,' Jones agreed. 'What a gaff.'

'I remember this place when it was a hospital,' Phillips replied. 'Came to see my grandad when we were back from Hong Kong one summer. He had emphysema after years of smoking Woodbines. Looks a bit different now.'

Jones leaned forward and peered up out the windscreen. 'The rent can't be cheap, based on the size of it.'

Phillips noted the vast number of BMWs and Mercedes

saloons parked around them, each one black, dark blue or grey. Company cars, by the look of it. 'Plenty of money in oil and gas,' she said, climbing out.

Inside, the building was just as impressive, with many of the original ornate Victorian features beautifully restored. In the centre of the triple-height reception area sat a tall and wide mahogany desk that Phillips considered could well have been part of the original hospital. If so, it had evidently been given a new lease of life more recently. Behind it sat two receptionists, both smartly dressed in matching dark purple blouses with yellow scarves that looked identically tied.

As they approached the desk, one of the women greeted them with a warm smile. 'Good morning, and welcome to GBOG. My name's Victoria. How may I help you this morning?'

Phillips placed Victoria in her early fifties, but she could easily have been mistaken for someone ten years younger, her skin flawless, her makeup subtle and clearly expensive. 'I'm DCI Phillips, and this is my colleague DI Jones, from the Major Crimes Unit. We're here to see Mr Bouché. He's expecting us.'

Victoria nodded before turning her attention to the monitor in front of her. 'Ah, yes,' she said before picking up the phone. A moment later she announced them to the person on the other end, waited, nodded and then replaced the handset. 'Mr Bouché's assistant is on her way down to take you through. If you'd just like to take a seat.'

'Thanks,' said Phillips before moving to the right of the reception desk, where she dropped gently onto an oversized charcoal-coloured sofa, with Jones a split second behind her.

About five minutes had passed by the time a tall, dark-

haired woman appeared wearing the same purple and
yellow combo. She too sported a beaming smile that
matched those of the receptionists, and Phillips wondered if
they were genuinely happy to work here – or more cynically
– if it was all part of a carefully crafted image GBOG was
keen to promote. Having seen how big conglomerates
worked in the past, she guessed it was likely the latter.

'DCI Phillips?' the woman asked as she approached.

Phillips and Jones stood in unison.

The woman held out her hand to Phillips. 'I'm Sinead,
Mr Bouché's executive assistant. Would you like to
follow me?'

Phillips and Jones fell in behind Sinead as she walked
quickly out of reception and set off down a long corridor
where the decor was more boutique hotel than energy
conglomerate. Large sepia photographic prints of refineries,
oil rigs and oil tankers adorned the walls around them –
each lit from above like works of art in a museum. If she
didn't know better, based on her experience of GBOG so far,
it would have been easy to believe the oil and gas industry
was a beautiful component of the world's ecosystem. It was
clear these guys really cared about their brand image.

After a few minutes of snaking their way through a
labyrinth of corridors and internal doors, they found themselves in the outer office of Pascal Bouché, which itself was
similar in size to an average conference room.

'If you could just wait here one moment,' said Sinead
before knocking on a thick oak door in the wall ahead of
them. After a second or two, she opened the door and leaned
inside. 'DCI Phillips and DI Jones are here.'

Phillips heard the sound of a voice inside the room, but
couldn't make out what was being said.

Sinead stepped back out and opened the door wide. 'Mr Bouché will see you now.'

As Phillips moved inside, she came face to face with Bouché, who had made his way around his desk. A slim, athletic man with wavy black hair and a dark single-breasted suit that was obviously tailored.

He greeted them both with a firm handshake, his brow creased, the eyes filled with sadness. 'It is a pleasure to meet you both.' His accent was French, but the English flawless. 'I wish the circumstances had been different.'

'We appreciate you making the time to see us so readily, Mr Bouché. Particularly as you've already spoken to our colleagues in the counter terrorism team.'

Bouché offered a faint smile now. 'Please, call me Pascal.' He ushered them to two leather seats opposite his gargantuan oak desk. 'Would either of you care for a coffee, or tea perhaps?'

'No, thanks,' said Phillips.

'I'm fine, thank you.' Jones took out his notebook and pen.

Bouché unbuttoned his suit jacket and took a seat in his high-back chair. 'So how can I help?'

Phillips sat forward slightly. 'As DI Jones explained to your assistant on the phone this morning, Major Crimes has taken over the investigation into the car-bomb attack on Ross Grayson.'

Bouché nodded. 'Does that mean you no longer think it was a terror attack?'

'No, we don't,' said Phillips.

Bouché's eyes narrowed. 'Then who did this terrible thing?'

'That's what we aim to find out,' she replied.

'I'll help in any way I can, and you have the full resources of GBOG at your disposal.'

Phillips smiled. 'We spoke to Ross's wife, Lynda, as well as his friend Kevin, who was with him just before the bomb was detonated. Both mentioned he had received emails previously from anti-oil protestors making threats against the company. Were you aware of that?'

'Of course,' Bouché replied. 'All the executives receive them from time to time. It's par for the course in this line of work.'

'Did Ross ever show you any of the emails he was sent?'

'All emails of that nature are passed straight on to our internal security team to be logged and monitored.'

'We'll need to see them.'

'Of course,' Bouché replied.

Jones scribbled in his pad.

Phillips took the lead once more. 'Can you tell us about Ross's role at the company?'

Bouché reclined in his chair now. 'He's responsible for the P&L of the business; globally he manages the finance teams in each of our territories around the world.'

'And what territories are those?'

'Venezuela, Saudi Arabia, Canada, Iran, Iraq, Kuwait and UAE,' Bouché reeled off. 'We were in Russia too, but we pulled out of there because of the war in Ukraine. A bad business we could not support.'

'That's admirable,' said Phillips.

'We do try to do the right thing at GBOG, despite what the environmentalists think.'

Phillips ignored the remark. 'Ross's friend Kevin told us he'd just brokered a deal in Norway. Is that right?'

'Yes, indeed. He's a fantastic negotiator and led the team

that won the rights to drill the Continental shelf. It was a real feather in his cap.'

Phillips shifted in her seat as she changed tack. 'Does he have any enemies that you know of?'

'Not that I'm aware of, no. He's a lovely guy and always great company. He's a very popular member of our team and well liked across the industry as a whole.' Bouché folded his arms. 'In fact, he was due to speak at the International Energy Conference at the Lowry later in the week as one of the keynote speakers. What happened to him on Saturday has shocked the energy sector worldwide.'

'I can imagine,' said Phillips.

Just then there was a knock on the door behind them, and Sinead popped her head in. 'I'm sorry to interrupt, Mr Bouché, but there's an urgent call for you, regarding the Norway deal.'

Bouché's face fell, concern etched in his brow as he returned his focus back to Phillips. 'I really need to take that. Is there anything else you need before I go?'

'Can we see Ross's office?'

'Of course. Sinead will show you the way.'

'Thank you.' Phillips stood before she and Jones turned and followed Sinead out.

Grayson's office was located just a few moments' walk away. About half the square footage of Bouché's, it was still an impressive size and military tidy. Aside from a couple of framed photos of Lynda and the girls sitting by the phone on the large desk, there were few real clues as to what kind of man Grayson really was.

After Sinead made her excuses, they spent the next ten minutes working their way methodically around the space. Exactly what they were looking for, Phillips wasn't totally sure, and this uncertainty made her growing frustration even more palpable. Twenty-four hours into the investigation they still knew very little about Ross Grayson or who might have wanted him dead. Given his role, the anti-oil brigade with their hatred for all things fossil fuel were the obvious choice, but attempted murder? That seemed extreme given their history of peaceful protests.

'Well, it all seems very unremarkable, guv,' said Jones when they'd completed their sweep of the office.

'Doesn't it?' She sighed.

'So what now?'

Phillips shook her head. 'I don't know – and that's half the problem. I have this feeling in my gut that the answers are staring us straight in the face, but for some reason, we're just not seeing them.'

'I know what you mean.'

'I think we've exhausted this place for now.' Phillips closed the desk drawer she'd been examining. 'Let's get back to the office, see what the guys have come up with while we've been out.'

9

The next day, Phillips and Jones's first visit was to the forensic lab, where they found senior crime scene investigator Andy Evans sitting behind his desk in the tiny glass box he called his office. It always tickled Phillips just how different he looked without his forensic suit and mask covering the majority of his body, his thick ginger beard offset by his black T-shirt and trousers, a security lanyard around his neck.

As they approached, he was staring intently at his laptop screen; evidently, he hadn't seen them enter the main lab.

With Jones standing at her shoulder, Phillips rapped on the open door. 'Morning.'

Evans appeared in a world of his own as he glanced up at her.

'Is this a bad time?' she asked.

'No, not at all.' He shook his head as he closed his laptop. 'Sorry, I didn't hear you come in. I have a tendency to hyper-focus when we're busy.'

Phillips was keen to get down to business. 'We were

hoping you might have an update on the SUV that was blown up outside David Lloyd's on Saturday.'

'Ah yes. The Lexus.' Evans got up from his chair and stepped around the desk. 'It's up on the hydraulic lift in the workshop; well, what's left of it is. Follow me.'

Phillips and Jones fell in behind him as he led them through a set of doors and into a large double-height workshop that housed a number of vehicles positioned around the cavernous space, each evidently at different stages of the forensic examination process.

Up ahead, Phillips spotted the black Lexus sitting on the lift about ten feet off the ground, the rear end pretty much intact, the front burned down to nothing but the frame.

Evans guided them under the car, stopping next to what had once been the fuel tank. 'This is where the explosive device was attached.' He pointed to a small area no larger than a cigarette packet where the metal had burned to a different shade compared to the rest of the charring. 'It was connected directly to the fuel line.'

Phillips stepped closer to get a better look. 'Any fingerprints?'

'No. Sorry. The fire put paid to that.'

'They obviously knew what they were doing,' said Jones.

Evans's face contorted slightly. 'I wouldn't go that far.'

'What do you mean?' Phillips asked.

'Well, whoever fitted it didn't actually do a very good job. If they had done, the whole car would have exploded, and the victim would have died instantly. As it was, the engine block took the brunt of the blast, and because these Lexuses are built like tanks around the chassis, it remained intact. In fact, if this car had been a diesel engine, he'd likely have walked away without a scratch on him.'

'So what was this?' asked Jones. 'Petrol?'

Evans nodded. 'Yep. Slightly better for the environment, but hellishly combustible.'

Phillips remained silent as she took in the whole car before turning her attention back to Evans. 'When you say it was a poor job, could an amateur have done this?'

'It's a possibility. It certainly appears homemade but then again, I'm no expert. I'm just telling you what Clara came up with.'

'Is she here?' Phillips asked.

'Yeah, in one of the testing labs,' replied Evans. 'Come on, I'll take you through.'

Once again Phillips and Jones fell in behind Evans as he guided them through a series of card-activated security doors, using his pass to gain access each time until finally opening the door to Lab 2B. Stepping inside, they found Clara, Evans's second in command in the CSI team, hunched over a bench, wearing safety glasses and a white lab coat, complete with purple latex gloves. A laptop was open to the side.

She turned her head, then straightened as they walked in, cutting a striking silhouette, standing at almost six feet tall with the broad athletic frame of an experienced swimmer. Her blonde hair was pulled back into a tight ponytail.

'I've just been updating the guys about the IED that was responsible for the Lexus,' said Evans.

Clara nodded.

'Andy says there's a chance it could have been homemade,' ventured Phillips.

'Looks that way to me.'

'In what way?'

'Here, I'll show you what I mean.' Pulling the laptop

closer, Clara tapped into the keyboard for a few seconds before turning it round so the screen was visible to the room. 'These are pictures I took of it when the car first came in. You can see the device is still attached to the engine block.' She hit return on the keyboard. 'And these are what it looked like when I'd removed it.'

Phillips and Jones both learned forward slightly to study the images up close.

Clara spun the laptop back to face her and began typing again. A moment later, she returned it to its former position, so it was visible to the room once more. 'These are examples of IEDs used by the Taliban in Afghanistan. I did two tours as a frontline medic out there and came across quite a few of these in my time. Thankfully, none of them detonated, or I wouldn't be standing here today.'

Again, Phillips and Jones scrutinised the screen.

Clara continued, 'It's quite hard to tell because the IED on the Lexus was subjected to so much heat, but looking at the different images, I'm convinced they're the same type of device.'

Phillips felt her face crumple. 'What? The attack on Grayson was down to the Taliban?'

'Maybe,' Clara replied.

'But the counter terrorism boys ruled them out,' said Jones.

'The only thing I am certain of,' replied Clara, 'is the fact the bomb was not the work of an expert. Plans for IEDs like this are all over the Dark Web. Anyone with a high level of computer literacy could have accessed them and built it.'

'Any chance we could trace someone downloading information like that?' Phillips asked.

'Unlikely,' said Clara. 'That's the whole point of the Dark Web: staying hidden.'

Phillips sighed heavily. 'So we're no further forward, then. No fingerprints and no signature on the IED.'

'Sorry, Jane,' said Evans. 'We still need to go through the rest of the car that wasn't affected by the flames. You never know, we might get lucky and find some trace evidence somewhere in there.'

'I won't hold my breath.' Phillips turned to Jones. 'Come on, I think I've had enough good news for one day,' she said sardonically.

10

'I'm starving,' said Phillips as they reached the car. 'You fancy an early lunch?'

Jones grinned. 'Any kind of lunch that doesn't involve pre-packed canteen sarnies is good by me.'

Phillips opened her door. 'There's a cute little pub just down the road. Adam and I have been there a couple of times before. Great food.'

'Sounds good.'

'My treat,' Phillips added.

'Even better,' replied Jones before climbing into the driver's seat.

Soon after, they were guided to their table in the dimly lit pub-cum-restaurant by the smiling waitress, who handed them each a menu before taking their drinks order while promising to return promptly to organise their food.

For the next few minutes, they both studied the menu in silence before Phillips placed hers on the table. 'I think I'll have the homemade steak and ale pie. Adam had it last time we were here, and it looked amazing.'

'I'll have the gammon steak,' said Jones, folding the menu away. 'Oh, by the way, I meant to tell you, I heard on the grapevine that Brown is being made acting chief constable down at Thames Valley.'

Phillips did a slight double take. 'Brown? You're kidding?'

Jones was of course referring to their former boss, who, for a brief and painful period had led the Major Crimes Unit. It was no secret there had been zero love lost between Phillips and Brown during their time working together. In fact, the entire team had breathed a collective sigh of relief when Brown was finally promoted to superintendent and moved across the Pennines to join the West Yorkshire police.

'God help them,' Phillips added. 'But I thought he was still in Leeds.'

'He was. Did a couple of years there before moving down to Thames Valley. Apparently, it's one of the best places to be if you want to be noticed by the top brass. Good links with the Met and all that.'

'Sounds like Brown; never happier than when he's climbing the greasy pole through the ranks. So how did you hear about that?'

'A guy I worked with in the Met back in the day. He recently moved out of London and joined Thames Valley as a DCI. Rumour has it the current chief constable has gone off with stress, so Brown's being bumped up temporarily.'

'Pah,' Phillips scoffed. 'There'll be nothing temporary about it. If I know Brown, he'll be making plans to get the job full time, whispering in the right ears at every possible opportunity.'

Jones shuddered. 'I wouldn't wish that horrible little bastard on my worst enemy.'

'Me neither.' Phillips chuckled. 'Which is ironic, really, given he was once actually my worst enemy.'

Jones laughed too as the waitress returned and placed two large Diet Cokes on the table, then pulled out her pad and pen.

'Are you guys ready to order?'

A minute later, with the waitress dispatched to the kitchen and 'Careless Whisper' by George Michael playing at a low level in the background, Jones scanned the room. 'This is a rare treat, I must say. I only ever get lunch bought for me when Sarah's trying to butter me up, or about to break bad news.'

Phillips forced a thin smile and did her best to avoid his gaze.

Jones's eyes narrowed as he stared back at her intently. 'Why do I get the feeling you're about to do the same?'

Phillips didn't respond and instead took a mouthful of Coke.

Jones kept his eyes locked on her. 'Why did you *really* bring me to lunch, guv?'

'You deserve it,' she replied. 'And besides, we were virtually passing this place; it'd be rude not to.'

He shook his head. 'No. We've just landed a case that has us all stumped. There's no way you'd break away from the investigation without good reason.'

She held his gaze, then sighed. 'Is it really that obvious?'

'Yes. I've known you a long time, and I can always tell when you're keeping something back. So what is it?'

Phillips exhaled loudly as she placed her glass back on the table. 'Do you remember during the Crowther case, when I promised I'd never keep anything from you again?'

'You mean the Fox stuff? Back when she was a DI?'

'Yeah,' replied Phillips. 'Well, something else happened during that investigation that I need to talk to you about.'

Jones frowned. 'Go on.'

'When the tapes went missing, the ones from Duval's place...'

'Yeah.'

'Well, I know who took them out of MCU.'

'Are you serious?' Jones recoiled now. 'And you *didn't* tell me?'

Phillips raised her palms in defence. 'Hang on. I'm telling you now, aren't I?'

'Who?' asked Jones flatly. 'Who took them?'

She paused. 'Entwistle.'

'Whistler? The Boy Scout.' Jones scanned the room. 'Is this a windup?'

'I wish it were,' said Phillips coolly. 'And there's something else you need to know, too.'

'Of course there is.' Jones folded his arms across his chest.

'Whistler removed the tapes because Fox threatened to ruin his career if he didn't.'

Jones stared back at Phillips, agog.

Phillips continued, 'There was something on those tapes that Fox clearly didn't want the world to see, so she blackmailed Whistler into handing them over.'

'And you know all this, how?'

'Because he confessed to me, about a week after they went missing. Offered to resign.'

Jones shook his head. 'And I'm just hearing about this now? I'm your DI. We're supposed to share everything when it comes to the team.'

'I know,' Phillips replied. 'And that's why I'm telling you

now. I promised no secrets, and I meant it. I just needed to get a few things clear in my head before I shared it with you.'

'Like what?'

'Like whether or not I wanted to keep Whistler on the team.'

'Well, surely you *don't*,' spat Jones. 'I mean, he clearly can't be trusted.'

Phillips sat forward. 'Look, I understand why you'd think that, but I honestly feel the opposite is true. He didn't have to confess. I mean, Fox was never going to let it slip that she forced him to lose evidence, was she? And none of us knew who'd taken them, so he could've just carried on as if nothing had happened. But he didn't; he owned up to it, knowing full well it would likely see him kicked off the force.'

'Does anyone else know about it?' Jones asked.

'Just Carter.'

'And what did he say?'

'Same as you. Asked me if I could really trust Whistler.'

Jones ran the long, bony fingers of his right hand through his thinning hair. 'And I really don't think you can.'

Phillips nodded. 'I know, and I get that, but I also know how manipulative Fox is. She as good as told him his career was finished if he didn't play ball. Threatened to expose something from his past.'

'Which was what?'

'I don't know. He wouldn't tell me,' said Phillips.

'Are you sure he's not just bullshitting you, guv?'

'I don't believe he is, and why would he? No, I just think he's a young lad who made a mistake. God knows, you and I have both made plenty of those over the years.'

Jones breathed heavily through his nose for a long

moment as he stared back at her. 'You should've told me as soon as he came to you with all of this.'

'Yeah, and I'm sorry, but like I said, I needed time to process it myself first.'

'And where does Fox fit in all this?' asked Jones. 'I mean, we can't just let her get away with it, can we?'

'We need evidence first.'

'What about Whistler? Can't he just go to the PCC?'

'And say what?' Phillips shrugged. 'He's a detective constable accusing the chief constable of evidence tampering. Who do you think the commissioner would believe?'

'But that's so shit,' said Jones. 'She's bent. They should throw the bloody book at her.'

'And, in time, hopefully they will, but until we have proper irrefutable proof, there's nothing we can do.'

'What, so we just act as if nothing happened?'

'For the time being, yes,' Phillips replied. 'But at least we now *know* for sure that she's corrupt.'

'And that's good news how?'

'Well.' Phillips grinned. 'As we understand better than most, there's *always* a trail of evidence somewhere, no matter how well someone tries to hide it. All we have to do now is find it.'

11

After what turned out to be a delicious lunch – albeit relatively light on conversation after the Fox and Entwistle revelations – Phillips and Jones returned to Ashton House. During the drive back to base, she had called and asked the guys to get the conference room ready for a full debrief on everything the team had found so far.

As soon as they arrived, after taking their seats around the conference table, Phillips and Jones spent the first five minutes updating Bov and Whistler on their conversation with Evans and Clara, which sadly had delivered little – if anything – of value. In fact, all it had really confirmed was that virtually anyone with a computer could have designed the IED detonated under Grayson's car.

'So we're really hoping you guys have had more luck,' said Phillips finally.

Entwistle pointed to the large screen fixed to the wall opposite, which again mirrored the laptop in front of him. 'Grayson's financials.'

'Anything that stands out?' asked Jones.

'Sadly, no. It seems he's a very well-paid executive with a salary payment going into his account of just under fifteen thousand each month.'

Bovalino whistled. 'That's his *take-home* pay?'

Entwistle nodded. 'Yep, plus he received a one-off payment of a hundred and fifty grand in April.'

'Jesus,' Bovalino muttered. 'How the other half live.'

'I spoke to the HR manager at GBOG this morning, and she confirmed the hundred and fifty grand was his annual bonus. Their tax year runs April to March each year, and they pay all bonuses in April.'

'So that won't include the bonus for the Norwegian deal he's just brokered,' said Jones.

'No. She said he'll get that next April on top of any other bonuses,' confirmed Entwistle. 'Other than that, he and his wife have a joint mortgage on their house in Altrincham, which is worth close to a million, as well as a couple of houses they rent out in Fallowfield, student-lets, by the looks of it. They also have a joint will with everything passing directly to the other spouse in the event of either of their deaths, and into trust until the kids turn twenty-one, should they both die before they reach that age.'

'Sounds very sensible,' said Jones.

'Yep. Everything you'd expect from a finance expert, right?' Whistler replied.

'What about the phone records?' asked Phillips.

Entwistle minimised the current window and opened another folder. An Excel spreadsheet filled with dates and times, as well as incoming and outgoing calls, appeared on the big screen. 'I've run all the numbers listed through the sequencing software, and there's nothing unusual in any of his call patterns. No increased or decreased activity connected to any specific numbers over the last three months. I haven't had a chance to go back any further as yet, but I plan to do that next.'

'I'm not sure it'll do much good,' Phillips volleyed back. 'If his attacker had made direct contact with him, I'm pretty sure it'd have shown up in the three-month data.'

Entwistle nodded. 'No harm in running them for the last twelve months, anyway. I can get it set up this afternoon, and we should have the results by the morning.'

'Why not?' said Phillips, turning her attention to Bovalino. 'How did you get on with the CCTV around the park?'

The big man straightened. 'I've found footage that shows quite a few individuals leaving the park through various exits in the two hours immediately after the attack. Nobody that I recognise, and certainly no one wearing hoodies like the gang spotted messing with Grayson's car.'

'Probably ditched them in the park,' said Phillips.

'That's what I'd do,' Jones added.

'Do we know if uniform checked the bins in the park on the night of the attack?'

'No, they didn't,' said Entwistle. 'The search area didn't reach that far.'

'Well, get another team down there today and check them. I'm sure they've probably been emptied by now, but you never know, cuts to the council budgets might actually work in our favour for once.'

'I'll get straight onto it.' Bovalino made a note in his pad.

Phillips reclined in her seat in silence for a time, her lips pursed before sitting upright again. 'What we need is facial-recognition software to track anyone coming out of the park. That'd speed up the search.'

'The only people who have access to that would be the security services,' said Entwistle.

Phillips turned sideways to face him, her eyebrows raised. 'Such as the Counter Terrorism Unit.' She reached into her jacket pocket and pulled out the business card Flannery had given her. Grabbing her phone, she keyed in the number and pressed the green call icon on-screen.

He answered almost instantly. 'Flannery.'

'Danny. DCI Phillips. I'm hoping you can help me out.'

'Sure, what do you need?'

'I don't suppose you have access to facial-recognition software, do you?'

'Indeed, we do.'

'And what databases do you filter against?'

'All known terror cells as well as the PNC,' he said, referring to the Police National Computer.

'Excellent. If we send over some CCTV footage from the park near the attack, would you be able to run it through both?'

'You found something, then?'

'We're not sure. That's why we need the software.'

'Not a problem at all,' he assured her. 'I'll get one of my tech guys onto it as soon as it arrives. You should have my email on the business card I gave you.'

'Yeah, I'll get one of the team to send it over in the next hour. Thanks, Danny.' She ended the call and passed Flannery's business card to Bovalino. 'Pull together all the footage you have and send it over to Flannery. His guys will be ready to run it for us as soon as it transfers over.'

Bov nodded as he took the card and checked out the details.

'Right, guys,' said Phillips. 'We're three days into this investigation, and so far, we've got nothing to show for our efforts. I want us to rectify that ASAP. Okay?'

'Yes, guv,' Bovalino replied.

Jones and Entwistle nodded.

Phillips stood now. 'Jonesy, Whistler, I need you both for a second,' she said as casually as she could before heading out of the room.

A minute later, she closed the door to her office as Jones took a seat opposite her desk and Entwistle perched in his usual position on the adjacent cabinet.

Phillips sat forward and folded her arms on the desk. 'I wanted you to know that I've shared with Jonesy what happened with you, the Duval tapes and Fox.'

Entwistle's shoulders sagged as his chin dropped to his chest.

'As my second in command, it's his business to know everything about the squad.'

Jones cleared his throat.

Entwistle lifted his head to face him. 'I'm so sorry, Jonesy. I honestly didn't know what else to do.'

'You should have come to us as soon as Fox approached you,' said Jones.

'I know, I know.'

'The guv and I know exactly what she's like; we could have helped you.'

Phillips watched on in silence.

'I came seriously close to coming clean at one point when she first approached me, but at the last minute I panicked. She made it really clear my career was over if I didn't do as she asked.'

'What does she have on you?' Jones asked. 'What's her leverage?'

Entwistle took a beat before replying, his eyes filled with sadness. 'I can't say.'

Jones held his gaze and nodded. 'Secrets and lies will always come out, Whistler. Whatever it is, you're better off being out in front of it rather than trying to hide it away.'

'I know.' Entwistle nodded sagely. 'But I really can't tell you. I made a promise a very long time ago, and I swore I'd take it to my grave. I'm sure it could well come back to bite me, but I have to keep that promise.'

'That's your call, I guess,' replied Jones. 'But know this: trust is the bedrock of MCU, and it's hard earned. You understand that as well as anybody.'

Entwistle nodded as he placed his hand on the back of his head – the site of a serious injury he'd suffered while working his very first MCU case. 'I still have the scars to prove it.'

Jones continued, 'You're not quite back to ground zero, but you've got a lot of work to do to fully regain my trust. You made us all look stupid, sneaking around behind our backs.'

'I know, and I truly am sorry for that.'

'As it stands, though, if the guv thinks you're worthy of a second chance, then the same goes for me, too.'

Entwistle exhaled sharply. 'Thanks, Jonesy. I promise I won't let you down again.'

'You'd better not, believe me.'

Entwistle's gaze shifted to the office outside, where Bovalino was now sitting back at his desk. 'What about Bov, does he know?'

'Not yet,' Phillips replied flatly. 'But if we do ever find evidence that proves Fox is bent, then it'll likely come out. If and when that happens, we'll bring him into the loop. As it stands, we have too much riding on the Grayson investigation, and we need the team focused. So, for now, it stays between us. Okay?'

'Of course.'

'We're getting nowhere fast at the moment,' said Phillips. 'Let's put this behind us and move on, shall we?'

Jones nodded as he stood up from the chair.

'Yes, guv,' Entwistle replied, matching him.

'Right, then,' added Phillips. 'Time to get cracking.'

12

By the middle of Friday afternoon, a carnival atmosphere had begun to build across Manchester city centre in anticipation of that night's game at Old Trafford between England and Italy, a European Championship qualifier between two giants of European football. Tens of thousands of Italian fans had flooded into town in the last twenty-four hours, and every corner of the city was awash with the blue shirts and tricolour flags synonymous with the Italian national side.

The sun was high in the sky, and a nervous excitement gnawed at Tex's gut as he guided Clem and Squeaky to a relatively secluded area on the patch of grass sandwiched between the Museum of Football and the Royal College of Music, a popular spot in hot weather, located just a hundred metres from Victoria train station. In an effort to blend in with the crowd, each member of the gang was wearing a white and blue England replica jersey, as well as sunglasses – in part to shield their eyes from the bright sunshine, but mainly to help conceal their identities. In addition to the shirts and glasses, Tex's face was hidden under a black AC/DC baseball cap. Clem had chosen a shoulder-length black wig to change her appearance, while Squeaky was sporting a bucket hat emblazoned with a St George's cross and pulled low over his forehead.

Tex scanned the area around him to ensure they couldn't be overheard. A large video screen attached to the nearby Corn Exchange – a Baroque-style Victorian building that contained a host of restaurants and a hotel – was blasting out current pop music mixed in with footage of some of the England football team's greatest moments in the build-up to the game. Satisfied no one was listening, Tex turned his attention back to the team. 'Remember, code names only. We have to be vigilant.'

Clem and Squeaky nodded.

'The orders have come through from Charlie,' Tex continued. 'We go again tonight as planned.'

Clem shook her head slightly, then averted her gaze.

'What's wrong with you?' Tex asked.

She continued staring at the nearby crowd basking in the sunshine of the adjacent Exchange Square, before turning her attention to him once more. 'I'm just not sure about all this. I mean, after what happened on Saturday, seeing that guy burning in his car. I didn't sign up for that.'

'So what did you sign up for?'

'Making a difference. Trying to save our future.'

'Which is exactly what we're doing,' replied Tex.

She shook her head. 'After seeing what happened to the guy in the car, I'm wondering if we're any better than the people we're trying to stop.'

'That's bullshit, Clem. We're doing all this for the greater good. They're doing what they do to satisfy their greed and desire for power.'

As was usually the case when they argued, Squeaky acted if he were somewhere else.

'I get the cause,' she replied. 'I really do. I'm just not sure the end justifies the means. Surely there has to be another way. A more peaceful way of making the change needed.'

'You know as well as I do, there isn't.' Tex glanced left and right before continuing, 'We've seen what happens with the peaceful protests: absolutely nothing. Stop the Drilling have been chucking paint around at events all over the country for years now, and oil production continues unabated. That's why Charlie started Terra – to take the fight to the next level. To hurt those who continue to abuse the planet so much that they have to listen.'

'But what if we get caught?' asked Clem. 'We're talking about murder. That's life in prison.'

He sat forward now and placed his hand on her knee. 'But we won't get caught. Not if we all stick to the plan. The boss has it all worked out. If we do exactly as he says, we can get away without a trace, like ghosts, moving in the shadows.'

Clem's bottom lip began to tremble as she looked back at him in silence for a time. 'If this is all about making people sit up and take notice, then why hasn't he taken credit for it? So far, nobody has a clue who planted the bomb, which totally defeats the object of what we're trying to do.'

'He wants to wait a while longer until he goes public,' said Tex.

'For what? If he really wants people to take Terra seriously, he should be shouting from the rooftops about it. About *Terra*.'

'All in good time,' Tex replied. 'He knows what he's doing.'

'It does seem a bit weird, like.' Squeaky finally joined the conversation. 'We took a massive risk on Saturday to then say nothing about it.'

Tex tried hard to maintain his composure. He was keen to activate tonight's plan rather than sit here and debate what had already been done. 'We have been told to wait to go public, so we wait. In the meantime, we action phase two this evening.'

'I don't think I can,' said Clem. 'I'm sorry, but I've changed my mind on all this.'

Tex glared at her, his jaw clenching with frustration. 'You've got no choice. If you walk away now, then you're as good as dead. Charlie will see to that.'

Clem recoiled. 'Says who?'

'Says Charlie,' Tex replied.

'What you talking about?' Squeaky cut in.

Tex averted his gaze.

'What do you mean we're as good as dead?' pressed Squeaky.

Tex exhaled loudly. 'He told me that once Operation Wild Fire was in play, if any of us tried to back out or compromise any of the future ops, he'd have no option but to nullify the cell.'

'Nullify the cell?' Squeaky's face twisted. 'What the fuck does he mean by that?'

'He meant we'd be his next victims.' Clem glared at Tex. 'Didn't he?'

'Yeah,' said Tex.

'Are you fucking kidding me?' asked Squeaky.

'No. I'm not.' Tex swallowed hard. 'Terra has a whole

bunch of active cells operating all over the UK. Any one of them could come after us.'

'And you're just telling us this *now*?' Squeaky was incredulous.

Clem bit her top lip as she fought back tears.

'I can't believe you didn't tell us this, man,' Squeaky raged. 'You're bang out of order.'

'Maybe so, but if I had, you'd never have gotten involved, would you?'

'And for good reason,' Clem growled.

'Damn fucking right,' added Squeaky.

Tex checked there was no one within earshot. 'Look, I'm sorry I kept that from you, but I couldn't do any of this without you both, and like I say, there's no need to worry. Charlie has everything worked out in minute detail. He knows where all the cameras are around tonight's location and made sure our exit routes will keep us out of sight of them. So as long as we hold our nerve and stay focused, we'll be home free.'

Clem glowered at him.

'Fuck's sake,' Squeaky muttered, shaking his head.

'Come on, guys,' said Tex. 'Remember the Terra mantra, "No retreat. No surrender".'

Clem was close to tears now. 'Jesus, Tex. This isn't a fucking game!'

He straightened. 'No, it's not. This is life or death.'

'Murder more like,' she spat back.

'It's not murder...' Tex checked himself, glancing left and right before lowering his voice. 'It's war. And if we don't fight for the greater good, for the future of our kids, then who will?'

Clem stared back at him in silence.

He held her gaze, then checked his watch: 4.03 p.m. 'Look, like it or not, we're in this to the end now, so come on. It's time to move out.'

NOT MUCH MORE THAN half an hour later, at just after 4.45 p.m., they arrived at St John's Gardens.

Standing together under the trees at the edge of the public park, away from any prying eyes, Tex ran through the plan one last time. 'As we know, Nixon is a creature of habit. He leaves the office every night at approximately 5.30 p.m. and enters through the south gate of this park five minutes later, on his way to catch the train at Deansgate station. We'll each take up our positions at the three remaining gates, north, east and west, and when I give the signal, we'll converge on him where the paths meet. We strike fast and hard and make our escape through the agreed exits. Clem, you leave by the south, Squeaky the east gate, and I'll take the west exit. No matter what happens, don't stop and don't look back. Got it?'

Clem and Squeaky hesitantly glanced at each other.

'Got it?' Tex growled.

Squeaky nodded.

Tex locked on Clem. 'Got it?'

'Yeah,' she said without conviction.

Tex continued, 'Right. Now remember, it's vital we follow our agreed exit routes to stand the best chance of staying off any CCTV cameras, okay?'

Clem and Squeaky nodded in unison.

'Then we stay dark for twenty-four hours. No contact whatsoever.'

'Why?' asked Clem.

'That's just the way Charlie wants it.' Tex checked his watch again. 'Right, he'll be here in seven minutes. Let's get ready.'

Right on cue Nixon appeared. He was a stocky man, almost as wide as he was tall. He was wearing a charcoal suit over a white shirt, which was open at the neck. His head was shaved, and his fleshy cheekbones and cauliflower ears suggested he had – or maybe even still – played rugby on a regular basis.

As he made his way through the park, Tex nodded and set off walking.

Clem and Squeaky reluctantly followed suit.

Thirty seconds later Nixon moved into range.

Walking directly towards him, Tex flicked open the knife in his right hand, which he'd had hidden behind his back. His heart felt like it would burst out of his chest as his adrenaline spiked.

Squeaky approached Nixon from behind, his arm in a similar pose.

Clem moved on him from the right.

Tex dropped his head and, as he passed Nixon, rammed the blade into his torso, once, twice, three times.

Nixon cried out in agony as Squeaky hit him from behind and Clem from the side.

Hardly breaking stride, Tex slipped the blade in his jeans pocket and continued walking at pace.

Behind him, he heard Nixon fall to the ground, shouting for help, telling anyone and everyone that he had been stabbed.

Tex continued, focused on the exit, trying his best to

resist the overwhelming urge to run. He could no longer see Clem or Squeaky.

From the shouts and screams that echoed around the park, it was evident that bystanders were now rushing to Nixon's aid.

As Tex stepped out onto the street, he caught sight of a man out of the corner of his eye, running at lightning pace to his right. Glancing across, his heart sank when he spotted the man chasing after Squeaky, shouting at him to stop.

Shit. Shit. Shit.

Tex continued to walk at pace, following his designated exit route, all the time glancing surreptitiously to his right.

The man had now caught up with Squeaky, who was doing his best to fight him off as another have-a-go hero rushed towards them both.

Fuck. For a split second Tex contemplated changing direction and racing to his friend's aid, but that could never be part of the plan. Charlie had been crystal clear on that. Casualties were a consequence of war, and it was better that he make his escape now, in order to fight another day. Squeaky was on his own, a foot soldier and a necessary sacrifice.

As the shouting and screaming ramped up another notch to his right, as more of the passing public got involved, Tex dropped his head again, walking away as fast as he could without drawing attention to himself.

13

The following day, Phillips was sitting on the back deck of the house, wearing her dressing gown, pyjamas and slippers, drinking coffee in the early morning sunshine with Adam, who in turn was leafing through the Saturday edition of *The Times*. An Abba medley was playing on the radio, and aside from that, Chorlton seemed unusually quiet but for the sound of distant planes and the light hum of nearby traffic. Floss had joined them a few minutes ago and now lay asleep on the grass, stretched out, purring away like a tiny pneumatic drill. Bliss.

'Any news on your application?' she asked.

Adam looked up from the paper. 'I've pretty much filled in the forms online. Actually, I wouldn't mind you taking a look at it for me, just to make sure I've not missed anything obvious.'

'Sure, I can do it later today if you like?'

'Perfect,' he replied. 'That way I can send it off this weekend and forget about it for a while. It's all I can think about at the minute.'

'You really want this job, don't you?' she asked.

'Yeah, I do,' he said as he took a sip of coffee. 'I'm not sure if I'm going through a bit of a midlife thing, but I'm frightened life's gonna pass me by and, before I know it, I'll be sleepwalking into retirement.'

'Steady on, babe.' Phillips giggled. 'You're only a couple of years older than me. Try not to pension us both off, not just yet.'

Adam smiled softly. 'After what happened to me, time feels too precious to waste. Seeing the things you do every day, I'm sure you understand.'

'Sadly, I do.' Phillips placed her mug down on the table. 'Life is terrifyingly fragile.'

A companionable silence descended, and soon Phillips's attention was drawn back to the radio as Abba faded out and a news jingle signalled the start of the 9 a.m. bulletin.

'*It's nine o'clock, and these are this hour's top stories. A man was stabbed in the city centre last night in what is believed to be an unprovoked attack...*'

Phillips stepped up from the chair and moved into the kitchen to turn it up.

The bulletin continued, '*Paramedics were called to the scene just after 5.30 p.m., and the forty-eight-year-old man was taken to the MRI, where he later died of his injuries. The police are asking for any witness to come forward...*'

Phillips sighed, then switched the radio off before returning to her seat outside.

'What were you saying about life being fragile?' Adam said, shaking his head.

'Sodding knives,' spat Phillips. 'They're bloody everywhere, and it doesn't matter what we do, we can't seem to solve the problem.'

'It's the same right across the country, love. I was reading a report the other week showing the number of patients admitted to UK A&E departments with knife wounds is up almost thirty percent year on year, with fatalities up by almost twenty-five percent.'

'It's a complete waste of life,' replied Phillips.

'I'm just grateful guns aren't legal in this country. I'd hate to think what damage could be done if any Tom, Dick or Harry could pick one of those up on the high street.'

Just then, Phillips's mobile began to vibrate on the table next to her coffee cup. A glance at the screen told her it was Carter. She held it up so Adam could see. 'This can't be good news,' she said before answering, 'Morning, sir.'

Adam poured them both fresh coffees from the cafetière.

'Jane, sorry to bother you on a weekend, but it's urgent.'

Her heart sank, and she closed her eyes for a long moment before answering, 'What are we looking at?'

'Did you hear about the fatal stabbing in the city last night?'

Phillips opened her eyes, her brow furrowed as her gaze locked on Adam's. 'I did, just now on the radio, as it happens.'

'Fox wants us to handle it.'

'A stabbing? With respect, sir, if it's gang related, then it's down to Serious Crimes, not us. And besides, we're stretched as it is, chasing our tails looking for the car bombers.'

'Sorry, Jane. Fox called me ten minutes ago and insisted you take it on as SIO. The victim's name hasn't been released to the public, but he has been identified as Robert Nixon. Based on initial witness statements, it looks like he was attacked by a gang of three who could well be a match for our Cheadle bombers.'

Phillips straightened. 'Seriously?'

'Yeah. Not only that but, like Grayson, Nixon was also a high-

powered executive – CEO of Opus Air, in fact – and a very well-known figure in the Manchester business community. Apparently, he played golf on occasion with the PCC's husband, so Fox is keen to get out in front of this one before it gets out to the press.'

'Of course she is,' said Phillips sardonically as she returned her gaze to Adam.

'And there's one more thing too.'

'Go on.'

'It seems there's an Energy Industry Expo at the Lowry happening next week, and Nixon was due to speak at it. The great and the good of the world's biggest energy companies are flying in, and the fact that one of the keynote speakers has been murdered in broad daylight doesn't paint the city in a very good light. Well, according to Fox, at least.'

Phillips could easily imagine the conversation Carter had had with Fox. If the chief constable had her mind set on MCU taking on the case, then resistance was futile. 'What would you like me to do, sir?'

'Fox wants a real show of force, so I need you and Jones down at the crime scene as quick as you can.'

'Which is where?' asked Phillips. 'I switched the radio off before they gave the location of the attack.'

'St John's Gardens, just off Deansgate.'

'I know it.'

'Evans and the team have been there since the wee small hours. He can brief you on what we have so far.'

'Understood. I'll call Jonesy now.'

'Thanks, Jane.' Carter sighed. *'Look, I know this will totally screw up your weekend, but I'll make it up to you at some point.'*

'Don't worry, sir,' she said, with a wistful glance at Adam reading the paper. 'It goes with the territory.'

'*I'd better let you get on,*' said Carter. '*Keep me posted, and thanks again.*'

Phillips ended the call.

'I'm guessing from all that, I won't be seeing you for the rest of the day, then?' asked Adam.

'Looks that way. Sorry, babe,' she said as she clicked on Jones's number. 'Time to share the bad news.'

14

'Mission accomplished,' said Charlie via the encrypted link.

Despite the distortion in his voice, Tex could tell he was smiling.

'It's headline news this morning. All local media outlets are talking about the fact that Nixon is dead, plus some of the nationals.'

Tex was struggling to control his rapid heart rate as he prepared to debrief on last night's compromised mission.

'You and the team are to be congratulated.'

'Thank you,' said Tex, 'but we have a problem.'

'Oh?'

'We may have suffered a casualty on our side.'

'What do you mean, *may* have suffered a casualty?' Charlie's voice was suddenly agitated. 'Who?'

'Squeaky.'

'What happened?'

Tex paused before answering, 'I think he was captured.'

'What? You mean you don't know for sure?'

'No. I don't. We followed the plan to the letter: we hit Nixon in unison and made our escape using different routes, but as we were leaving the park, a member of the public chased after Squeaky, and they got into a scuffle. I was trying to see what was going on without drawing attention to myself, and then another bystander joined in. The last thing I saw was the two guys wading into Squeaky, who was doing his best to fend them off.'

'I see,' replied Charlie flatly.

'Has there been any police chatter about him being arrested?'

'No, but that doesn't mean he wasn't.'

'So, what do we do now?' asked Tex.

'Have you reached out to him in any way since last night?'

'No,' Tex replied. 'As ordered, we all agreed to have no contact of any kind until tomorrow.'

'If he has been arrested, will he talk?'

'I don't think so.'

'You'd better hope for all your sakes that he doesn't,' spat Charlie. 'I warned you at the very beginning of all this, there would be no room for mistakes. If he utters so much as one word about Terra and our plans – just one word – it'll be the end of all you, including Clem. I make no concession for the fairer sex. Do I make myself clear?'

'Crystal.' Tex nodded furiously. 'And he won't talk, I'm sure of it.'

Charlie's avatar stared out from the screen, but he remained silent for a time before speaking. 'It pays to remember we're at war, soldier, and we must all make sacrifices to ensure we achieve our ultimate goal.'

'I understand.'

'The war we're waging has only just begun. Can I count on you to continue the fight to preserve our world for the next generation?'

'Absolutely. I know what's at stake, and I won't let you down.'

Charlie nodded. 'Good. In that case, I'll see if I can find out what happened to Squeaky. In the meantime, you and Clem are to remain dark until tomorrow as planned.'

'Understood.'

'You both need to stay alert and be ready. I'll send details of the next target in a few days.'

'We'll be waiting,' said Tex.

A second later, the link was severed.

15

After a quick shower, Phillips was soon on the road, arriving at the crime scene at bang on 10.15 a.m. A host of police patrol cars with flashing lights as well as forensic vehicles were positioned around the perimeter of St John's Gardens.

As she pulled the Mini Cooper to a stop next to the railed park, she spotted Jones's squad car in her rear-view mirror, approaching from behind. A second later as he parked up in the adjacent spot to her left, she waved, then jumped out of the car into the summer sunshine.

'Morning, guv,' he said, sounding brighter than she had anticipated.

'You're in a surprisingly good mood, given the circumstances. I thought you'd be seriously pissed off having to work on a Saturday.'

Jones shrugged. 'That's because you're comparing my twenty-year marriage to your two-year relationship. Whereas you still yearn for time off with Adam, I'll do whatever I can to get time away from Sarah and the girls.'

Phillips chuckled. 'I don't believe that for a second.'

'Maybe you're right,' Jones replied with a wink. 'In all honesty, I've long since given up getting annoyed when we're called in unexpectedly. We're murder detectives – comes with the job.'

'I can't imagine Sarah was quite so philosophical when you told her.'

'Not quite, no,' said Jones. 'Put it this way, I'm rather hoping we'll be working *all* weekend, because I'm going to need every bit of overtime I can get to pay for the fancy meal I promised her as a peace offering.'

Phillips glanced sideways into the park at the blue and white police tape that surrounded the location of last night's knife attack. 'Well, I think you might be in luck, if that's the case. From what Carter said on the phone this morning, I have a funny feeling this is not going to be a straightforward stabbing.'

Jones followed her gaze. 'Yeah, I think you might be right.'

A minute later, a uniformed officer standing guard at the entrance of the park lifted the police tape so they could pass underneath before making their way to where Evans and his team were hard at work, suited and booted in their forensic overalls.

Evans turned to face them as they approached, pulling down his hood and removing his face mask. 'Morning.' He smiled brightly. 'I have to say, I certainly wasn't expecting to see you guys assigned to this one.'

'Neither were we,' replied Phillips. 'So, what are we looking at, Andy?'

'Robert Nixon. Forty-eight-year-old IC1 male. Stabbed multiple times in the chest, stomach and back. Treated here at the scene by paramedics before being transferred to A&E at the MRI. Died of his injuries soon after.'

'Any trace evidence of value?'

Evans pointed towards a dark red patch – almost black now – on the path that led further into the park. 'As you'd expect, given his injuries, we have large quantities of blood where he fell to the ground. Also a few fibres, which may have come from his attackers, but we can't be certain at this stage. Naturally we'll check them for any DNA and see if there's a match in the system.'

Jones rubbed his chin. 'Doesn't give us a huge amount to go on, does it?'

'No, but this might be of interest.' Evans pointed towards Clara, who was crouching down a few feet away. 'We also found a partial shoe print on the edge of the flower bed. When I say shoe print, it looks more like it came from a trainer of some kind. Clara's in the process of making a cast from it as we speak.'

Phillips moved to get a closer look. 'I wouldn't hold my breath if I were you. This is a popular park, especially on sunny days like yesterday. It could belong to any one of a thousand different people.'

Evans shrugged. 'You never know, Jane.'

Phillips nodded absentmindedly.

'There's also blood at the location of the second knife attack,' Evans added.

She flinched before staring at him. 'What second knife attack?'

Evans's brow furrowed. 'You didn't know?'

'No.'

'Follow me.' Evans guided them out of the park and

through a nearby gate onto the street where a small area of the pavement had been cordoned off with police tape.

'So what happened here?' asked Phillips.

'Witnesses said they saw a gang of three people set about Nixon,' Evans replied. 'Two males and one female, by the looks of it. After the attack, it seems they each made their escape by different gates, and on the way out, one of the gang was confronted by two members of the public, just here, but he managed to get away.'

Phillips gazed down at the bloodstains on the pavement as Evans continued, 'He turned whatever blade he'd used on Nixon onto the two men who tried to stop him. I don't have the full details, but from what I understand, he stabbed them both a number of times before they let go.'

'Were they badly hurt?' said Jones.

'You're probably better talking to the uniform boys who were first on scene, but as far as I'm aware, their injuries were minor. Slash – as opposed to knife – wounds.'

'It would have been nice to know all this before we arrived,' said Jones, his tone facetious.

'Par for the course these days,' replied Phillips. 'Thanks to Fox's staff cuts, the left hand has no idea what the right hand is doing half the time.'

Jones nodded. 'I'll head over and get the victims' names from uniform. With a bit of luck, they got close enough to give us a detailed description of the suspect.'

'Okay,' said Phillips. 'And make a note of all the surrounding buildings with CCTV fitted.'

'Will do,' he replied, then turned and headed off back towards the patrol vehicles.

'Any idea who's doing Nixon's postmortem?' she asked.

Evans shook his head. 'I don't, sorry.'

'Not to worry.' Phillips pulled her phone from her pocket. 'Let me know as soon as you get anything concrete that I can share with the rest of the team, won't you?'

'Of course,' said Evans before heading back into the park.

Next Phillips sent a short message to Dr Tanvi Chakrabortty, the chief pathologist.

> Hi Tan. Sorry to bother you on a Saturday, but I was hoping you could tell me who's handling the Nixon PM next week and when it's scheduled. I'd like to sit in. Thanks. J.

A whoosh signalled the message had been sent, so she headed back to the car in search of Jonesy.

At that moment, her phone began to vibrate in her hand. 'This is Phillips.'

'Jane. Danny Flannery. Looks like we've got a facial-recognition hit on the cameras around Bruntwood Park you asked us to look at.'

'Wow, that was fast.' Phillips spied Jones walking back towards her. 'Is *everyone* working the weekend?'

'Weekend?' Flannery chuckled. *'They don't exist in counter terrorism.'*

'Nor Major Crimes at the moment.'

'Anyway, the guy's name is Adrian Firth. IC1 male, twenty years of age. Got seven years for arson when he was just fifteen and was released on licence nine months ago after serving three and half.'

'And what time was he spotted?' Phillips asked.

'Er...' Flannery took a moment to answer. *'Looks like it was thirty minutes after the bomb went off.'*

'I don't suppose you managed to pull his full file, did you?'

'I did, actually.'

'You are a legend, Danny,' said Phillips.

He chuckled. *'Always happy to help when it comes to rounding up bad guys. I'm emailing it over as we speak, along with the stills from the CCTV we used to find him in the system.'*

'Thanks, Danny. I owe you one.'

'My pleasure,' he replied. *'If you need anything else, just shout.'*

'Oh, I will. Don't you worry about that. You're a good man to know.'

'Take care, Jane,' he added before ending the call.

Just then Jones arrived. 'Right, so I've got the name and address for Robert Nixon's wife, Carrie, which is out in Prestbury.'

'We should probably get over there as quick as we can,' replied Phillips.

'Yeah. I also got the name and addresses of the two bystanders who were stabbed in the melee, so I called Bov, and he's happy to come in and speak to them both.'

'Top man.'

Jones thumbed over his shoulder. 'Uniform are doing a sweep of the area, looking for any private CCTV cameras. Once we have the names of each of the businesses, Whistler's going to try to track down last night's footage.'

'So the full team's now working a Saturday?'

Jones put his notebook away and smiled. 'Had to be done, boss.'

Phillips returned his smile as she opened her phone and pulled up the email from Flannery. 'The anti-terror boys have found a match on CCTV footage from the park.'

'Really? Who?'

She presented the mugshot on-screen. 'This guy, Adrian Firth. Was given seven years for arson. Served three and a half and was released eighteen months ago on licence. Says here he lives in Rusholme.'

'Arson?' Jones's face wrinkled. 'Really? I'm not sure I'm buying that.'

'Why, what you thinking?'

'Well, I mean, I can see the link between the bomb and the fire it caused, of course, but it's the running away from the scene that doesn't make sense to me—'

'Because arsonists always stay to watch their handiwork,' Phillips cut in. 'It's where the thrill comes from, right?'

'Exactly. Not to mention the fact arsonists tend to be loners. It's unlikely you'd ever see them working in a gang like the guys who did Grayson.'

'I hear what you're saying, but we still need to check him out.' Phillips glanced at her watch. 'Ideally, I'd like to speak to Nixon's wife first, but as we're so close to Rusholme, why don't we check out what Firth has to say for himself, and then we can head over to Prestbury.'

'Sounds like a plan, guv.'

Just then Phillips's phone beeped, signalling a message had landed. Checking the screen, she could see it was from Chakrabortty.

> Hi Jane. You're not bothering me at all. I'm working today, anyway. Catching up on paperwork. Re Nixon's PM. That's me, 9 a.m. Monday. See you then and in the meantime, enjoy the rest of your weekend – if you can – :-) Tan

'Everything all right?' said Jones.

'Yeah, just Tan letting me know Nixon's PM is happening first thing Monday morning.'

'Ooh goodie.' Jones hated postmortems and turned a lighter shade of grey every time he attended one.

She patted him on the arm and grinned. 'It's all right, mate. I'll look after you.'

16

According to his file, Firth lived in a second-floor council flat in the middle of Rusholme, a suburb located just three miles south of the city centre, where crime rates were high and employment was low.

As Phillips and Jones walked side by side along the exposed, second-floor communal walkway, they could hear a cacophony of different TVs blaring out through the open windows of the surrounding flats – a frenetic mix of different programmes at varying volumes. Dogs barked in the distance, and groups of kids could be heard shouting between one another on the concrete area below.

'There's no place like home,' said Jones as they reached flat number twenty-five.

Phillips scanned the area around them. 'Quite.'

'Let's see if anyone's in, shall we?' Jones rapped his knuckles on the flimsy front door.

A minute passed with no answer, so Jones knocked again. Harder this time.

Thirty seconds later they heard the sound of a chain being released inside, and the door opened.

'Yeah? Whaddaya want?' A woman – Phillips placed her in her mid-thirties – wearing a white vest and denim skirt, stood staring back at them. Her hair appeared to have been dyed jet-black, and her makeup was thickly layered, so much so that the skin on her face appeared almost orange.

Phillips presented her ID. 'DCI Phillips and DI Jones. We need to talk to Adrian Firth.'

The woman sneered. 'What's the little bastard been up to now?' Her speech was slurred, and she'd clearly been drinking despite the fact it was only just after midday.

'And you are?' asked Phillips.

'Nicki, his mum, worst luck. Nothing but trouble that boy—'

'Is Adrian in?' Jones cut her off.

Nicki pulled a pack of cigarettes from the pocket of her skirt and placed one between her lips before pulling out a lighter. 'No. He's not,' she slurred before sparking up.

Phillips was already tiring of the woman. 'Do you know where he is?'

Thick smoke billowed from her nostrils and mouth as she spoke. 'With that bitch of a girlfriend, Kat, most likely.'

'And where might that be?'

'Moss Side.'

Phillips exhaled sharply. 'Any chance you could be a little more specific?'

Taking another long drag on the cigarette, Nicki ran her hand through her lank hair. 'Opposite the Claremont pub. The house with the old washing machines out front.'

Phillips forced a thin smile. 'Well, I suppose that's better than nothing.'

'His dad left me because of that little shit, you know,' Nicki muttered. 'We were all right until Adi came along and ruined everything. After that, he wanted nowt to do with me. Buggered off with another woman, he did.'

Phillips had heard the same self-pitying bullshit a hundred times before and was in no mood to listen to it again. Glancing at Jones, she nodded her intention to leave.

He nodded his agreement.

'Thanks for your time, Nicki,' she said. 'We'll let you get back to whatever you were doing.'

Nicki appeared not to have heard her. 'That boy's a total waste of space. I mean, heaven forbid he should get a job and help out with the bills or buy me a pack of fags once in a while.'

Phillips didn't respond. Instead, she walked briskly back along the walkway, with Jones following close behind.

———

DIRECTLY OPPOSITE THE Claremont pub in Moss Side, Phillips and Jones stood on the pavement outside the redbrick terraced house with their backs to a bustling Claremont Road. The tiny yard to the front of the property contained what appeared to be at least four disused washing machines, as well as parts and spares for many more.

'Looks like this is the one, boss,' said Jones.

Phillips nodded, then stepped up to the front door and pressed the old bell fixed to the adjacent brickwork, which rattled on the other side.

As they waited for a response, Phillips leaned back and took in the rest of the house.

Just then the net curtains in the window to the right of

the front door were pulled back, and a girl in her late teens or early twenties peered out.

Jones, standing closest, flashed his ID. 'We need a word.'

The girl stared out in silence for a moment before disappearing back behind the curtain.

A minute later, the door opened, and the sickly sweet smell of cannabis wafted out of the house. The same girl from the window stood barefoot in the doorway, dressed in black leggings and a blue hooded top. She couldn't have been more than five feet tall with pink hair and a plethora of piercings protruding from her face and ears. 'Yeah?'

'You must be Kat,' said Phillips.

The girl stared back in silence.

'We're looking for Adrian Firth.'

'He ain't 'ere.'

'I see.' Phillips folded her arms. 'Mind if we come in and see for ourselves?'

'I do, as it goes.'

Jones took a step forward and sniffed loudly. 'What's that smell?'

The girl stared back defiantly. 'Dunno, I've got hay fever. Can't smell anything.'

Jones sniffed again, then glanced at Phillips. 'Smells like cannabis to me. Doesn't it you, guv?'

Having worked with him for so long, she knew where he was going with this and was happy to play along. 'Yeah. It does. Skunk if I'm not mistaken.'

'Remind me, what's the maximum prison term for possession of a Class B drug with intent to supply?' he asked.

'Well, as I recall, according to section five of the misuse of drugs act, 1971, I think it's fourteen years.'

Jones stared intently at the girl. '*Fourteen* years. And what with your boyfriend being on licence n' all, it doesn't bode well for his chances of staying out of the nick now, does it? So with that in mind, we'll start again, shall we? Are you Kat?'

She nodded.

'And can we come inside? Or do I need to get my mates from the drug squad down here to turn this place over?'

A snarl formed on the girl's top lip before she relented and opened the door wide. 'Be my guest.'

Once inside, Phillips followed Jones along the darkened hallway to the back of the house, where it sounded as if someone was playing a video game at full volume.

As they moved into the back room, Phillips instantly recognised Adrian Firth. He was lying flat on a battered old couch, manipulating a games control in his hand. The smell of cannabis was even more pungent in this part of the house.

'Adrian Firth?' she asked.

'Who wants to know?' His eyes remained fixed on the screen.

Even lying down, it was evident that Firth was a tall, muscular young man. His shaven head, coupled with the intricate tattoo that encircled his neck, gave him an air of menace.

Jones walked over to the TV and pulled the plug out of the wall, killing the picture and sound instantly.

'Hey, you prick!' Firth suddenly sat upright on the sofa. 'Man was up to level ten, innit.' His accent was unmistakably Manchester, mixed in with the affected style of a London gangster; it was a way of talking that seemed to have become the norm for wannabe bad boys across the UK these days.

Jones turned to face him. 'Remember you're on licence, so show some respect, please.'

Firth glowered back as Kat dropped onto the sofa with him.

Phillips moved into the middle of the room to stand next to Jones. 'Where were you on Saturday night?'

'Don't remember.'

Kat giggled, drawing a self-congratulatory grin from Firth.

'Between eight and nine o'clock,' added Phillips.

Firth shrugged. 'Like I say, man, don't remember.'

Phillips fished her phone from her pocket, opened up the email attachment from Flannery and presented Firth with the CCTV still of him leaving the park. 'This is you walking out of Brentwood Park at 8.50 p.m. What were you doing there at that time?'

'Going for a walk.'

'Where?'

'Nowhere. Just exercising, innit?'

'Funny, you don't look the exercising kind to me,' quipped Jones.

'Man gotta look after himself, bruv. You know what I'm saying?' Firth looked Jones up and down, then burst out laughing. 'Oh, my life. Of course you don't.'

Jones glared back.

Ignoring the cockiness, Phillips continued, 'Have you ever been to the David Lloyd leisure club at Cheadle?'

'Every week, innit.'

Firth and Kat both laughed again.

Phillips was tiring of his game so cut to the chase. 'You may have heard on the news that a bomb was detonated under a car outside David Lloyd just before 8.30 p.m. on

Saturday, causing it to burst into flames and inflicting life-threatening injuries on the driver.'

Firth shrugged. 'So?'

'So, *you*, Mr Firth – with your record for arson – were spotted in the vicinity of said bombing just thirty minutes later. Which means *you* are a serious person of interest in an attempted murder investigation.'

Firth's face fell, and the blood seemed to drain out of him now. The cockiness was suddenly evaporating.

Kat was silenced too.

Phillips continued, 'That's a life sentence, Adrian.'

Firth swallowed hard but said nothing.

'If you think a three-and-a-half stretch was tough in that young offenders holiday park,' Jones cut in, 'wait till you get to Hawk Green. There's some seriously nasty bastards in there.'

'Yeah. *Proper* gangsters,' added Phillips. 'Who would eat you – you little wannabe – for breakfast.'

'That fire was nuffin to do with me, right?' Firth finally found his voice again.

'And what about six o'clock last night?' Jones asked. 'Where were you then?'

Firth flashed a knowing smile. 'Here, all night, together.'

'Is that true, Kat?' said Phillips.

'Yeah.' She giggled. 'We was together all night, making sweet lurve.'

Firth straightened in the chair, his confidence clearly returning. 'Look, lady, I know my rights.'

'Oh, I've no doubt you do,' said Phillips.

'And unless you're here to arrest me, I'd like you to piss off, right now.'

Phillips didn't respond as she turned to Jones. 'Get the girl's details. I'll meet you outside.'

Jones nodded.

'I'll be seeing you, Adrian.' Phillips glared at Firth one last time before heading out of the room and back towards the front door.

17

Sitting in the driver's seat of the Mini, Phillips stared out at the house as the net curtain in the front window twitched. She couldn't see who was hiding behind it, but she guessed it would likely be Kat, checking to see if they had gone.

Jones, who was parked up in the squad car in front of her, signalled his intention to join the traffic running along to their right. Determined to travel in convoy, Phillips fired her ignition and a moment later tucked in behind him as he pulled out and accelerated away in the direction of Prestbury.

A few minutes had passed when her hands-free buzzed into life – Jones was calling. She hit the green icon on-screen. 'What's up?'

'Just thinking about Firth, the cocky little shit.'

'What about him?'

'I'm sitting here trying to figure out when it was that all these northern lads started pretending they come from London?'

Phillips could see him glancing in his rear-view mirror ahead. 'I dunno,' she said, 'but at the same time, I wouldn't quite describe how he speaks as cockney. More plastic gangster.'

'All that "man" and "bruv" and "innit". Makes my bloody teeth itch.' His car began to slow up ahead as they approached a set of traffic lights on red. 'As far as I'm concerned, if you're born and bred in Manchester, you should talk like you bloody come from Manchester – not sodding London.'

Phillips chuckled as she pulled the Mini up behind the now stationary squad car. 'Sounds like someone's getting grumpy in their old age.'

'God. Don't. Sarah said the same thing to me just the other week.'

The light turned green, and they set off again in unison.

'Seriously, though, guv. Little shits like Firth piss me off. I mean, the guy's out on licence, yet he made no effort to hide the fact he's smoking weed in there. No bloody respect or shame, whatsoever. I've a good mind to call Sammy K, over at the drug squad, and tell him all about it. Firth'd be back inside before lights out.'

'I hear you, and I get your frustration, but I'd rather keep the little scumbag to ourselves for now. If he gets sent back to the nick, then it just complicates things.'

'I guess you're right.'

'For now, it's better to let him think he's won so we can keep an eye on him. See where he goes, who he connects with.'

'Okay,' said Jones as he moved into the outside lane of the Princess Parkway. 'If that's how you want to play it, boss. Oh, and by the way, the girl's name is Katarina Holmes. I've asked

Whistler to take a look at her file. If she's been hanging out with Firth for any length of time, I'm pretty sure she'll be in the system too.'

'Yeah, no doubt.' Phillips followed him into the outside lane.

They each said nothing for the next few minutes as they headed south towards Prestbury. Finally, as they approached the turn-off for the A34, Phillips broke the silence. 'So, what do we know about Nixon's widow?'

'Nothing at all, really, other than the fact her name's Carrie.'

'I take it uniform have done the official death notification?' asked Phillips.

'They didn't have to. Apparently, she was called into the hospital last night, not long after the attack, and was there when he died.'

'Jesus,' whispered Phillips. 'It doesn't bear thinking about, does it?'

'Life's really shit at times.'

'Yeah, it bloody is.'

Twenty minutes later, Jones guided them down a wide, tree-lined avenue replete with large, well-appointed houses.

After parking the Mini behind the squad car, Phillips jumped out into the heat of the afternoon sun, which was high overhead. 'Bet this cost a few quid,' she said as she glanced over at the enormous white house located at the end of the long driveway.

'Footballers, TV stars and bankers,' said Jones. 'The only people who can afford to live round here.'

'True,' said Phillips before making her way up the drive.

After ringing the bell, they stepped back and took in the immaculately manicured lawn to the front of the property.

Soon after, the door opened, and a short-haired woman in her sixties wearing a pink blouse and chinos stood looking at them, her expression grave, the eyes red and watery. 'Can I help you?'

Phillips held up her ID wallet. 'DCI Phillips and DI Jones from the Major Crimes Unit. We were hoping to speak to Carrie Nixon. Are we in the right place?'

'Yes,' said the woman. 'She's my daughter.'

'Is it possible to speak to her?'

'Sure. She's in the back. But I must warn you, she's not in a good way.'

'Which is understandable,' Phillips replied softly.

'I'm Margaret, by the way,' said the woman as she ushered them inside before heading off down the hallway.

As they followed her into the kitchen, Carrie came into view, sitting on a stool next to a large cooking island – a slim middle-aged woman with shoulder-length brown hair, wearing an oversized plain grey sweatshirt. She was staring into space, her face clearly puffy from crying, and she was cradling a scrunched-up tissue in her right hand.

'These people are from the police, Carrie,' said Margaret. 'They need to talk to you.'

Carrie's gaze shifted robotically towards them, but she said nothing.

Phillips offered a soft smile. 'Hi, Carrie. I'm DCI Phillips, and this is DI Jones. We're very sorry for your loss.'

Again, there was no response.

Phillips continued, 'We know this must be a very difficult time for you, but we need to ask you some questions about Robert. Would that be okay?'

Carrie stared back blankly, then finally nodded.

'Would either of you like a tea or coffee?' asked Margaret.

'No, thank you,' Phillips replied.

'Not for me, thanks,' added Jones.

'Well, let me know if you change your mind.'

Margaret sat down next to her daughter as Phillips pulled a stool out from under the island and took a seat opposite Carrie. Jones sat down next to her.

'We know this is the last thing you want to do, but anything you can tell us might help us find the people who did this to your husband.'

Carrie's face creased. 'I don't understand. Why would anyone want to hurt Robert?'

'That's what we intend to find out.'

Margaret squeezed her daughter's hand.

Phillips was acutely aware she needed to choose her words carefully. 'Did Robert ever mention feeling worried for his safety at all?'

'No.'

'And do you know if he had any enemies or disputes with anyone recently?'

Carrie shook her head. 'He was a good man. Everybody liked him.'

'I've no doubt,' said Phillips.

'Well, almost everyone,' Carrie added. 'You don't get to be CEO without upsetting a few people along the way.'

'That's understandable. Do you know if he had any issues at work at all?'

'Not that I know of. I mean, he loved his job.' Carrie's face contorted, and fresh tears flowed.

Phillips's heart went out to her, knowing only too well how lucky it was that Adam had survived a similar knife attack. *There but for the grace of God*, she thought.

'How had Robert been in himself, lately? Anything unusual in terms of his behaviour?'

'Nothing. He was fine. Very happy, actually.'

'I see,' said Phillips. 'And did your husband walk through St John's Gardens regularly?'

'Every day. His office is just round the corner, and he liked to walk through the park on his way to catch the train from Deansgate.'

'So that was his regular route?' Jones asked.

'Yes.'

'And what time would he usually get the train home?' Phillips cut back in.

'He liked to get the five fifty-six so he could be home just before seven to spend time with the boys.' Tears welled in Carrie's eyes once more. 'They don't even know he's gone.'

'They're at Michelle's, my other daughter's,' explained Margaret. 'They've been there since Carrie got the call last night.'

'How am I going to tell them their dad's dead?'

Phillips offered a soft smile. 'A grief counsellor once told me the best way to tell kids about the loss of a parent is to be as honest and straight with them as you can. They're a lot more resilient than we give them credit for, most of the time.'

Carrie's tears flowed once more, her shoulders heaving as she broke down.

Phillips placed a reassuring hand on her wrist. 'We'll do everything we can to catch the people who did this. I promise you that.'

Carrie continued to sob.

Phillips turned her attention to Margaret. 'Can we have a quick word outside?'

'Of course.'

A minute later, Phillips, Jones and Margaret gathered by the front door.

'I'm going to organise a family liaison officer to come and support Carrie,' said Phillips. 'We refer to them as FLOs, and they're specialist officers trained to deal with families in situations like these. She can expect a call later today.'

'Would it be okay for them to ring me instead?' Margaret asked. 'I'll be staying with her for the time being, and as you can see, she's in no fit state to make any kind of arrangements at the moment.'

'Of course.'

'I'll give you my number.'

Jones made a note of it in his pad.

'Do you know when the body will be released?' Margaret asked. 'I'm just thinking of the funeral.'

'The postmortem will take place on Monday,' said Phillips. 'Once that's done, the FLO will be able to help organise access for whichever funeral director you choose.'

'Thank you.'

'We'll leave you alone now,' said Phillips as she handed over her business card. 'If you or Carrie need anything, please call me, day or night.'

Margaret nodded.

With that, Phillips and Jones headed back to their cars.

'Where to now?' Jones asked as he deactivated the central locking on the squad car.

'Home.' Phillips exhaled loudly. 'I don't know about you, but I've had enough for one day. We can start early again in the morning.'

'Sounds like a plan.' He pulled his phone from his pocket. 'I'll give Bov and Whistler a call. Let them know they can get off too.'

Phillips pulled open the driver's door to the Mini, then stopped to cast her gaze back to the house. She could almost feel the grief emanating from within. Turning back to Jones, she waved. 'See you tomorrow,' she said, then dropped down behind the wheel, closing the door on the brutal world outside.

18

'And you're sure Squeaky's in the clear?'

'One hundred percent,' Tex replied. 'We spoke yesterday on the burner phones.'

'What did he say?' asked Charlie over the encrypted video link.

'It seems he was walking away after we'd done Nixon, trying not to draw attention to himself, when some guy began yelling after him, telling him to stop. Obviously, he wanted to get out of there as fast as he could, so he started running. But Squeaky's a big lad and not very quick. And the guy caught up to him, shouting to anyone who would listen that he'd stabbed someone. Squeaky pleaded ignorance, but the guy was having none of it, grabbing him and screaming to people walking past that he needed help. Squeaky was doing his best to fend him off when another bloke jumped in to restrain him, saying he was making a citizen's arrest, so Squeaky pulled the knife and started swinging it.'

'What? He stabbed them?' asked Charlie.

'Yeah, but he's pretty confident their injuries weren't serious. Not life threatening, anyway.'

'And did either of these two men see his face?'

'He didn't say so,' replied Tex. 'He was wearing sunglasses and a hat.'

'But you don't know *for sure*?'

Tex paused before answering, worried what reaction it would elicit from Charlie. 'No. I don't.'

'That's most unfortunate,' said Charlie flatly. 'Did he at least stick to the planned route out of the city centre?'

'I don't know. I was so relieved to hear he was okay, I forgot to ask about the specific roads he took to the train station.'

The avatar stared out grimly, silently from the screen.

'I'm sure he will have done,' offered Tex, fearing the opposite was true, knowing how Squeaky acted under pressure.

'He's put us all at risk,' Charlie said. 'If his face shows up on any of the city centre CCTV, the police could easily track him down. And if they find him, it's only a matter of time before they figure out his connection to you and Clem, which could jeopardise all the plans I've put in place.'

'I'm sure that won't happen,' said Tex, without conviction.

'We can't take the risk. Squeaky needs to lie low and stay out of the way until the rest of the plan has been executed. Is that clear?'

Tex nodded. 'I'll speak to him.'

'You'd better. For *all* your sakes,' said Charlie. 'I made it clear right from the start that failure would not be tolerated, from anyone. If Squeaky's actions *have* jeopardised what we're trying to do, there will be no place on this earth he can hide where Terra soldiers can't find him. And when they do, he'll wish to God he could switch places with Nixon.'

'I'll make sure he understands.'

'See that you do,' Charlie shot back. 'And stay alert. The next phase of the plan will need to be actioned later this week. You'll receive full instructions in the next twenty-four hours.'

'I'll be ready.'

'Good, and make sure Clem is too,' said Charlie. 'I have something extra special planned for her.'

'Clem?' Tex felt himself recoil slightly, an uneasy feeling clawing at his gut. 'What do you want her to do?'

'You'll see,' replied Charlie. 'All in good time.'

A moment later the link went dead.

19

It was just after nine o'clock on Sunday morning when Phillips wandered into the offices of MCU carrying a handful of breakfast sandwiches, Jones bringing up the rear with a tray of steaming hot drinks. Considering the team had each given up their weekends without a single word of complaint, the least she could do was feed them.

'Just what the doctor ordered.' Bovalino grinned as he took delivery of his favoured 'Belly Buster' – a large sub roll filled to the brim with bacon, sausage, black pudding, two eggs and a large serving of fried mushrooms.

'You're a stroke waiting to happen, you are,' said Entwistle as he gazed at the gargantuan sandwich.

'Heart of a lion.' Bovalino banged his chest before taking his first bite of the sub roll.

Phillips smiled, seeing the contentment on the big man's face. She'd never met anyone who enjoyed his food quite as much as Bov.

For the next few minutes, they sat in relative silence as they each made a start on their breakfast. When she was satisfied everyone was relatively content, Phillips began running Bov and Entwistle through the details of their various conversations with Andy Evans and Flannery, as well as with Adrian Firth and Kat, and finally with Nixon's widow and her mother, Margaret.

Ten minutes later, with everyone up to date, she zoned in on Bov. 'Did you manage to speak to the guys who stepped in to tackle one of the suspects?'

'Yeah, caught up with them both yesterday afternoon.'

'And?' asked Jones.

'Nothing much to report, really. Both told me pretty much the same story: they stepped in to try to stop the guy getting away, but he ended up turning the knife on them.'

'Were they badly hurt?'

'Both suffered superficial slash wounds to their hands and wrists that required stitches, but nothing life threatening.'

'Did either of them get a good look at the guy with the knife?' Phillips asked.

'I'm afraid not. Seems he was wearing dark sunglasses and an England bucket hat to hide his face, but they both described a big man, at least six two, possibly six three. Very strong and most likely in his early twenties.'

Phillips glanced at Jones. 'How tall is Firth, do you reckon?'

Jones shrugged. 'Hard to tell, as he never stood up while we were there, but could be six two.'

She turned to Entwistle. 'Can you bring up his file and check for us?'

Entwistle obliged. 'Six feet two,' he revealed thirty seconds later.

Bovalino jumped back in. 'Both victims are coming in to go through mugshots tomorrow.'

'In that case, let's make sure they get a good look at Firth's,' replied Phillips.

'No problem, guv.' Bovalino made a note in his pad.

Phillips turned her attention to Entwistle. 'What about Firth's girlfriend?'

He passed across a police mugshot. 'Katarina Holmes. Eighteen years old with several convictions for minor drug offences. Nothing major and no jail time to date.'

'Give it time,' said Jones sardonically.

'Have we had any updates on how Ross Grayson's doing?' asked Phillips.

'I called the ICU about an hour ago. The nurse I spoke to said he's stable but very heavily sedated and that the biggest risk at the moment is infection.'

'Poor bugger,' muttered Bovalino through a mouthful of bacon.

'Stay in regular contact with the ICU team,' urged Phillips. 'Anything changes, I want to know about it, okay?'

'Of course, guv.'

Phillips continued, 'And what about the CCTV from around St John's Gardens? Any joy with that?'

Entwistle nodded and opened his notepad. 'I've managed to track down a chunk of footage from the private cameras listed by uniform, but as it's Sunday, it's taking a little longer to track down the council cameras.'

'I have a good contact over at the CCTV hub who might be able to help,' said Bovalino. 'Not sure if he's working today, but I can call him and see if there's anything he can do to speed things up.'

'Great idea,' said Phillips.

'To be honest,' Entwistle cut in, 'there must be about twenty hours of footage from the private cameras, so I think I've got enough to be going on with for today.'

'Call him anyway, Bov.' Phillips took a mouthful of tea. 'Get him to speed things up for us.'

'No problem.'

'And I'll tell you what else you can do,' she added. 'Take another look at the CCTV around Bruntwood Park at the time we spotted Firth. See if you can find any footage of Kat Holmes on there. If Firth *was* involved in the David Lloyd attack, chances are she was too.'

'Sure,' said Bovalino.

'We also need a full background on Robert Nixon, as well as Opus Air,' added Phillips. 'If we *are* looking for the same gang for both attacks, we need to work out if either of them are in any way connected to Grayson or GBOG.'

'I may as well follow that up too.' Entwistle typed into his laptop. 'I've already done some of the background work you asked for on GBOG.'

'And?'

'So far, from what I can see, there are three GBOG territories that have had issues with security over the years.'

'What kind of issues?' Jones asked.

'Violent attacks by locals, in the main targeting staff at GBOG's refineries in Carabobo in Venezuela, Ahvaz field in Iran and Basra in Iraq.'

Phillips's interest was piqued. 'Basra? Wasn't that once an ISIS stronghold?'

'I think it was, yeah,' Entwistle replied.

Jones's brow furrowed. 'Can't see Firth and his missus as Jihadists, can you, boss?'

'Probably not, but Clara did say the device they pulled off

Grayson's car was very similar to those used by the Taliban.'
Phillips drummed her fingers on the desk, deep in thought
for a moment. 'Might be worth giving Flannery a call, Jonesy.
See if the counter terrorism boys have any intel on active UK
groups that are still linked to Iraq.'

'Yeah, of course. I'll see what he says.'

'Great. Looks like we've got a very busy day ahead of us.'
Phillips stood. 'The answers are out there, guys; we just need
to find them, okay?'

Each of the men nodded in unison before Phillips
headed for her office and her least favourite task of all –
updating the decision logs on the investigation so far.

A COUPLE of hours passed before Bov's massive frame filled
the open doorway to her office.

'What's up?' Phillips asked.

'I've found footage of Kat Holmes on the cameras outside
of Brentwood Park.'

'Show me.' Phillips got up from behind her desk and
followed him back through to the office.

As Bov took a seat in front of his PC, she moved to stand
at his back.

His interest clearly piqued, Jones joined her a few
seconds later.

'This is taken from the camera positioned at the north
exit to the park.' The big man hit play on-screen.

A second later, Kat Holmes could be seen walking out of
the park at pace.

'What time was this?' Phillips asked.

'Dead on 8.52 p.m.'

'More or less the same time as Firth was spotted on the other camera,' said Jones.

'And this is *definitely* the same day as the Grayson car bombing?' Phillips asked.

Bovalino tapped the time and date on the screen with his pen. 'Yes, guv. Saturday night.'

'Bingo!' Phillips patted him on the shoulder as she turned to face Jones. 'I think it's time to arrest the pair of them, *bruv*, don't you?' she said, mimicking Firth's fake London accent.

A broad smile spread across Jones's face as he clapped his hands together. 'Abso-bloody-lutely, *bruv!*'

20

T hree hours later, Phillips and Jones made their way to the custody suite to interview Firth and Holmes separately. Entwistle and Bovalino would watch via video link from the observation suite.

With Jones dispatched to Interview Room Three to tackle Holmes, Phillips stepped inside Interview Room Two, where she found Firth sitting behind a small metal-legged table accompanied by his court-appointed solicitor, Julie Simpson. Simpson was a regular visitor to Ashton House and was rumoured to make a half-decent living from representing literally any waif and stray in Manchester who couldn't afford to retain their own legal counsel. As per usual, her face was fixed with an austere expression that matched her trademark dark suit and straight black hair, which today was tied in a tight bun on the top of her head. A thick leather-bound notepad and pen were laid out on the table in front of her.

Phillips took the seat opposite and placed a manila folder on the table between them. 'Hello again, Adrian,' she said as she stared him straight in the eye before acknowledging Simpson. 'Julie.'

Simpson offered a thin smile but said nothing.

Firth stared back in silence. His hands were stuffed into the belly pocket of his black hoodie; the hood was pulled up over his head.

After explaining the protocols that ensured the interview would be taped on both audio and video, she pressed record on the DIR – the digital interview recording – and after a long audible beep, she got started. 'What can you tell me about the car-bomb attack at the David Lloyd leisure centre on Saturday, Adrian?'

Firth shifted in his seat. 'Noffin.' The gangsta twang remained in place.

'So you had nothing to do with it?'

'Nope.'

Phillips opened the folder and took out one of the CCTV still images of him walking out of Bruntwood Park, turning it 180 degrees to face him. Even though she'd quizzed him earlier about his movements on the night of the bombing, she needed to repeat the process to be able to use his response at a later date in court. 'What were you doing in Bruntwood Park so soon after the explosion went off?'

Firth sniffed defiantly. 'Like I told you yesterday, I was out for a walk.'

'Often go walking up there, do you? I mean, it's a long way from Rusholme or Moss Side.'

'Walk where I like. Free country, innit?'

Phillips paused before pulling out another CCTV still, which again she turned and passed across. 'For the purpose of the tape, can you tell me who that is in the photograph?'

Firth glanced down briefly. 'Kat.'

'And how do you know her?'

'She's my lady.'

'Your girlfriend?' Phillips asked.

'That's what I said, innit?'

'So, bear with me, Adrian, but this is what I'm finding a little confusing. If she's your girlfriend, then why did you both leave the park at the exact same time on Saturday night, but by different exits?'

'I don't remember.' Firth exhaled loudly, sounding bored. 'Maybe we had a fight or something.'

'Argue a lot, do you?'

'What can I say?' Firth flashed a lopsided grin. 'We is passionate. Know what I mean?'

Phillips held his gaze. 'If I didn't know better, Adrian, I'd say you deliberately separated so as not to be seen together. Now why would you do that, unless of course you were deliberately trying to avoid detection?'

'Like I say, I was just chilling, taking a walk on a sunny day. I can't remember what Kat was doing. Got a bad memory, like.' He grinned. 'Too much weed, innit.'

'Do you know what *I* think?' Phillips asked.

Firth shrugged.

'I think you and your girlfriend were trying your best to look casual while running away from the David Lloyd club. I think you were back to your old fire-starting ways and had just detonated an incendiary device that turned Ross Grayson's car into a raging fireball.'

Firth chuckled. 'That's insane. I was nowhere near the place.'

'But you were though, weren't you?' She tapped the photos with her pen. 'These were taken twenty minutes after the explosion, and David Lloyd is less than a fifteen-minute walk from that spot, which by my reckoning puts you and Kat *firmly* in the frame.'

Firth glanced at Simpson, who drew him into a huddle. A second later he sat upright and turned his focus back to Phillips.

'I'll ask you again, Adrian. Why did you and Kat leave Bruntwood Park by different exits on Saturday night?'

'No comment.'

'Really? You're going down that route, are you?'

Firth shrugged nonchalantly as he stared back.

'I see,' said Phillips. 'So, let's talk about Friday evening. What were you doing in St John's Gardens in the city centre?'

'No comment.'

'Why can't you answer that question? You didn't seem to have a problem when I asked you that yesterday.'

'No comment.'

'So, what? You weren't actually at home as you and Kat claimed?'

'No comment.'

Phillips passed across another CCTV still that Entwistle had uncovered just thirty minutes previously, this time of the man accused of stabbing Nixon and slashing the two other men. 'Recognise him?'

'No comment.'

'Is that *you,* Adrian, in the bucket hat?'

'No comment.'

'Did you stab Robert Nixon in St John's Gardens on Friday night?'

Firth pulled his hands from the pocket of his hoodie and folded his arms across his chest. 'No comment.'

And so it continued for the next thirty minutes as Phillips worked her way through a list of questions the Crown Prosecution Service required answers for, should Firth end up being charged. As expected, he maintained his 'no comment' stance throughout.

Finally, having exhausted the list of questions, she gathered the photos together and closed the folder. 'DCI Phillips terminating the interview at 2.12 p.m. on Sunday the eleventh of June.' She pressed stop on the DIR and stood. 'One of the detention team will escort you back to the cells.'

Firth grinned, and Simpson began packing away her things as Phillips took her leave.

A few minutes later, she joined Bovalino and Entwistle in the observation suite.

Bovalino was waiting for her, his headphones resting around his thick neck. 'Well, he wasn't giving much away, was he, guv?'

'No, but to be honest, I'm surprised he didn't opt for no comment from the very start.'

'Yeah,' replied Bovalino. 'Especially with Simpson representing him. That's her normal route.'

Entwistle, who'd been watching Jones interview Kat Holmes, also removed his headphones.

'How's Jones getting on?'

'Just wrapping up,' he said. 'No comment all the way, I'm afraid.'

'Same as Firth, which is to be expected. These guys have been here plenty of times before.' Phillips glanced at the screen behind Entwistle, where she could see Jones making his way out of Interview Room Three. 'Both their fingerprints and DNA are in the system. Get them over to Evans as a matter of urgency, and let's see if he can connect them to either crime scene.'

'Of course,' said Entwistle. 'I'll do it now.'

'Thanks.' Phillips pulled out her phone. 'I think it's time I called Carter,' she said as she headed for the door.

———

21

During their call, Carter, being Carter, had offered to come in and help the team in any way he could, but Phillips had assured him they had everything covered for now. She knew only too well that Fox would be prowling around looking for signs of progress when she arrived first thing tomorrow morning, and that Carter would be the best line of defence. She could see no real benefit to him in interrupting his weekend when they were yet to make any real breakthrough on either attack. Having assured him she would call the moment they had anything of value to share, she finished the call and turned her attention back to the mountain of paperwork that needed updating to ensure both investigations were compliant and in line with the correct protocols. It was the one part of the job she had little time for. Ironic, given the fact it seemed to devour so much of her schedule on a weekly basis.

A couple of hours passed before she reached the point where she felt sufficiently up to date to take a break. Pushing her chair back with relish, she stepped up and stretched her arms out wide before wandering out into the main office. Each of the team appeared lost in their own worlds, staring intently at their respective screens, brows furrowed, eyes narrow. 'Does anyone need a coffee?' she asked as she approached the bank of desks. 'My round.'

Jones, Bov and Whistler broke away from their computers in unison, each of them appearing grateful for the momentary distraction and all too keen to accept her offer.

After making a note of their drinks orders and agreeing to Bovalino's request for some sweet treats to keep up their energy, she made her way down to the canteen on the first floor. As expected – and was most often the case on a Sunday – it was ghostly quiet with just a few uniformed officers sitting in pairs in quiet conversation at tables dotted around the room. Watching them for a moment, she was transported back fifteen years to her time as a beat cop when life seemed simpler and much more straightforward. A life without the daily burden of office politics. Happy days, she thought.

Rounding up the drinks and biscuits on a tray, she headed back to MCU with renewed hope of a breakthrough.

As she approached the bank of desks, Jones leaned back in his chair and stretched his arms above his head.

'Just what the doctor ordered,' he said as he gratefully accepted his mug of peppermint tea.

Entwistle also seemed excited to receive his double-shot latte.

Bovalino, on the other hand, was unusually quiet, his eyes still locked on his computer screen.

'Everything all right, Bov?' she asked as she placed his black tea on his desk.

The big man appeared to be in a trance-like state.

'Bov?' Phillips repeated.

Suddenly he was back in the room. 'Sorry, guv,' he mumbled as he turned to face her.

'Whatever you're looking at must be bloody interesting to keep *you* from a plate of biscuits.'

'Check this out.' He pointed to the screen with his pen.

She moved to his shoulder.

'I've been going over the city centre CCTV footage my mate Dave sent over, and I've managed to track the bucket-hat guy we spotted in St John's Gardens across various camera feeds all the way to Piccadilly station.'

Phillips stared at the screen as Bovalino pressed return and the video played. Sure enough, the guy in the bucket hat, the one suspected of stabbing Nixon, could be seen walking across the street just in front of the Malmaison hotel before making a right turn and heading up to the station concourse at pace.

'Do we have access to the cameras inside the station?' Phillips asked.

He shook his head. 'They belong to Network Rail, so sadly not.'

'Do we know anyone over there?'

'We don't, but I'm sure my mate Dave will. I can give him another call and see who we need to speak to.'

'Do that.' Phillips felt a surge of energy coursing through her veins as she sensed they were closing in on their first suspect. 'We need to know where he went after that as a matter of urgency.'

Bovalino picked up the desk phone and began dialling.

'I've got a bit of background for you on Nixon and Opus Air, boss,' said Entwistle.

He had her full attention now.

'Looking at various articles online, everything points to Nixon being a no-nonsense bloke who first joined as the marketing manager, quickly working his way up to CEO a couple of years ago. Other than that, there's very little info on the man himself. No social media presence to speak of, and the only content I can find that features him directly is all related to Opus. The most recent being an interview he did with the *Financial Times* where he was talking up the fact that they'd just secured investment to purchase fifty new planes to service new routes to China, Asia, Australia and New Zealand. Apparently, their share price hit an all-time high a few days later.'

'Anything to link Opus to GBOG?' Jones cut in.

'Nothing directly, no, but digging a little deeper, it appears GBOG supply fuel to a company called Transcorp, and Transcorp in turn provide a chunk of airports in the UK with aviation fuel. Maybe there's a connection in there somewhere?'

Phillips turned to Jones. 'Can you look into that?'

'Sure.' He made a note in his pad. 'Just send over everything you have so far.'

Entwistle nodded.

'What about Nixon's financials?' Phillips asked.

'They're still on my list to do,' replied Entwistle. 'As well as his phone records.'

'Okay. Get onto those as quickly as you can. We also need to see if he's connected in any way to the anti-oil brigade. Airlines get a lot of stick from environmentalists because of their carbon footprint. The fact that Nixon and Grayson both worked in fossil-fuel-based industries seems like a natural link between the two of them.'

Just then, Bovalino put the phone down.

'Any joy?' asked Phillips.

'Dave's given me the number of a guy over at Network Rail, called Gavin Matthews. He's an ex-copper, apparently, so hopefully he'll be happy to help.' He picked up the phone again. 'I'll call him now.'

Phillips dropped into the seat at the spare desk and for the next few minutes watched the big Italian at his charming best. She'd always known he was a great copper, but it was a reminder of just how effective he could be, seeing him in action now.

Finally, he put the phone down, a satisfied grin spreading across his face. 'I can have full access to everything they've got first thing in the morning, guv. He starts at seven, so I'm meeting him then.'

She felt herself smiling like a proud parent. 'Great work, Bov. Well done.'

The big man appeared to blush slightly.

Phillips checked her watch. It was almost five. 'Okay. Let's call it a day and regroup first thing tomorrow, shall we?'

'Sounds good to me,' said Jones.

'What do you want to do about Firth and Holmes?' Entwistle asked.

Phillips considered their options for a moment before answering, 'Leave them where they are for now. Let's see if a night in the cells can loosen their tongues.'

'I'll call custody and let them know.'

'Good work, guys,' said Phillips with renewed vigour. 'We're getting close to a breakthrough. I can *feel* it.'

22

E arly next morning, Phillips and Jones made their way to the mortuary at the MRI in readiness for Robert Nixon's postmortem. After being buzzed through the secure outer doors, they wandered along the corridor towards the office of chief pathologist Dr Tanvi Chakrabortty. At that moment, Phillips's phone began to vibrate in her pocket. Fishing it out, she could see it was Bovalino calling.

'Bov?' she asked, activating the speaker function so Jones could hear.

'Morning, guv. I'm down at the Network Rail offices, and I wanted to let you know I've been able to track the bucket-hat guy onto a train headed for Wilmslow.'

'Do we know where he got off?'

'Not yet, but it's a Northern train, so they're my next call. The guy I'm with down here, Gav, reckons that all trains have CCTV fitted these days, even the old bone rattlers, so we should be able to see where he ended up easily enough.'

'Excellent. We're about to head into Nixon's PM, but call as soon as you find out. I can easily step away for a minute.'

'Ha, any excuse to get out of it.' He chuckled, then ended the call.

'Looks like the net is closing on the bucket-hat guy,' said Jones.

Phillips grinned. 'Certainly seems that way.'

Just then, Chakrabortty came out of her office, looking as tall and elegant as ever in her spotless green medical scrubs paired with a pair of white clogs, her dark hair tied back against her head. 'I thought I heard you two.' She passed across a couple of plastic aprons. 'Nice weekend working again, was it?'

'Sadly, yes,' said Phillips as she pulled the apron over her head.

'Me too,' Chakrabortty replied. 'Not enough hours in the day at the moment.'

'We know the feeling,' Jones added as he tied the apron around his waist.

Chakrabortty placed her right hand on his left shoulder. 'You ready for this, my friend?'

It was widely known that Jones had a weak stomach when it came to postmortems. He exhaled sharply. 'No, but if we wait until I am, we'll be hanging round here for an awfully long time.'

Chakrabortty gestured in the direction of the examination room. 'In that case, let's go in, shall we?'

As was usually the case, Chakrabortty took up her position on the far side of the examination table where Nixon's greyish-white body was laid out, a green surgical sheet covering his legs and torso. Phillips and Jones stood opposite her as she slipped on a pair of purple latex gloves.

'Right, then.' Chakrabortty pulled back the sheet, which she folded so it just covered the pelvis, then grabbed a large scalpel from the metal trolley to her right. 'Let's get started.'

For the next hour, Phillips and Jones watched on as Chakrabortty narrated each section of the postmortem – carefully working her way around the body.

Of particular interest to Phillips, owing to the nature of Nixon's death, were the cluster of knife wounds to the left side of the torso, and the single slash to the right-hand side.

After taking measurements of each entry point, Chakrabortty pointed to the purple blemishes that surrounded the deeper cuts on the right. 'Each wound is more or less the same diameter, and by the looks of it, the blade used to inflict these here on the left was smooth on either side, and judging by the depth of the wound, I'd say similar in size to a switchblade. However, as you can see here' – she moved her attention to the left side of the body – 'the width of the slash wound is slightly smaller. Add to that the fact the angles of impact are different between the cluster of wounds and the gash and it's pretty clear that two separate knives were used in the attack.'

'Which fits with the eyewitness accounts that he was set upon by more than one assailant,' said Phillips.

Chakrabortty nodded. 'He was stabbed from two opposing directions.'

Phillips stared down at Nixon's body, trying to imagine the attack as it happened in real time.

Chakrabortty continued as she pointed to a wound under Nixon's ribcage to the right of the torso. 'What I can say with absolute certainty is that this one here would have been the killer blow. It ruptured his liver, and unless an injury like that is treated almost immediately, the outcome for the victim is inevitably fatal.'

'Poor sod never stood a chance,' said Jones.

'This one went through his lung.' Chakrabortty pointed to another deep wound higher up. 'Which, although it would have been horrifically painful, was an injury he could likely have survived on its own.'

'So we're looking for at least two attackers,' said Phillips.

'I'd say so, yes,' Chakrabortty replied.

'Is there any way to tell if it was more than that? Say, three, for example?'

'Hard to say definitively, but in my opinion, based on the tight cluster of wounds on the right, and the single gash on the left, I'm pretty certain you're looking at two attackers.'

'Eyewitnesses said they saw three people set upon him,' mused Phillips.

'Well, if that's the case, I'd say one of them must have missed.'

'Or maybe didn't strike at all.'

'I hope you don't mind me asking,' ventured Chakrabortty, 'but since when did street crime fall under Major Crimes?'

'Since the victim started playing golf with the PPC's husband,' quipped Jones.

'Ah, I see.' Chakrabortty nodded. 'Say no more.'

'Plus, we suspect the people who did this' – Phillips pointed to the battered torso – 'may also have been involved in the car-bomb attack at David Lloyd's last Saturday.'

Chakrabortty's brow furrowed. 'I'd heard you got lumbered with that investigation. I thought that would be a counter terrorism gig, all day long.'

'So did we,' said Jones.

'How come you got it, then?'

'It's a long story,' Phillips replied.

'So how are a car bomb and a knife attack connected?' Chakrabortty raised her eyebrows. 'I must say, I would never have thought to put the two together.'

'Neither would we,' said Phillips. 'But each of the attacks was carried out by three assailants, and both victims were connected to fossil-fuel-driven industries.'

Chakrabortty did a slight double take. 'Far be it from me to tell you your jobs, guys, but that seems one helluva leap?'

'Massive, we know,' said Phillips, 'but it's all we've got right now.'

'Fair enough.' Chakrabortty placed the scalpel back on the trolley, then reached for the circular saw used to open up the head.

Phillips turned to Jones. 'I think we've seen enough, don't you?'

Jones swallowed the lump in his throat as his eyes locked on the gruesome tool in the doctor's gloved hands. 'Yeah. I do.'

Chakrabortty grinned. 'I'll finish up without you, then.'

'Thanks, Tan,' said Phillips.

'One of the team will email across the full report later today or first thing tomorrow.'

'Perfect.' Phillips glanced back at Jones before nodding towards the door. 'After you, then.'

'Thanks,' he managed to mumble before turning on his heel and rushing for the exit.

Phillips locked eyes with Chakrabortty and chuckled before following him out.

23

A s Phillips stepped into the revolving front door of Ashton House, with Jones just behind, her phone began to ring. Glancing at the screen, her heart sank, as she realised it was the *Manchester Evening News* reporter Don Townsend. After a recent spate of challenging events involving the investigative journalist, she knew better than to ignore his call.

'Don?' she said without feeling.

'Jane, how the devil are you?'

It never ceased to amaze her how quickly – and regularly – Townsend seemed to forget the level of grief his stories had inflicted on her team over the years. Just a few months ago, he'd written a series of articles highlighting the shortcomings of the Greater Manchester Police and ultimately called for Fox's head, which had caused no end of issues for Phillips and Carter. Shit always rolled downhill when it came to the chief constable.

'What do you want, Don?'

'Information.'

'So what else is new.' She was struggling to hide her contempt for the man.

'I heard a rumour that you might be looking at the same suspects for the David Lloyd car-bomb attack as for Friday night's fatal stabbing in the city.'

'That information has not been released to the press,' she shot back.

'So, it's true?' He sounded as smug as ever.

The anger Phillips felt was instant and burned hot in her stomach. She'd known for some time that Townsend had a mole working within the force who was feeding him sensitive information, but despite her best efforts to track that person down, whoever it was remained a mystery.

'You know better than anyone I can't talk to the press about an ongoing investigation.'

Townsend chortled. *'Come on, Jane. Do we have to go down this route every time? The terms of our deal were very clear: I get the exclusives ahead of everyone else, and in return the truth about Fox soliciting false confessions back when she was a DCI never makes it into the paper.'*

'I'm well aware of the agreement,' Phillips growled. 'And when there's something to share, you'll be the first to know, okay?'

'I'd better be.' The undertone was menacing.

'Piss off, Don.' She sneered, then hung up.

Jones, who had clearly overheard the conversation, stared at her with one eyebrow raised. 'I'm telling you, guv, Townsend is a snake. Always has been, always will be. You'd be better off telling him to do one, and letting Fox take her chances. After all, *she* was the one who played fast and loose back in the day, not you.'

Phillips set off walking at pace.

Jones soon caught her up.

'Trust me,' said Phillips as they started up the stairs. 'If I thought it was the right thing to do, I would, but after the inevitable public outrage that would ensue, she'd just resign and sail off into the sunset with her massive pension.'

'The wonderful world of police politics and saving face, hey?'

'Yeah. And I'm not having it.' Phillips marched upwards. 'When Fox goes down, she goes down in flames.'

Jones exhaled sharply. 'Remind me never to upset you, guv.'

Phillips chuckled. 'Don't worry, Jonesy. The difference is, I *like* you.'

A few minutes later they wandered into the MCU offices.

'Guv!' Bov beckoned them over to his desk.

'What have you got?' asked Phillips as they moved next to him.

Bov tapped his screen with his pen. 'Bucket-hat guy got off the train at Wilmslow.'

Phillips peered at the still image on the screen of their number one suspect opening the back door of a taxi. 'How did you find this?'

'It was on Network Rail's system. The guys at Northern Trains helped me follow him to Wilmslow station, and then Gav at Network Rail found this.'

'We need to speak to the taxi firm,' said Jones.

'Already have.' Bovalino looked down at his notes. 'The driver confirmed he took our man to 37 Hough Road, about ten minutes from the station.'

Phillips felt her pulse quicken. 'Don't suppose he paid on card, did he?'

'No, but it *was* charged to an account registered to a

Meredith Heppingstall.'

'Doesn't sound like our guy?'

'No, guv. Quite the opposite. According to the electoral role, Meredith is a seventy-five-year-old widow who's been at the address for over forty-five years.'

'Maybe bucket-hat guy lives with her?' suggested Jones.

'Or he cloned the account?' Entwistle cut in. 'Easy enough to do these days.'

Phillips scrutinised the figure on the screen. 'Have you been able to contact the old lady at all?'

'Not yet, no. I've called a couple of times since I got back to the office, but it keeps going to answer machine.'

Phillips placed her right hand on Bov's left shoulder. 'Can you print off some stills of this guy? Jonesy and I will head out to Wilmslow and see if we can track down Meredith. With a bit of luck, she might know who he is.'

'I'll do it now.' Bovalino busied himself at his laptop.

'Before you go, guv,' said Entwistle, 'Evans has sent through some preliminary results from the Nixon crime scene.'

'Any joy?'

'Yes and no.' Entwistle picked up a sheet from his desk. 'The bad news is, there's no DNA or fingerprint matches for Firth or Holmes at the scene.'

'Doesn't mean they weren't there,' said Jones. 'Could've been wearing gloves.'

Phillips nodded. 'And what's the good news?'

Entwistle passed across another sheet. 'This is the plaster cast taken from the footprint left in the flowerbed where he was stabbed.'

Phillips stared down at the white composite on the page.

'According to Evans, it belongs to a...now, let me get this

right, a "Nike Court Vision Low Next To Nature".'

'Catchy,' said Jones sarcastically.

Entwistle passed over another printout. This one contained a professional profile shot of a black trainer with white soles and the ubiquitous Nike swoosh. 'I got this off Nike's official website. Apparently, it's one of very few trainers on the market made entirely from sustainable materials.'

'Which could potentially fit with our environmentalist theory,' said Phillips.

'That's what I was thinking,' Entwistle agreed. 'And whoever left the print wears a size thirteen.'

Phillips raised her eyebrows. 'Thirteen?'

'We're looking for bloody Sasquatch!' Bovalino chuckled.

'This is great,' said Phillips, slapping her hand on the printout. 'Evans has really come up trumps with this one.'

At that moment, Bovalino jumped up from his chair and headed for the printer.

'One more thing before you go, boss,' said Entwistle. 'What do you want us to do with Firth and Holmes? Their twenty-four hours is almost up.'

Phillips glanced at the clock on the wall. 'Cut them loose for the time being, but I want their local cop shop to keep tabs on them.'

'No worries,' said Entwistle, standing. 'I'll head over to the custody suite and sort out the paperwork now.'

Bovalino returned, clutching a fresh bunch of A4 print-outs, which he passed across.

'Thanks,' said Phillips before turning to Jones. 'Looks like we're off again.'

Jones threw his car keys in the air, catching them a split second later. 'Ready when you are.'

24

The sun was high in the sky when Jones parked next to the grass verge in front of the large, detached house belonging to Meredith Heppingstall. From her position in the passenger seat, Phillips could see an elderly lady wearing a sunhat, a blue flannel shirt and cream shorts, kneeling on the lush grass of the well-maintained garden, tending to a blooming pink hydrangea in front of her.

'Looks like she's in,' said Jones as he killed the engine.

'Yeah.' Phillips tapped the folder containing the CCTV still images in her lap. 'Let's see what she has to say about these, shall we?'

A minute later, as they walked up the smartly paved block-work driveway, the woman straightened, but remained on her knees, a pair of glasses hanging on a cord around her neck.

'Can I help you?' Her voice was slightly shrill, the accent neutral.

Phillips flashed her credentials. 'DCI Phillips and DI

Jones from the Major Crimes Unit. We're looking for Meredith Heppingstall.'

The woman frowned. 'That's me.'

'We were hoping we might have a word.'

'The police are wanting to speak to me?' Heppingstall's eyes narrowed. 'Well, that's a first. What's this about?'

'It might be better if we talk inside,' replied Phillips. 'Somewhere more private.'

'Very well, but bear with me.' Heppingstall slowly got to her feet, groaning as she did. 'My knees aren't what they used to be, I'm afraid.'

Phillips and Jones fell in behind as she led them down the side of the property towards the rear of the house.

'Will this do?' she asked, gesturing towards the open doors of a large conservatory overlooking the expansive back garden.

'That'll be fine,' Phillips replied.

A moment later, Phillips and Jones took a seat on a small wicker sofa facing Heppingstall, who dropped gingerly into the matching armchair.

'How can I help you?' said Heppingstall, resting her hands on her lap.

'Do you have a taxi account with Wilmslow Cars?' Phillips asked.

'Yes, I do.' She smiled. 'I use them to go to the shops and when I'm out seeing friends – I don't drive, you see. I took one this morning, in fact, when I went to Tai Chi at the village hall. They're ever so good, very reliable and quite reasonable.'

Jones made a note in his pad.

It was evident that Meredith liked to chat, as she continued unabated. 'It was my late husband's idea, you see

– God rest his soul – because I couldn't drive, and he got fed up of taking me everywhere.' She chuckled. 'Said he'd worked too long and too hard all his life to become *my* taxi driver when he retired and—'

'Does anyone else have access to your account?' Phillips cut in, trying to steer the conversation back to the reason for their visit.

'No. Just me. It's ever so clever. I have a password, you see, so when I call up to book, they know it's me, and I pay by standing order every month, which means I don't have to carry cash.'

Phillips opened the folder and passed across an image of the bucket-hat guy getting into a taxi at Wilmslow station. 'Do you recognise this man?'

Heppingstall scrunched up her nose as she put on her glasses, scrutinising the image for a moment. 'I can't be certain, but it does look a bit like Sebastian. Same build, but it's hard to say for sure because of the hat and sunglasses.'

'And who is Sebastian?' Jones asked.

'My grandson.'

'And when did you last see Sebastian?' asked Phillips.

'This morning, at breakfast. He lives with me.'

Phillips straightened in the chair. 'He lives *here*?'

'Yes. For the last couple of years, actually.'

'Where is Sebastian now?'

'At school, of course.'

Phillips flinched. 'He's *school* age?'

'Yes.' Heppingstall nodded enthusiastically. 'He's doing his A Levels at St Bartholomew's grammar school in the village. His father – my son, Jeremy – got a promotion which involved a move to Dubai. Must have been about eighteen months ago now. Anyway, it was decided that Sebastian would stay here to do his exams next year. Jeremy and Tiggy – that's my daughter-in-law – thought it would give him a better chance of getting into Cambridge to do law.' She wrinkled her nose. 'As opposed to going to one of those local Arab schools over there.'

'Could Sebastian have used your taxi account on Friday night?' Phillips asked.

'I guess so, yes.' Heppingstall's brow furrowed. 'Why do you want to know about Sebastian and my taxi account?'

Phillips avoided the question. 'What time did he come home on Friday night?'

'I don't know. I didn't ask, but he was here when I got back from bridge at about 9.30.'

'How did he seem that night?' Jones asked.

'Fine. His usual, sullen, teenage self.' Heppingstall folded her arms across her chest now. 'What's this all about? Why are you so interested in my grandson?'

Phillips sat forward. 'Look, Mrs Heppingstall—'

'Please, call me Meredith.'

'Meredith.' Phillips held up the image of the bucket-hat guy. 'We have reason to believe that the man in this picture was involved in a violent crime that took place on Friday night in the city centre.'

Heppingstall was aghast. 'Well, in that case, that *can't* be Sebastian in that picture. Seb's a good boy.'

Phillips held her gaze. 'We were able to trace this man from the scene of the crime, right through the city, then onto the train and all the way to Wilmslow, where he got into a cab that dropped him off at this house.'

Heppingstall stared back with wide eyes, but remained silent.

'I think we all know that the man in this picture is Sebastian,' Phillips said flatly.

'Oh, God.' Heppingstall placed her hand to her open mouth. 'I can't believe he's in trouble again.'

Phillips raised an eyebrow. 'Has he been in trouble before?'

'Yes.'

'With the police?'

'No. Nothing like that, but he was suspended from school earlier this year.'

'What for?' Phillips asked.

'One of the other students accused him and a couple of his friends of bullying. The school suspended him while they investigated. Jeremy had to fly back from Dubai and smooth things over at St Bart's. He was livid. Gave Sebastian a terrible hiding. Heaven only knows what he'll do when he hears about this.'

Phillips pulled out the picture of the Nike trainers and held it in front of Heppingstall. 'Does Sebastian own a pair of shoes like these?'

She peered at it for a few seconds. 'He has so many shoes, I have no idea.'

'Do you know what size feet he has?' Jones asked.

Heppingstall eyed him suspiciously. 'Why on earth do you want to know that?'

'It's just a line of inquiry we're following,' he replied.

'I really couldn't say, but he's tall like his father and has his big feet too.'

Phillips glanced at Jones. She could tell he was thinking the same thing. If they could find those trainers, they could put him at the exact spot where Nixon was stabbed. She turned her focus back to Heppingstall. 'Would you mind if we take a look in his room?'

'Do I have a choice?'

'Of course you do,' replied Phillips. 'You're not under arrest, and neither is Sebastian.'

Heppingstall took a moment to respond. 'If it'll help get all this cleared up, then I'm sure it can't hurt.' She made to get up from the armchair, clearly finding it a challenge.

'No need for you to put yourself out.' Phillips stood. 'We're detectives; we can find it on our own.'

Jones led the way into the main body of the house, and it didn't take long for him to locate Sebastian's room. Having teenage daughters of his own was clearly an advantage in a situation like this.

The room itself was a decent size and decorated as you'd expect a seventeen-year-old's bedroom to be: dark painted walls, posters of rock bands Phillips had never heard of and an electric drum kit positioned in one corner of the room. It also had a unique aroma Phillips couldn't place. 'What's that smell?' she asked as they both slipped on latex gloves.

Jones turned to face her and laughed. 'Eau de teenage boy. A mixture of sweat, weed and, well, you know...' He paused as if trying to find the right words.

'Don't go any further.' She waved him away. 'I get it.'

For the next ten minutes they methodically worked their way around the room, looking for any sign of the Nike trainers, the bucket hat or the sunglasses. Despite finding a number of items that closely resembled what they needed, any actual evidence was nowhere to be found.

Phillips cast her eyes around the room as she checked off the list of places they'd searched. 'So we've looked inside the wardrobe, on top of it, behind it and under it. The drawers, under the bed, behind the curtains. Nothing. Not a bloody thing.'

'I know, which is very un-teenage behaviour,' replied Jones. 'My girls just chuck everything in a pile in the middle of the room. I swear to God, guv, some days I feel like I'm living in an episode of *Ultimate Hoarders*.'

'So where would a teenage boy hide something that he wouldn't want to be found?'

'Beats me.' Jones shrugged. 'I have enough on my plate trying to understand the wonderfully chaotic minds of teenage girls.'

Phillips walked slowly around the bedroom, checking each and every nook and cranny, but still she found nothing.

'What now?' asked Jones.

Phillips let out a loud sigh of frustration. 'I guess we'd better tidy up.'

For the next few minutes, they both did their best to put everything back the way they'd found it.

'Best shove that bottom drawer back in.' Phillips nodded beyond Jones.

He followed her gaze, then bent down and attempted to get the drawer closed. 'It's stuck,' he muttered as he jiggled it back and forth.

Phillips moved next to him. 'Probably just needs a bit of muscle behind it.'

Jones craned his neck towards her. 'I know I'm not Bov, but I'm not a bloody weakling either. I'm telling you, this thing ain't budging.'

Phillips dropped to her haunches. 'Pull it right out.'

Jones obliged, and as the drawer came free from its surround, Phillips grabbed it, spinning it around so they could both see the back.

'Bingo,' said Jones.

They both stared at the switchblade taped to the back panel of the drawer.

Phillips pulled it loose and held it lightly between her gloved thumb and forefinger. 'Now what have we got here?'

'Exactly the type of knife Chakrabortty said was used on Nixon.'

Phillips sucked her teeth. 'Well, well. I think a bollocking from his absent father is going to be the least of Sebastian's worries.'

25

'We need a warrant to search the whole house, Bov,' said Phillips through the in-car phone system as they raced to St Bartholomew's school.

'And you're pretty sure the knife you found was used on Nixon?'

'Based on the fact we know the kid was there when the attack happened and we found it hidden away in his room, it has to be.'

'No problem. That should be enough for the paperwork. I'll call my mate Jonny at the Magistrates' Court now.'

'Make sure you stress how urgent this is. We need the old lady's house locked down tight before she starts cleaning his room and removing all the forensics.'

'I'll call Jonny now and then book in the CSIs.'

'Great. And get yourself over to the house as well. I want you ready to go in as soon as the warrant is approved.'

'On it.'

'We're also going to need a uniform team at the school to take him into custody.'

'*No worries. I'll ask Whistler to sort that.*'

'Thanks, Bov.' Phillips ended the call.

'We should be there in two minutes,' said Jones.

Phillips nodded. 'I just hope his grandmother hasn't called ahead of us.'

'Why would she? We didn't tell her about the knife. As far as she's concerned, we found nothing.'

'Which worries me slightly.'

'How do you mean?'

'Well, she must be in her mid-seventies,' said Phillips. 'How's she gonna react when Bov knocks on her door with a full forensic team in tow? She could end up having a bloody heart attack.'

Jones glanced left. 'I hadn't thought of that.'

Phillips pressed redial.

Bov answered promptly. '*Guv?*'

'I want you to take PC Lawford with you to the Heppingstall house.'

'*Okay. Anything I need to be aware of?*'

'The old lady needs handling with care. I'm worried we could scare the crap out of her when we turn up mob handed. Lawford's job is to take care of Mrs Heppingstall and make sure she's okay. It's all going to come as quite a shock. Lawford has a good nature; she'll be able to keep her calm.'

'*I've just seen her come in a few minutes ago. I'll go and speak to her now.*'

'Good stuff.'

Jones indicated left as they approached the sign at the entrance to the school.

'Right, we're at St Bart's. Let me know as soon as the warrant is approved.'

'*Will do.*'

Phillips rang off and gazed out through the windscreen towards the school sitting at the end of the long drive. It was a gargantuan stone building that looked like it belonged in a Harry Potter movie.

'Bit posher than my girls' school,' said Jones.

'Bit more expensive too.'

'How much do you reckon?'

'Well, back in the dim and distant past when we moved back from Hong Kong, my dad talked about sending me and my brother here to do our A Levels. That was until he realised they wanted twenty grand a year for the pair of us. And that was way back when.'

'Nothing wrong with a good old-fashioned state school.' Jones pulled the car into a visitor's space directly in front of the building. 'I mean, it didn't do me any harm, did it?'

Phillips raised an eyebrow as she turned to face him. 'You sure about that?'

'What do you mean?' Jones protested.

Phillips flashed a wry grin. 'Come on. We've got work to do.'

The inside of the building matched the exterior, dark and foreboding. High ceilings sat atop tall stone columns, and the walls were a mixture of painted render and oak panelling. The intricate tiled floor caused their footsteps to echo around the cavernous entrance hall.

Following signs for the admin block, they soon found themselves facing an imposing double-width oak door – the words 'school office' emblazoned in gold across the middle. Phillips knocked, and a moment later the door opened.

A woman Phillips guessed was in her fifties appeared. She looked every bit the clichéd British schoolmistress, with greying hair, beige and brown clothes and half-rimmed glasses perched on the end of her long nose. The name plate on her desk suggested she was called Mrs Drabble. 'Can I help you?'

Phillips held up her ID badge. 'DCI Phillips and DI Jones. We need to speak to the headmaster, please.'

'I'm afraid *Mrs* Freeman is busy at the moment.' Mrs Drabble appeared to sneer slightly.

'Aren't we all?' replied Phillips, in no mood for games. 'This is an urgent police matter, and I'd appreciate it if you could let her know we're here. We won't be leaving until we speak with her.'

Mrs Drabble stared back, contempt etched around her thin lips. 'Wait here.' With that, she headed back into the office.

A minute later, she returned. 'Mrs Freeman said she can see you now.' Beckoning them inside, she gestured towards another door on the opposite side of the office, labelled 'Headmistress'. 'Please go through.'

Phillips led the way, and pushing open the second door, she stepped into an opulent room with double height ceilings that looked more like a chapel than an office. Freeman was sitting in a high-backed, maroon leather Chesterfield chair, behind a vast oak desk. She was a slim woman, her long face framed by a sharp dark bob, her mouth turned down at the sides. Everything about her screamed austere and entitled.

'I hope this won't take long. I've just had to cancel a very important call,' she almost spat as she remained seated.

Phillips was more than happy to skip the small talk as

she moved to stand in front of Freeman with Jones at her shoulder. 'We need to speak to Sebastian Heppingstall as a matter of urgency.'

Freeman's eyes narrowed. 'I take it you have permission from the boy's parents?'

'No. I don't.'

'In that case, I'm afraid you've had a wasted journey. Without parental consent, I am not permitted to let you or anybody else speak to any of our students.'

Phillips fished in her pocket before holding her badge open in front of Freeman's face. 'I am a detective chief inspector in the Major Crimes Unit, and this badge allows me to talk to every single student in this place if I so choose.'

Freeman shook her head. 'Not without parental consent, you can't. If you can come back in twenty-four hours, I can speak to Sebastian's father, and if he agrees to it, I will organise access for you.'

Phillips glanced at Jones, whose frustrated expression matched her own. She turned back and took a step closer to the desk. 'Okay. Here's the deal. We're investigating one case of murder and another of attempted murder. Sebastian is a person of interest in both investigations. We're not here to simply talk to him – we're here to *arrest* him.'

'That's preposterous!' Freeman was incredulous. 'St Bart's doesn't produce criminals.'

'We'll be the judge of that,' replied Phillips. 'And either *you* take us to him right now, or I'll call in a small army of uniformed officers, under blues-and-twos, to lock this entire school down in thirty minutes flat. We'll even cordon off the gate on the main road with lots of eye-catching blue and white police tape for good measure – just to make sure *everyone* knows something big is going down here. I'm sure that will do wonders for your intake rates in September.'

Freeman glared back but remained silent.

'So.' Phillips flashed a thin smile. 'Best you get off your backside and take us to him.'

Freeman shoved back the chair and stood bolt upright. 'I'll need to find out which lesson he's in,' she muttered. 'I'll be back in a moment.'

Once she'd left the room, Phillips turned to face Jones.

'Bloody hell, guv,' he whispered. 'That told her.'

'Too harsh?' she whispered back with a wry smile.

Jones shook his head. 'Nah. Spot on. Snooty cow.'

A moment later, Freeman returned. 'According to the timetable, he's in History with Dr Bell. It's on the other side of the school. If you'd like to follow me, I can take you there.'

'Thank you,' said Phillips, trying her best to appear magnanimous.

The walk through the old building to Dr Bell's class took five minutes as they zigzagged through a maze of corridors, each turn carrying them deeper into the belly of the school. After climbing two flights of a wide stone staircase, they finally stopped outside a classroom where the top half of the door had been fitted with a glass panel allowing sight of the lesson taking place inside.

'If it's okay with you, and to minimise disruption to the rest of the class, I'll go in and get him,' said Freeman. 'I'll need to let Dr Bell know what's happening. Discreetly, of course.'

'That's fine,' replied Phillips.

'And if you do insist on arresting him, could you do it away from prying, impressionable eyes?'

'Of course. We'll be equally discreet.'

'Thank you,' said Freeman before heading in.

Phillips watched as the headmistress made her way to the front of the class, where she stopped and appeared to whisper to Dr Bell, who frowned and glanced at Phillips and Jones. Next, Freeman pointed to a young man sitting in the middle of the class with his back to the door and gestured for him to get up.

'So that's bucket-hat guy,' said Jones.

The young man stood up and turned to face the door. Shock flashed across his face as he spotted Phillips and Jones.

'Doesn't look very pleased to see us, does he?' Jones added.

Phillips kept her own counsel as she watched the tall youth lumber his way towards the exit, his head down, shoulders sagging.

As Freeman stepped through the door, Heppingstall moved out into the corridor alongside her.

Dr Bell wasn't far behind. 'Mrs Freeman has briefly explained to me why you're here, and I simply must protest,' he said as the door closed behind him. 'There is no way Sebastian would be involved in anything like you're suggesting.'

Phillips ignored his protestations as she stared at Heppingstall. 'I think we know different, don't we?'

Heppingstall avoided her gaze.

Jones placed his right hand behind the young man's elbow. 'Come on, son. Let's do this outside, away from your pals.'

'Don't worry, Sebastian,' said Freeman. 'I'll call your father at once. He'll know what to do.'

Jones set off, guiding Heppingstall down the stone steps.

'You're making a huge mistake,' Bell protested once more.

'Let's hope you're right,' replied Phillips. 'For his sake.' With that, she followed Jones out.

As soon as they reached the ground floor, Jones cautioned Heppingstall and placed him in handcuffs, ready for the walk back to the main entrance and the uniform team stationed out front.

Phillips glanced at the boy's shoes now. 'Jones,' she said, nodding down at them.

He followed her gaze.

'Black Nike trainers with a white sole and swoosh,' said Phillips.

'They look pretty big to me, too.'

'Yeah,' she replied. 'About a size thirteen, rather like the footprint left behind when Robert Nixon was stabbed.'

26

As they neared Ashton House, Phillips's phone rang.

'Bov,' she said, accepting the call, 'did you get the warrant?'

'Yeah. I'm at the Heppingstall house now.'

'Is Lawford with you?'

'Yes, guv, and I have to say, she's been brilliant with the old lady.'

'Does Meredith know we've arrested her grandson?'

'Yeah, Lawford was about to tell her when her son called from Dubai and beat her to it. By the sounds of it, he was raging on the phone. Apparently, his lawyer is en route to Ashton House as we speak.'

'Do we know who it is?'

'No, boss. Just that whoever it is, is on their way.'

'Judging by the school fees he's willing to pay, I'm sure we can expect a big hitter.'

'Yeah, no doubt.'

'So how did Meredith take the news of Sebastian's arrest?'

'Not great at first, as you can imagine, but Lawford did a great job of calming her down and explaining what was happening with the search, and they're both in the conservatory having a cuppa at the moment.'

'Excellent. And what about forensics?

'Arrived about fifteen minutes ago. They're setting up as we speak.'

'Is it Evans?' Jones chipped in.

'No, mate. Clara's leading this one.'

'Well, when you speak to her, tell her we think we've just found a match on the shoe print they found next to Nixon.'

'Really? Is it the boy's?'

'Yeah, he was wearing an identical pair to the ones Whistler showed us.'

'Looks like this one could be a slam dunk, then?'

'We'll see. It's early days yet,' Phillips cut in. 'Right. We're nearly back at base, so keep us posted on any developments at the house as soon as they come through.'

'Goes without saying, boss.'

Phillips dropped the call.

An hour later, back in MCU, Jones tapped on Phillips's door as she was updating the decision logs.

'Seems we're going up against David Collins with the Heppingstall boy, guv.'

Phillips sat back in the chair. 'A big hitter *indeed*.'

'We're gonna need our wits about us on this one. If anyone can dig Sebastian out of his current predicament, it's Collins.'

Phillips took a moment as she considered what lay ahead. She'd been up against Collins on several occasions, and he was a formidable foe. In fact, only last year, thanks to him, what appeared to the whole world to be a stone-wall conviction had ended with a not-guilty verdict. That result had seen a very dangerous gang boss walk free despite the overwhelming amount of evidence against him.

'I've just spoken to Sergeant Walsh in custody,' Jones continued. 'As you'd expect, Collins has taken the lad off for a private consultation. I'm guessing it'll be at least another hour before we can get in front of him.'

Phillips had already carefully planned out the interview. 'Thankfully for us, the evidence is potentially damning. If we can link the knife to the attack on Nixon, and match the shoe print, then, with the CCTV footage, I'm not sure even Collins could find any way to refute it.'

'Let's hope so, guv.'

'I'm sure of it. The challenge, however, will be trying to crack the inevitable no-comment stance Collins is so fond of using.'

'Walsh said he'd call me when they're ready.'

'Okay,' replied Phillips. 'As soon as he does, we'll get cracking.'

JUST OVER AN HOUR LATER, Phillips and Jones entered Interview Room Three.

Sebastian was sitting behind a small table, wearing a grey tracksuit that had been provided by the custody team, his eyes bowed, shoulders sagging once more. Collins, by contrast, sitting next to him, exuded confidence and opulence in a crisp hand-tailored navy suit matched with a bright red tie. His tanned skin was accentuated by his thick silver hair, coiffed and lacquered to within an inch of its life – and by the diamond-encrusted Cartier watch on his left wrist, glistening in the light.

Phillips and Jones took the seats opposite them.

'Well, this is a pleasant surprise, David,' said Phillips, her tone facetious.

Collins flashed his trademark toothy grin. 'Likewise, Chief Inspector.'

For the next minute or so, Phillips explained the process and procedures in place for recording the interview before finally switching on the DIR. 'Sebastian, why don't you start by telling us where you were on Friday evening, at approximately 5.45 p.m.?'

Sebastian glanced at Collins, who barely nodded, then turned back to face Phillips. 'No comment.'

Phillips felt her jaw clench. Even though she'd been expecting this response, it didn't make it any less frustrating. 'I see.' She pushed across a CCTV still of him running from the scene of the Nixon murder. 'Is this you in the picture?'

'No comment.'

She passed across another image, this time of Sebastian stepping onto a train at Piccadilly station. 'How about this one? Is this you in the photo?'

Sebastian shuffled in his seat. 'No comment.'

She glared at him in silence, but he refused to make eye contact as she passed over a third image, this time of him getting into the taxi at Wilmslow station. 'Is that you in this photograph, Sebastian?'

'No comment.'

Collins and his client were playing a well-worn game of cat and mouse: a legal strategy that was becoming more and more prevalent in interviews these days. By answering no comment, Collins could assess the case against his client before conjuring up – quite literally at times – his defence. She totally understood it made sense for lawyers to do it this way, but it seriously annoyed her that she was still required to ask the full gamut of questions in order for the evidence to be admissible in court.

She passed over a closeup photograph of the cluster of stab wounds inflicted on Nixon. 'Do you know what caused these wounds?' she asked.

'He can't possibly know what he's looking at, Chief Inspector,' Collins shot back. 'It could be a photograph of anything.'

Phillips turned her gaze to Collins. 'It's a photo of a number of stab wounds found on Robert Nixon's body. A man we believe your client attacked on Friday night, along with his two associates.'

Sebastian swallowed hard as he stared down at the photo.

Phillips turned her focus back to him. 'Do you know what made those incisions?'

Sebastian glanced at Collins – who shook his head ever so slightly. 'No comment.'

'We found this knife taped to the back of a drawer in your bedroom.' Phillips pushed across a photo of the switchblade. 'It's being forensically tested for DNA as we speak. The postmortem revealed that the blade used in the attack on Nixon was the same shape and size as a switchblade. If we can match *that* knife to *those* wounds, you're in a whole world of trouble, Sebastian.'

The boy remained silent.

'This isn't a game, son,' Jones cut in. 'You're looking at life in prison for this.'

'He's right,' added Phillips. 'The best years of your adult life, locked up with the scum of the earth, day in, day out, constantly watching your back, wondering if they're coming for you. A rich boy like you in prison? You won't know what's hit you. Is that what you want?'

'May I remind you, Chief Inspector,' said Collins, 'that my client is still legally classed as a minor, and as such, this threatening line of questioning is totally unacceptable.'

Phillips was struggling to hide her contempt. 'And may I remind you, Mr Collins, that your client is sixteen years old and suspected of murdering a father of three. Not only that, but we have reason to believe he was also involved in a car-bomb attack that left another father in Intensive Care, fighting for his life.'

'Based on what evidence?' Collins spat back.

Phillips opened her folder and fished out a photo of the gang taken outside David Lloyd at the time Grayson was attacked. 'Based on the fact that the same three individuals were captured on CCTV at both locations. One of whom we believe is Sebastian.'

Collins glanced down at the image for a few seconds, then shrugged. 'All I see is a bunch of people wearing hoodies and scarves. That could be anyone in that photo.'

Phillips retrieved the image. 'Well, we'll just have to let a jury decide, won't we?'

'This will never get to court and you know it,' sneered Collins. 'It's circumstantial at best.'

Phillips recoiled. 'A knife hidden in the boy's room is circumstantial?'

'It will be by the time I've finished with it. I mean, for starters, you'd have to prove it actually belonged to *Sebastian.*'

'Well, who else would have put it there?' Phillips countered.

'Not for me to say,' replied Collins nonchalantly. 'Not at this stage, anyway.'

Phillips could feel her face twisting, knowing full well that Collins was more than capable of sowing seeds of doubt in the minds of even the most robust members of a jury, but there was little to be gained from taking him on at this stage of the investigation.

'This is your last chance, Sebastian,' she urged. 'Come clean and tell us everything you know, and we can put in a good word with the CPS when it comes to sentencing. In the long run, that could be the difference between a Cat B holiday camp and Hawk Green maximum security.' She leaned in closer to him now. 'Come on, do the right thing for everyone. Tell us what you did, and let us help you get out of this mess you're in.'

Sebastian lifted his head, revealing eyes filled with fear, his mouth open, as if ready to speak.

Collins placed his right hand on the boy's left wrist. 'Sebastian will be maintaining his no-comment stance at this moment in time. I'm sure you understand.'

Phillips sighed as she looked up at the clock on the wall. 'Very well. In that case, DCI Phillips is terminating this interview at 4.17 p.m.' She gathered her files and stood. 'You're making a big mistake, Sebastian.'

The boy stared back like a frightened puppy.

Phillips focused on Collins. 'No doubt, we'll be seeing you again very soon, David.'

He flashed that same toothy grin. 'I look forward to it.'

Phillips turned, then headed for the door.

27

Ten minutes later, Phillips made her way into Carter's outer office, where she found his PA, Diane, working away.

'Is the boss in?' Phillips asked.

Diane glanced up from her PC screen and smiled. 'Yes, and he's free for the next half an hour, so go right in.'

'Thanks,' said Phillips before stepping through the open door to Carter's main office.

Her boss appeared lost in a pile of paperwork and hadn't noticed her enter.

Phillips cleared her throat to attract his attention.

He glanced up and peered over the top of his glasses. 'Hello, Jane,' he said warmly.

'Have you got a minute, sir?'

'Of course,' he said before removing his glasses, which he laid on the desk. 'In fact, I was about to call you.'

'Oh really? What about?' Phillips took the seat opposite him.

'I understand we have a teenager in custody.'

Phillips frowned. 'News travels fast.'

'Yes.' Carter sighed. 'I just got off the phone to Fox about that very thing, as it happens.'

'Fox? How the hell does she know we have someone in custody? We only arrested him a few hours ago.'

'Turns out the boy's father is very well connected.'

'Of course he bloody is,' Phillips shot back. 'She'll be telling me to let him go next.'

Carter sat forward. 'Not quite, but she did make it very clear we should tread carefully. In her words, "He's still only a child, and we don't want to be seen to be too heavy-handed with him."'

'A child?' Phillips was incredulous. 'He's sixteen. And have you seen the size of him? He could give Bovalino a run for his money. The kid's a giant.'

'I know, I know,' Carter said, raising his arms in surrender. 'I don't like it any more than you do, but she's the boss, and while she didn't say it definitively, she gave me the distinct impression that she's personally connected to his father, Jeremy Heppingstall, in some way.'

Phillips dropped her chin to her chest for a moment before looking up again. 'Why does that not surprise me?'

Carter linked his fingers together on the desk. 'So, what have we actually got on the Heppingstall kid?'

'Firstly, CCTV footage of him running away from the Nixon murder.'

'Well, that's a good start.'

'We also found the potential murder weapon in his bedroom.'

'Anything else?' asked Carter.

'Yeah, a partial shoe print in the mud next to Nixon's body. Evans identified it as a black, size thirteen, Nike trainer, identical to a pair Sebastian Heppingstall was wearing when he was arrested. We also have two potential eyewitnesses.'

'Have they identified the lad yet?'

'Not yet, no. We're in the process of organising the line-up.'

'And what about the knife and trainers? Do we know for sure they were both connected to the Nixon murder?'

'No, but Evans is testing each of them as we speak.'

'How long before we get the results back?'

Phillips shrugged. 'I don't know for certain, as I've not spoken to Evans, but I'm hoping later today or first thing in the morning at the latest.'

'And what about Adrian Firth and his girlfriend? Do we know if they're in any way connected to Sebastian?'

'Not yet, no. And while it seems odd that a rich kid like Sebastian would be in cahoots with a pair of clowns like Firth and Holmes, we can't rule it out just yet.'

'I see.' Carter fell silent, evidently deep in thought.

'What you thinking, sir?'

'I'm wondering the best way to play this with Fox.'

'How'd you mean?' Phillips asked.

'Well, we both know what she's like once she sets her mind to something. If she wants us to tread carefully, we need to let her think that's exactly what we're doing, even if we aren't.'

'So how do we do that? I'm not about to let him go, sir.'

'I should hope not.' Carter chuckled. 'No, I'm thinking maybe we just leave him alone for a while, no more inter-views for the time being. Allow him to speak to his parents, give him some food, let him get a bit of kip, that sort of thing.'

Phillips felt her jaw clench. 'We wet-nurse him?'

'Not quite how I would put it, but yes. Just *until* we get the results back from forensics. If they prove he's our guy, then he's all yours.'

'Of course, sir. If that's what you want.'

'None of this is what I want, Jane,' replied Carter, 'but we are where we are when it comes to managing the chief constable's expectations.'

Phillips exhaled loudly. 'I know, sir, and I totally get it, but I'm really struggling taking orders from her, knowing what she did to Entwistle.'

'I know, and I feel the same way as you,' said Carter. 'But the reality is, until we can prove she did *any* of it, we're stuck with her.'

Phillips nodded sagely as she stood. 'And that's what I'm afraid of, sir.'

28

A couple of hours later, Phillips pulled the Mini Cooper onto the drive next to Adam's red coupe. Switching off the engine, she took a moment to gather her thoughts as she stared out at the clear evening sky. Her head was pounding, and she was struggling to shake the grubbiness she felt having to kowtow to Fox and her cronies within the Manchester elite. Not for the first time, she wondered if she'd made the right decision going back after almost a year out of the job. Was it worth the hassle? If Fox was as crooked as she suspected, would she forever be fighting a losing battle?

With no answers forthcoming, she got out of the car and headed inside.

Stepping into the hallway, she was immediately struck by the delicious aromas filtering through from the kitchen. It seemed Adam was cooking up another storm.

She spotted him next to the stove, dancing with his back to the room as he cooked, James Brown's 'Get Up Offa That Thing' playing on the smart speaker.

He hadn't heard her come in, so she crept up behind him. 'Hey, babe,' she whispered in his right ear.

Jumping with fright, he span round to face her. 'Jesus! You scared the shit out of me.'

'Sorry, couldn't resist.' She laughed, drawing him into a long hug and savouring his unique scent.

'How was your day?' he asked, resting his chin on her head.

Phillips gripped him tighter. 'Don't ask.'

'That bad?'

She released her grip and looked up at him. 'To be honest, I haven't got the energy to talk about it. I just want to switch off and forget about Major Crimes for one night.'

Adam kissed her on the forehead. 'Sounds like a great idea. Why don't you grab a shower, and by the time you get back down, this'll be ready.'

'What are we having?'

'Spicy seafood noodles.'

'Sounds delicious,' she said before kissing him on the cheek and heading off upstairs.

Twenty minutes later, having washed the day away, she slipped on an old, faded T-shirt and jogging bottoms and made her way back down to the kitchen.

Adam smiled as he handed her a glass of her favourite Pinot Grigio.

'God, I need this,' she said, taking a mouthful. 'How long will dinner be?'

'About five minutes.'

Slipping onto one of the breakfast stools next to the kitchen island, she watched as he busied himself pulling everything together. She'd never been much of a cook herself. Long days in the office usually finished with some form of microwave meal or a takeaway on the way home, so it was a real treat to have him cook on the rare evenings he wasn't working at the hospital. She allowed herself a smile as the wine kicked in, and she finally started to relax.

A minute or so later her phone began vibrating on the countertop: Don Townsend was calling.

Adam glanced across. 'Who is it?'

'Nobody important,' she replied, rejecting the call.

As Adam began plating up, the phone vibrated again.

'Whoever it is, they really want to speak to you,' said Adam.

Phillips took another mouthful of wine, then rejected the call once more. 'Well, I don't want to speak to them.'

It wasn't long before Townsend's name appeared on-screen for a third time as the phone vibrated once more.

In that moment, it was as if every frustration Phillips had felt throughout the day crashed over her like a tidal wave. Who the hell did Don Townsend think he was? Ringing her day and night whenever he felt like it. She was off duty and about to have a lovely dinner with Adam. Unable to control her temper, she grabbed the phone and pressed the green answer icon. 'What the hell do you want?'

'Nice to speak to you too, Jane,' he said sarcastically.

'Seriously, Don. This has got to stop. I have a life outside of work, you know.'

'Yeah, sure you do,' he scoffed. *'Rumour has it you're holding a kid from St Bart's in relation to the car-bomb attack and Robert Nixon murder.'*

How the hell did he know that?

'Your silence would suggest it's true.'

Phillips felt like she was boiling inside. 'That is confidential information known only to a select number of people. How did you find out about it?'

'*So it is true?*'

'Don, I'm not going to keep playing this game with you.'

Townsend chuckled. '*But it's such a fun game, Jane. And you're so good at it.*'

Phillips glanced at Adam, who was staring at her, his brow furrowed. 'You okay?' he mouthed silently.

She nodded back. 'This conversation is over, Don.'

'*Not if you want to keep the chief constable's past out of the paper, it isn't.*'

Phillips felt ready to explode. 'Do you know what, Don? Write what the fuck you like. I'm past caring,' she growled, terminating the call. She'd had it with protecting Fox's shitty reputation.

29

The team were in early the next morning, and as Entwistle handed around hot drinks, Phillips updated them on the details of her call with Townsend the previous night.

'So, realistically, where *could* he be getting the information from?' Jones asked as he removed the lid from his steaming peppermint tea.

'That's what we need to figure out,' replied Phillips, taking a sip of her coffee as Entwistle sat at his desk. 'Who in the chain of arrest had access to that information?'

'Us four,' replied Bovalino, 'plus the uniform team, forensics and the custody crew.'

'Which uniformed guys picked him up at the school?' asked Jones.

Bovalino checked his notes. 'Jennings and Hussain.'

'And what about forensics?' Jones added. 'Who was at the Heppingstall house for the search?'

'Clara, Aziz and Frankie. And me of course. I was there too.'

Phillips nodded. 'And who were the custody officers yesterday?'

'Walsh, Ali and Benson,' Entwistle cut in.

'Any of them on your list of potential moles?' said Phillips.

'Give me a sec, and I'll check.' Entwistle scanned the list of people connected to the previous investigations that Townsend had managed to source sensitive information on. 'From a forensic point of view, Clara and Aziz.' He scanned further down the list. 'And we're looking at Sergeant Walsh and Ali in the custody team.'

Phillips took another sip of coffee as she considered if any of those names were likely mole suspects. The truth was, she had no idea; and, without a good reason, there was little chance of being able to officially investigate any of them either.

Just then, Evans's name appeared on-screen as her phone began to ring. Picking it up, she made her way into her office before answering, 'Andy, I'm hoping you've got good news for me.'

'*I do, as it goes. We have a clear match on the knife.*'

'Really? That's brilliant.'

'*Nixon's DNA was all over it, along with Heppingstall's. There's little doubt it was used in the knife attack. Plus, we found traces of the boy's DNA on Nixon's suit jacket.*'

Phillips held her breath in silent hope.

'*And there's more.*'

'Go on.'

'*We've also matched the shoe print left at the scene to the trainers you took from Heppingstall. Size thirteen, Nike Court Vision Low Next To Nature.*'

'We've got him.' Phillips clenched her fist and punched

the air in triumph. 'Not even Collins could refute that kind of evidence.'

'*Collins?*' Evans asked. '*Who's Collins?*'

'Never mind. This is first-rate work, Andy, first rate.'

'*We always aim to please in forensics.*'

'Yeah, well, you've really come up trumps this time.' She paused before continuing, 'By the way, Andy, who in your team was aware the suspect was a student at St Bart's during the testing process for the knife and trainer print?'

'*Why do you ask?*'

'No reason, really, just wondering.'

'*All of us, actually. It's not usually the case, but because of the house search, it came up. The school photos on the wall gave it away.*'

'So you, Aziz, Clara and Frankie?'

'*That's right.*'

'Okay, thanks.'

'*Is anything wrong?*' Evans asked.

'No, no, not at all,' Phillips lied. 'It's all good. In fact, it's more than good. I should get going so I can put your excellent work to good use.'

'*I'm sending the reports over as we speak. They're quite big files, so may take a couple of minutes to land.*'

'Perfect. Thanks, Andy.'

Phillips moved to the window and stared down onto the Ashton House car park as she processed the call and the mixed feelings it had stirred up. On the one hand, the evidence against Sebastian was damning, but on the other, could one of the forensics team really be the mole? It didn't bear thinking about, but her suspicions also couldn't be ignored. Turning round, she headed back out to the main office.

'Evans has just confirmed the DNA found on the knife we took from the bedroom is a match for Nixon and Sebastian.'

'Get in!' Bovalino clapped his hands together.

'Not only that,' she continued, 'they've also matched the shoe print found in the mud to the Nike trainers we took off him when we picked him up.'

'Slam dunk, guv,' said Jones, an elated grin on his face.

'Yeah, certainly looks that way. But I still want to be certain. How are we getting on arranging the line-up for the guys who tried to stop him getting away?'

'Still working on it, boss,' said Bovalino. 'It's not that easy finding lads his age and size.'

'Make it a priority, okay?'

'Of course.'

Phillips said nothing for a moment, her mind wandering back to the call with Evans.

Jones's eyes narrowed. 'Everything okay, guv?'

She rested her hands on the back of the spare chair and pursed her lips. 'No, it's not.'

'So, what's the problem?'

'On the call just then.' She thumbed back towards her office. 'Evans confirmed that because of photos they spotted at the house search, *every* member of his team knew Sebastian went to St Bart's.'

Jones sat forward. 'Which potentially puts each one of them in the frame as our mole.'

'Exactly,' said Phillips.

'Bloody hell, boss.' Jones blew out his lips. 'That's not good.'

'No, it's really not. Look, I hope I'm wrong on this, but from now on, I want us *all* to be extra vigilant when it comes to information leaving this department. Until we can prove otherwise, we have to assume anything and everything can and will be leaked to Townsend if we share it outside of this group. So, unless specified, everything is on a need-to-know basis for the time being, okay?'

Each man nodded.

'Right.' Phillips unlocked her phone screen. 'Time to call Derek Rogers and see if the CPS will authorise murder charges against Sebastian.'

'Well, based on the evidence, if they don't, we might as well all go home,' said Jones.

Phillips offered a thin smile as she dialled Rogers's number and marched back towards her office.

30

After collecting his decaf Frappuccino with oat milk, Tex chose a table to the rear of the Starbucks coffee shop, as far away as possible from any prying eyes and ears. Thankfully, the music playing through the PA system was quite loud, which made it difficult to hear any of the conversations happening at the tables around him. Taking his seat, he scanned the room for anyone he might know, and when he was finally satisfied he didn't, he settled down to wait for Clem.

She arrived five minutes later, her face strained as she scurried from the door to join him.

'Are you not getting a drink?' he asked before taking a mouthful of his own.

Clem shook her head. 'I don't want anything.'

Tex felt his brow furrow. 'What's up? You look nervous.'

'That's because I am,' she growled under her breath. 'Seb's in custody, for fuck's sake!'

'Ssh!' Tex glanced left and right to check if anyone had

heard. Thankfully it appeared not. 'Code names only, Clem. You know that.'

She bit her lip as tears welled in her eyes, and when she spoke, her voice was low. 'This has gotten totally out of hand. First the car bomb that went wrong, then Nixon dies, and now Se—' She caught herself. 'Now Squeaky's been arrested. It's totally messed up. I want out.'

'You can't get out now. It's way too late for that.'

'But what if Squeaky talks?'

'He won't. He knows what's at stake.'

'Really?' Clem's eyes darted around the room. 'You know how easily led he is. If the cops get inside his head, he could tell them everything. We could all go to prison for the rest of our lives.'

'He won't say anything. He's a soldier. He knows the drill.'

'Jesus!' spat Clem. 'He's *not* a soldier, he's a dumb teenager who got caught up in something that's now totally out of control. Do you *really* think he's gonna keep his mouth shut? Cos I don't.'

'Yes, I do,' he replied calmly. 'Because if he doesn't, Charlie will make sure he stays quiet forever. He as good as told me Seb's dead if he grasses.'

'How?' Clem was incredulous. 'He's locked up in a police cell, for God's sake.'

Tex shrugged. 'Charlie can get to him wherever he is. He as good as told me that yesterday – said there's nowhere on the planet Squeaky can hide where he won't find him. Charlie can get to anyone, anywhere.'

'This is so fucked up.' She dropped her head into her hands.

'We knew what we were getting into when we started all

this, Clem.'

She lifted her head. 'No, we didn't. *You* did. I thought we were trying to do something good. Making some noise to get people's attention before it was too late for the planet. If I'd have known what you and Charlie were really planning, I'd never have got involved in any of it. And I wouldn't have let you, either.'

Tex leaned in across the table and whispered, 'You must have known people were going to get hurt. We planted a bomb under a car, for God's sake.'

'I know that, but I had no idea Grayson wouldn't be able to get out of the car when it went off. I always thought the plan was to destroy the engine, to scare him.'

'And what use is scaring people? If we want people to wake up to what's happening, there has to be casualties. That's how you win the war, by destroying the enemy.'

Clem swatted away a tear as it streaked down her cheek. 'I'm scared, Tex. I don't want to do this anymore.'

He reached across and held her hand. 'We don't have a choice, babe. We're in this until the end now.'

Her bottom lip began to tremble.

'Take a few deep breaths,' he said softly. 'We've got this.'

For the next few minutes, silence descended as Clem did her best to steady her breathing and calm herself down.

When she had finally relaxed a little, Tex opened his phone. 'Charlie sent through the instructions for the next target and Operation Navaho.'

She closed her eyes.

'He's given us very specific instructions on how he wants it to go down tonight.' He passed across the phone. 'We're to take down the target as soon as he arrives at the Ollerton Hall Hotel. Think you can do it?'

Opening her eyes, she stared at the message. 'Are you for real? That's insane. I'm not doing that. No way.'

'You have to.'

'No, I don't. I hear what you're saying about Charlie, but I'd rather take my chances with some online lunatic compared to the murder squad. I want nothing more to do with this.'

Tex dropped his chin to his chest before looking up again. '*I* can't do what he wants, Clem. It *has* to be you.'

'No.' She folded her arms tightly across her chest. 'I'm sorry, and I love you, I really do, but no.'

'Well, then, we're both as good as dead,' he said flatly. 'If we don't action the operation tonight as planned, he'll kill us both, and all of this will have been for nothing.'

Clem recoiled. 'It *has* all been for nothing. I mean, not one single person knows that Terra is behind the attacks. Nobody has the first clue that all this is about trying to stop climate change – attempting to save what's left of our planet. Have you ever stopped to ask why that is?'

Tex straightened. 'He's waiting for the right time.'

She shook her head. 'And when will that be?'

'When Charlie says so.'

Clem banged her fist on the table, drawing puzzled looks from nearby patrons. 'Stop being such a puppet!' she growled.

Tex could feel the muscles in his jaw tensing. 'Are you gonna help me or not?'

She stared back in silence before shaking her head. 'No. I'm not.' She pushed the chair back and stood. 'I'm sorry, but I just can't,' she added before spinning on her heel and marching towards the door.

S	ebastian was looking tired and dishevelled by the time PC Ali from the custody team escorted him back to Interview Room Three to meet with Phillips and Jones for a second time. Sitting at his side, Collins, by contrast, looked as bright as a button in another tailored suit, this time a charcoal pinstripe.

'How are you feeling today?' asked Phillips.

Sebastian grunted as he dropped into the plastic seat opposite.

Collins wasted no time. 'My client has written a letter, which he has requested I read on his behalf, if I may?'

Phillips fired up the DIR. When the loud beep had passed, she folded her arms and sat back in the chair. 'Be my guest.'

Collins cleared his throat, then began reading from the page in his hand:

'On the evening of Friday the ninth of June at approximately 5.45 p.m., I was walking through St John's Gardens in Manchester city centre when I saw someone come to blows with a man on the path in front of me. I quickly realised that one of the men – whom I now know to be Robert Nixon – had been seriously injured, and I ran to help him. When I reached Mr Nixon, it was obvious he had been stabbed, as there was a knife protruding from his side. In my haste to help him, I removed the knife and shouted for someone to call for an ambulance. It was at that point that two bystanders, who were walking by the park at the same time, mistakenly believed me to be the attacker and shouted at me to put the knife down. Realising they thought I had stabbed Mr Nixon, I panicked and attempted to flee the scene, at which point the same two men tried to stop me by blocking my path and grabbing me. Scared the police would also think I was responsible for the attack, I fought the two men off and made my way to Piccadilly station, where I got the train to Wilmslow, followed by a taxi home. I was in shock, and it was only when I arrived at my grandmother's house that I realised I was still in possession of the knife. Not knowing what else to do, I hid it behind the drawer in my bedroom, which is where the police found it. I did not commit the knife attack on Robert Nixon, and I have no knowledge of any similar such attack, which I'm told took place at the David Lloyd leisure club in Cheadle on Saturday the third of June.'

Collins looked to Phillips. 'That concludes my client's statement, and I must tell you he now wishes to invoke his right to answer any further questions with no comment.'

Phillips chuckled. 'And you expect us to believe that fairy tale, do you?'

'Believe what you like, Chief Inspector.' Collins flashed his wide grin. 'It's what happened.'

Phillips held his gaze for a moment before turning her

attention to the boy. 'Sebastian, despite what Mr Collins may have told you, we now have enough evidence to put you in prison until you're a middle-aged man. Please forget all this no-comment nonsense and tell us what *really* happened in the park that night. It's the best chance you have of securing some kind of future for yourself.'

Sebastian stared down at the table in silence as Collins scribbled in his expensive notepad.

Phillips continued, 'Don't throw your life away by letting this get to court. *We* know you stabbed Nixon, *you* know you stabbed Nixon – and any jury in the land *will* believe you stabbed Nixon. So do yourself a favour and tell us what really happened. I promise it'll be better in the long run. If you carry on playing this game, you could easily end up spending the best years of your life locked in a cell at Hawk Green for eighteen hours a day.'

Sebastian didn't respond.

Phillips glanced at Jones, who raised his eyebrows.

She sighed. 'Very well, then. If that's how you want to play it, we'll organise for PC Ali to escort you back to the custody suite, where you'll be formally charged with the murder of Robert Nixon.'

Sebastian suddenly looked up, his eyes wide as he turned to Collins.

'Now hang on,' Collins protested.

'For what?' Phillips asked.

'Well, as I've just explained,' Collins said, 'Sebastian is an innocent party in all of this.'

'Come on, David, even *you're* not buying that bullshit story. We have Sebastian's DNA on the knife *and* on the victim's clothes, his footprints in the mud where Nixon died, plus CCTV footage of him fleeing the scene – not to mention eyewitness statements. Once we have the line-up sorted, we're looking at a slam dunk conviction, and your client is going to prison for the next ten to fifteen years, *if* he's lucky.'

Sebastian opened his mouth to speak but seemed to think better of it.

Phillips spotted it. 'If you've got something to say, now is the time to say it, son.'

Sebastian looked to Collins, then back to Phillips.

She sensed he just needed one more nudge. 'If you tell us what really happened, you can get out in front of this. *Or* you can grow old in jail. It's up to you, buddy.'

Sebastian stared at her in silence for a few seconds before mumbling in a low voice, 'I was only following orders.'

'That's enough, Sebastian,' said Collins. 'You don't know what you're saying.'

Phillips flinched slightly. 'You were given *orders* to stab Nixon?'

'Yeah.'

'And who gave you those orders?'

'Seriously,' Collins cut in again. 'Enough of this nonsense.'

'Never mind Mr Collins here.' Phillips glared at Sebastian. '*Who* gave you the orders?'

'Charlie.'

Collins slammed his pen down on his pad. 'I must insist on speaking to my client in private.'

Phillips glared at Sebastian. 'Is that what you want, Sebastian, to go away and make up more lies? Spend even more time in prison? Or do you want to tell us what's *really* going on?'

Sebastian's eyes were wide again now, his mouth partially open. He clearly didn't know which way to turn.

'We can help you, Sebastian, but you've got to start telling the truth.'

The boy continued to stare back in silence.

'Can you do that?' asked Phillips. 'Can you help yourself and tell us what really happened in St John's Gardens?'

'Yes,' he said finally.

'I really must insist,' Collins cut in again.

Phillips turned her focus to the flashy lawyer now. 'The boy has made it clear he wants to talk. I suggest you let him.'

A slight snarl appeared on the man's lips as he stared back. 'I'll allow it.'

'That's very good of you,' Phillips volleyed back, her tone sardonic.

'But,' Collins countered, 'I want it on record that I do not agree with this line of questioning. The boy is clearly not in his right mind, and as such is not aware he's being coerced into incriminating himself.'

Phillips glared at him. 'Are you quite finished?'

Collins nodded.

'Good.' Phillips turned back to Sebastian. 'So, who's Charlie?'

'I don't know. I've never met him.'

'Oh, come on,' Jones cut in. 'You can't expect us to believe that.'

'Honestly, I don't know who he is. He sends the orders via encrypted email, and we carry them out, that's it.'

'We?' asked Phillips. 'Who's *we*?'

'Erm...not we, I mean...I mean me.' He stumbled. 'Me, I carry out the orders.'

'That's not true, is it?' said Jones. 'We *know* there were

three people involved in the knife attack on Nixon, as well as three people who planted the bomb under Grayson's car.'

'He's right,' added Phillips. 'We've got clear CCTV footage to prove it. So who else did this with you?'

Sebastian shook his head. 'I can't say.'

'Can't, or won't?' asked Phillips.

The boy averted his gaze.

Phillips continued, 'Was one of them Adrian Firth?'

Sebastian remained silent.

'Or Kat Holmes?'

Again, no response.

'Look, Sebastian.' Phillips leaned in closer. 'Your mates – whoever they are – are in serious trouble, and believe me, you're really not helping them by staying quiet. The longer this goes on, the worse it'll be for them. So please do them a favour and tell us their names so we can stop this nonsense once and for all.'

'You can't stop it.' Sebastian shook his head. 'Charlie will see to that. He won't stop until the corruption stops.'

Phillips straightened. 'What corruption?'

'The corruption that exists everywhere.' Sebastian's chest puffed now, his confidence returning. 'Politicians turning a blind eye to the untold damage being done by big business on a global scale – trading the planet's resources for thirty pieces of silver. Burning up the Earth's atmosphere in the name of profit. Our world is on fire, our future is in jeopardy, and the people in power are sleepwalking towards Armageddon while everyone looks the other way. That's why the fight has to continue, and that's why Charlie won't stop until everyone truly understands the power of Terra.'

'Terror?' Jones asked. 'What's Terror?'

'Not terror, Terra, T-E-R-R-A,' Sebastian corrected him.

'It's Latin for earth. A movement created to build a new world order. Time is running out for the planet, and our generation has to do something before it's too late.'

'And is that why Grayson and Nixon were targeted?' said Phillips. 'Because they work with fossil fuels and burned up the world's atmosphere, as you put it?'

Sebastian shrugged. 'I guess so.'

Jones recoiled slightly. 'What? You mean you don't know?'

'I only knew the time, the target's location and method of attack. Nothing more. I'm just a soldier carrying out my orders.'

'Jesus,' Jones muttered, shaking his head. 'Is that the best you can come up with? An unknown mystical figure made you murder people in the name of climate change? Do us a favour.'

'It's true!' he spat back.

'Sure it is,' said Jones.

'You'll see. This isn't over just cos I'm locked up in here. Not by a long shot.'

Phillips leaned forward across the table. 'Are you saying there are more attacks planned by this Charlie character?'

'I don't know for certain, but probably, yeah.'

'Who?' said Jones. 'Who are they going after next?'

'Like I keep telling you, I *don't* know. I was given instructions for the stuff I was involved in. I've got no idea about anything else.'

Phillips studied his face for any signs he was lying, but it appeared he was telling the truth. 'So how many are there of you in this Terra group?' she asked.

'I don't know. Charlie wanted it that way.'

'But there were three of you in the gang that attacked Grayson and Nixon?' Phillips insisted.

Sebastian looked at his lawyer for help.

Collins leaned in and whispered in his ear before straightening.

'No comment,' said Sebastian a second later.

32

Once it became obvious that Sebastian was no longer talking, Jones organised for him to be sent back to the custody suite, where he would be charged and sent to a high-security young offenders institute later that evening – his home for the next six months while he awaited trial for the murder of Robert Nixon.

As yet, Derek Rogers, head of the Crown Prosecution Service in Manchester, was not convinced they had enough to add charges for the attack on Grayson, but Phillips was determined that they would find the necessary evidence in time.

Once back in MCU, Phillips and Jones wasted no time in briefing Entwistle and Bovalino on Sebastian's revelations.

'And do you think he's telling the truth about being ordered to kill Nixon?' Bov asked. 'I mean, it's quite a story, like.'

'It is, yeah,' replied Phillips, 'but it would go some way to explaining why a teenage boy with no history of crime or violence would go on a killing spree.'

'And teenagers are big on the whole climate crisis thing, too,' said Jones. 'My girls are always giving me a hard time about not recycling enough, or asking me when I'm going to swap the diesel car for an electric one.'

'Yeah,' Bovalino cut in. 'But it's a long way from reducing emissions to committing murder.'

'True,' agreed Phillips.

'So if he claims he never met this Charlie fella, how did he give the orders?' asked Entwistle.

'He wouldn't say,' Phillips replied. 'Only that they were sent via email and included the time, the target's location and method of attack. Nothing more, or so he claims.'

'And do we believe him?' asked Entwistle.

Phillips ran her hand through her hair. 'I don't know is the honest truth. I mean, with modern technology, it's possible the orders were sent remotely, but that doesn't explain how this Charlie character managed to get far enough inside the lad's head in the first place to convince him to kill.'

'Maybe Charlie's an influencer of some kind?' offered Entwistle. 'If that's the case, we could be looking for someone on TikTok or maybe Snapchat.'

'That would make sense.' Jones nodded. 'My girls are never off their bloody phones these days. If they're not watching shite, they're filming themselves *doing* shite.'

'Well, let's start with Sebastian's phone. If he's telling the truth about Charlie sending the orders via email, digital forensics should be able to find his trail.'

'I'll call them now,' said Entwistle.

Phillips continued, 'And see what you can find on this group Terra.'

Bovalino scribbled in his pad. 'I'll take that.'

'And we need to find out who his pals are as a matter of urgency,' said Phillips. 'He was giving nothing away when I asked him about Firth and Holmes.'

Jones shook his head. 'I don't see that connection, boss. I mean, teenagers move in like-minded packs. Everything they do is geared up to garner mutual approval, and I'm not sure a rich kid like Sebastian would have anything in common with pond life like Firth and Holmes. I think it's far more likely his co-conspirators are from his own circle and most likely pals from school.'

'What?' said Bovalino. 'You think *three* spoiled brats have gone rogue?'

'Yeah. Why not? I mean, having seen the place and the way the headmistress and that history teacher talked to us, I'm guessing most of the kids are entitled, think they're God's gift to the world and that mummy and daddy will dig them out of any and all shit when they screw up.'

'Well, when you put it like that...' Bov grinned.

'Right,' said Phillips. 'Looks like we're going back to school, then.'

33

Phillips and Jones arrived at St Bart's just after 2 p.m. and made their way to the headmistress's rooms. As they arrived, Freeman was standing in the outer office, talking to her secretary, Mrs Drabble. A petite teenage girl with jet-black hair and matching eye makeup and lipstick was sitting on a chair next to Freeman's open door.

'Could we have a word?' said Phillips as she strode in.

Freeman turned to face them, irritation etched on her face. 'Can it wait? I'm about to deal with a disciplinary issue.'

'No, I'm afraid it can't.'

Freeman's nostrils flared. 'Very well.' She turned to the girl. 'Isabelle, as I've said a thousand times before, this is a school not a nightclub. Get yourself to the toilet and wash that muck off your face, then come straight back here. I'll deal with you in a minute.'

The girl huffed, then stood and marched past them and out of the room.

'You'd better come in,' said Freeman as she headed into her office.

As soon as the door closed behind them and with no offer of a seat forthcoming, Phillips got straight to the point. 'We thought you should know that Sebastian has been formally charged with murder.'

Freeman's eyes widened as she touched her fingers to her open mouth. 'Oh no.'

Phillips continued, 'He's being remanded to a young offenders institute this evening, and his parents have been made aware by his legal team.'

'But Sebastian is such a quiet boy,' Freeman muttered. 'A gentle giant.'

In no mood to indulge her, Phillips ploughed on. 'We believe he has two accomplices who helped him carry out the murder, two people who are most likely his friends, which is why we're here.'

Freeman shook her head. 'I'm not following you.'

'We need to know who he was friends with here at St Bart's.'

Freeman was incredulous. 'You don't seriously think any more of our students were involved, do you?'

'We believe it's more than likely, yes.'

Freeman sat to attention now. 'This school has created government ministers, captains of industry, knights of the Realm, for heaven's sake. And you expect me to believe three of our students have committed murder. I'm sorry, but I'm not accepting that.'

Phillips stared her down. 'We're not interested in your roll of honour, Mrs Freeman, we simply need to know who Sebastian was friendly with.'

'We have strict rules regarding student safeguarding, and as far as I'm aware, I'm not compelled to give you that information.'

'Look.' Phillips hunched forward, placing both hands on Freeman's desk. 'This is a murder investigation, and we have good reason to believe that whoever helped Sebastian commit that murder may be looking to target more innocent people in the coming days. We don't have time to mess about playing games. We need to know who his friends are, *now*!'

A snarl formed on Freeman's top lip as she stared back. 'Jonathan Marsh and Veronica Blake are the two he's closest to, but I can't believe either of them would be involved in any form of crime whatsoever. They're both first-rate students from very respectable families.'

'We need to speak with them,' said Phillips.

'And do you have any concrete evidence to suggest Jonathan and Ronnie have done anything wrong?'

'I don't need evidence. As I've said before, I'm a detective chief inspector, and all I'm asking is to speak to them as part of our enquiries.'

'I'm afraid school rules won't allow that,' Freeman said defiantly. 'Not without their parents' permission.'

'Well, you can give us their numbers, and we'll call them now.'

'Not possible. It's against GDPR regulations. The school could be fined tens of thousands of pounds for handing that kind of information over, not to mention the damage to our reputation as one of the country's premier schools.'

Phillips was struggling to keep her cool. 'We don't have time to worry about data protection, Mrs Freeman.'

'That's as may be, Chief Inspector, but *I* do, and as you should know better than anybody, the law is the law.'

'I'm beginning to lose my patience,' said Phillips.

'However,' Freeman cut in, 'I am willing to call Jonathan's

and Veronica's parents and explain the situation on your behalf.'

Phillips paused as she considered the different options available at that moment. 'Fine,' she said eventually.

'If you wouldn't mind waiting outside?' Freeman gestured towards the door.

Phillips nodded reluctantly before leading the way out.

The black-haired girl, Isabelle, had returned from the toilet and was sitting back in the chair, her face reddened where she'd evidently scrubbed hard to get rid of the makeup. She looked different mused Phillips, younger and more childlike.

Phillips and Jones stood in awkward silence as they waited, the only sound the ticking of the giant grandfather clock standing up against the wall on the opposite side of the room.

'Are you the police?' Isabelle asked out of nowhere.

Mrs Drabble shot her a look. 'That's none of your business, Isabelle.'

Phillips eyed the girl for a moment, then nodded. 'Yes, we are.'

'You're here to talk to her about Sebastian, aren't you? About what he did.'

'Be quiet, Isabelle,' Mrs Drabble hissed.

Phillips and Jones exchanged glances.

'And what *exactly* is it you think he did?' Jones asked.

'Jenny Hayes said that he stabbed a man.'

'I won't tell you again, Isabelle.' Mrs Drabble glowered at her.

The girl had their full attention now. 'And where did Jenny hear that?' said Phillips.

'Her brother works for the police.'

'Isabelle!' Drabble hissed again. 'Hold your tongue!'

Phillips waved the woman away. 'Actually, I'd like to hear what she has to say. Jenny's brother, I see. You don't happen to know what job he does for the police, do you, Isabelle?'

The girl shrugged. 'No. Just that he's a copper.'

'Is he in uniform?' Jones asked.

'I dunno. I don't know him. It's just what I heard.'

'Right,' said Phillips.

'He's a total head case, you know,' Isabelle continued.

'Who is?' Phillips asked as neutrally as she could. 'Jenny's brother?'

'No.' Isabelle shook her head. 'Seb Heppingstall.'

Phillips took a step closer. 'What makes you say that?'

'Everybody thinks he is – *serious* daddy issues and takes his rage out on everybody else.'

'Isabelle, that's gossip pure and simple,' Drabble cut in again. 'And you know only too well that Mrs Freeman does not tolerate gossip in school.'

'It's not gossip if it's true,' Isabelle shot back.

Ignoring the scowling Drabble, Phillips probed the girl once more. 'What do you mean when you say he takes it out on everybody else?'

'He's a bully,' Isabelle replied.

'Really? In what way?'

'Physical, mental...' Isabelle lowered her eyes for a second before looking up. 'Whatever he thinks will hurt the most.'

'And has he ever bullied you?'

'All the time.' She nodded. 'He and his mates do it to all the scholarship kids.'

'So *you're* on a scholarship?'

'Yes. The only one in my year.'

Phillips eyed her in silence for a moment, her mind flashing back to her own difficult times at school when she first returned from Hong Kong. 'These friends of Sebastian's. Can you tell us their names?'

Drabble glanced towards the closed door to Freeman's office. 'I really don't think that's something you should be talking to Isabelle about, Chief Inspector.'

Phillips turned and offered a thin smile. 'Do you know what, you're right. That would be very unfair of me. I shouldn't have asked her to tell me their names.'

Drabble visibly softened.

Phillips continued, 'Not when I'm pretty sure their names are Jonathan Marsh and Veronica Blake.' Before Drabble could protest, Phillips turned back to Isabelle. 'Am I right?'

She nodded.

Just then Freeman's door opened, and the headmistress stepped out, her eyes locking on the girl. 'You can go in, Isabelle. I'll deal with you in a moment.'

Isabelle did as instructed.

Freeman moved closer to Phillips and Jones now, her voice low as if trying to avoid being overheard by Isabelle. 'Right. I've spoken with both sets of parents, and as expected, they want to be present when you speak to Jonathan and Veronica.'

Phillips could feel her frustration boiling up inside. More delays.

Freeman continued, 'We've agreed that they can meet you here, with the children, at 8 a.m.,'

'Tomorrow?' spat Phillips. 'Why not now? Or, at the very least, this evening.'

'Detective Chief Inspector.' Freeman's tone oozed condescension. 'Jonathan and Veronica's parents are incredibly busy people. They can't just drop everything and come running.'

'You've got to be kidding.' Phillips shook her head. 'This isn't a bloody PTA meeting they've been invited to.'

Freeman's eyes bulged. 'I'd appreciate it if you could control your language in front of the students.'

The truth was, Phillips was struggling to control a lot of things, especially her anger, but, based on experience, she knew only too well the best thing to do right now was to walk away and regroup. After all, there was always more than one way to skin a cat. 'Very well,' she said curtly. 'We'll see you tomorrow.'

A moment later and with Jones beside her, she marched back towards the car.

34

About a mile away from Ashton House, the in-car screen burst into life. Phillips immediately accepted the call. 'Whistler.'

'How far away are you, guv?' His voice oozed concern.

'About five minutes. Why? What's up?'

'It's Sebastian Heppingstall—'

'What about him?'

'He's tried to hang himself in his cell, boss.'

Phillips looked to Jones. The disbelief etched on his face matched her own. 'How? He's supposed be under twenty-four-hour surveillance, for Christ's sake!'

Jones immediately fired the siren, and the car accelerated rapidly.

'Apparently it happened when they were trying to calm down another prisoner who was kicking off,' replied Entwistle. *'They'd just opened Sebastian's door so he could make a phone call, and because they're short-handed today, they took their eye off him while they sorted it out. They found him unconscious a couple of*

minutes later. He'd ripped his T-shirt to pieces, wrapped it round his neck and hooked it over the corner of the open door.'

'Is he dead?' asked Phillips.

'No, but he's in a very bad way. The custody boys are giving him CPR at the moment, and the paramedics are en route.'

'We'll be there in two minutes,' Jones added as they streaked past a line of cars that had pulled over to the left to get out of their way.

'Where are you now?' asked Phillips.

'Just outside his cell.'

'Stay there and don't take your eyes off the boy until we get there.' With that, she ended the call and turned her attention back to Jones. 'If anything happens to that kid, I'll never forgive myself.'

A few minutes later, Jones screeched to a halt in the car park that serviced the custody suite, an array of patrol cars and vans surrounding them.

As Phillips leaped out of the car, she could hear the paramedics' siren wailing in the distance. Setting off running with Jones at her back, she burst through the entrance doors with all the force of a SWAT team. Thirty seconds later she arrived in the custody block to find Entwistle standing outside one of the cells, staring intently inside.

Phillips moved quickly to his shoulder and followed his gaze. Ahead of them, PC Ali was kneeling on the polished concrete floor, performing chest compressions on a motionless Sebastian. Sergeant Walsh was kneeling to the side, holding his chin and nose, ready to blow into his mouth.

'Is he responding?' Phillips asked, fearing the worst.

'He has a faint pulse,' replied Walsh, 'but he's still not breathing on his own.'

'Shit!' Phillips linked her fingers behind her head as she turned to face Jones.

He stared back in stunned silence.

A second later, the paramedics appeared at the entrance to the custody block.

Phillips stepped away from the cell and gestured for Entwistle and Jones to do the same.

As the lead EMT made his way inside the cell – a tall man with a shaven head – Phillips spotted the name badge on his chest, Clark. His 'oppo', a short woman following closely behind, was called Li.

With a flurry of movement, they got to work on the floor as Walsh and Ali moved out of the way and got back to their feet.

Li took over the CPR.

'How long since you found him?' asked Clark as he opened his bag and pulled out an intubation tube.

'Twelve minutes,' Ali replied.

'And did you start resuscitation straight away?'

'Pretty much, yeah.'

'Okay. Good. We'll take it from here.' Clark placed defibrillator pads on Sebastian's bare chest, then focused on Li. 'Let's see if we can get a shockable rhythm.'

Phillips stared into the cell as they attempted to stabilise Sebastian so as to transport him to A&E.

Ten agonising minutes had passed by the time Clark suggested Li fetch the stretcher from the ambulance.

'What are his chances?' Phillips asked as they waited for her to return.

Clark's brow furrowed. 'I just don't know. We've managed to stabilise him, but his pulse is still very weak, and his blood pressure is dangerously low.'

Silence descended for the next few minutes as Clark prepared Sebastian to be moved.

Li returned soon after, pushing the wheeled trolley along with the scoop stretcher needed to lift him from the ground.

Phillips watched, praying they could save him.

With Sebastian's neck secured in a spinal head block, Clark and Li moved the scoop stretcher under his back, bottom and legs, and then, on a count of three, lifted him carefully onto the trolley. Next, they took a few moments to secure his arms and legs with straps. Lying there, motionless now, his massive frame seemed to have diminished, a vulnerable, broken young man left in its place as they rolled him, still unresponsive, out of the cell and back down the corridor towards the ambulance.

'Fingers crossed, boss,' said Entwistle, standing a few feet away.

Phillips turned to Jones. 'I need to brief Carter before Fox finds out.'

Jones nodded. 'Want me to come with you?'

'No.' She exhaled sharply. 'This one's on me.'

'OH, GOD,' said Carter, dropping heavily into his office chair, his expression grave.

Phillips took a seat opposite his desk.

'Do his parents know?'

'No. I came straight to see you.'

'Well, if you get me their details, I'll call them as soon as we're done here.'

'Thank you, sir.'

'I take it Fox doesn't know either?'

'Not yet, but as we both know, news travels fast in this place.'

'Jesus.' Carter grimaced. 'She'll go postal when she finds out. How could this be allowed to happen? He was supposed to be under constant surveillance.'

'It seems that another prisoner kicked off when he was released from his cell. A big lad, by all accounts, who started throwing punches around, and it took the full team to subdue him. While that was going on, the boy strung himself up.'

'On what?' Carter was incredulous. 'The cells have *zero* objects to attach anything to – to stop this very thing from happening.'

'I know, sir, but it looks like it was a case of bad timing.'

Carter frowned. 'How do you mean, bad timing?'

'Digging a little deeper, it turns out PC Ali had just opened Sebastian's door so he could go to the charge desk to make a phone call to his grandmother before being transferred to the young offenders. Seems that when it all kicked off with the other prisoner, Ali forgot to lock Sebastian back in his cell, and in the few minutes it took to control the ruckus, the lad managed to hang himself off the open door.'

'Jesus. That's negligence, Jane, pure and simple. If his parents find out what happened, the fallout could be career ending for all of us.'

Phillips nodded gravely. 'I know, but in fairness to the custody guys, they were dangerously short-staffed today. PC Taylor called in sick, and because Fox has put an overtime ban on uniform this month, they were a body down, which is just asking for trouble.'

'We both know Fox won't see it that way.' Carter shook

his head. 'Did Sebastian ever give any clue that he could try something like this?'

'No, sir. Certainly not in my dealings with him. I mean, he was quiet and a bit withdrawn, but nothing unusual for a teenage boy. And according to the custody team, there were certainly no suicide markers.'

'That's something at least,' said Carter. 'The real question is, why did he do it?'

'The only thing I can think of was he was scared about being remanded and eventually ending up in Hawk Green. Maybe that was what tipped the balance for him.'

'So what are his chances? Did the paramedics give you any indication?'

'I'm afraid not. They just said he was in a bad way and needed to get to A&E as quickly as possible.'

Carter sat back in the chair and exhaled loudly. 'Where are we at with the investigation?'

'Until all this happened, I felt we were getting some-where with the CPS agreeing to charge Sebastian. Plus, we have a couple of strong leads on who his two co-conspirators are.'

'Really? Who?'

'Two of his friends from school.'

Carter raised his eyebrows. 'St Bart's?'

'Yes, sir.'

'God, that's all we need. More rich kids whose parents could be connected to Fox.'

'I thought the same,' said Phillips, 'but, seriously, what can she say if we're simply following the trail of evidence?'

'Who are we looking at?'

'Jonathan Marsh and Veronica Blake. Sebastian's best mates.'

'Certainly matches the profile of the gang,' said Carter. 'Two males, one female.'

'Exactly.'

'Are you bringing them in?'

'Not yet, no. It's a long story, but the school refused to give me permission to speak to the kids without their parents being present.'

'And we can't arrest them?'

'No, not really. I mean, so far all we have to connect them to the attacks on Grayson and Nixon is the fact they go to school with Sebastian. Plus, they're minors, which makes it even more complicated. Without probable cause, I'll just have to wait until the meeting, which is happening first thing tomorrow morning with the headmistress, Mrs Freeman.'

'I see.' Carter sat forward. 'Look, Jane. In light of what's just happened to the Heppingstall boy, you don't need me to tell you how fragile this investigation has suddenly become.'

'No, sir.'

'I know you will anyway, but tread carefully around these two kids and their parents. We can't afford any more mistakes.'

'I'll be careful, I promise.'

'Thank you.' Carter flashed a weak smile. 'Is there anything else before I go and speak to the chief constable?'

'Actually, there is one thing, sir, but I'm not sure of its credence, if I'm being honest.'

'What's that?'

Phillips shifted in her seat. 'During his second interview, Sebastian made a claim that he'd been *ordered* to kill Nixon.'

Carter flinched. 'Ordered? By whom?'

'Some guy called Charlie.'

'Do we have a last name?'

'No, sir, just Charlie.'

'And do we have any idea who this Charlie is?'

'Nothing as yet. All Sebastian would say was that he'd never actually met him and that the orders for the hits were sent via encrypted email.'

Carter's face wrinkled. 'Sounds like a teenage fantasy to me. I mean, why would a teenage boy suddenly start committing heinous crimes based on the word of someone he'd never met?'

'My thoughts, entirely,' replied Phillips, 'but we're looking into it all the same. Digital forensics are going over his laptop as we speak. After all, who really knows what goes on in the minds of teenagers these days.'

'Quite,' said Carter. 'Life was a lot less complicated before the internet.'

'Totally.'

'Right.' Carter looked at his watch. 'Is that it?'

'For now, sir, yes.'

'In that case, I need to speak to his parents and then go and update the chief constable.'

'Would you like me to come with you and explain what happened?' Phillips asked.

'No, not at all.' Carter waved her away as he got up from the chair. 'Your time is much better served focused on the investigation.'

Phillips stood.

'And besides,' he added, walking around from behind the desk, 'there's no sense two of us getting a bollocking, now is there?'

'No. I suppose not,' said Phillips.

35

Tex unlocked the garden shed and quietly stepped inside before pulling the door closed behind him. 'Where are you?' he whispered, casting his gaze around the space. 'Where does she keep you?' he repeated as he moved deeper into the darkness.

Careful not to make any unnecessary noise, he spent the next few minutes rummaging through the array of boxes and bags that covered the floor, until finally he spotted the bag he was looking for wedged up against the wall next to a storage rack. Pulling it out, he crouched down and placed it on the floor before releasing the zipper and peering inside. 'Bingo!' he whispered.

The door opened behind him suddenly, filling the space with light.

He turned to find Clem standing in the doorway.

'What are you doing in my dad's shed?' she asked in an agitated whisper.

He pointed to the bag. 'Looking for this.'

'What the hell for?'

'Operation Navaho.'

'Ssh! My mum's in the kitchen; she'll hear you,' she whispered again as she stepped inside and closed the door. 'You're not seriously going ahead with that ridiculous plan, are you?'

'Yeah, I am, and it's not ridiculous.'

She rolled her eyes. 'But you don't know the first thing about firing a bow and arrow.'

'It can't be that hard,' he replied. 'And besides, I've seen *you* do it often enough.'

'Yeah, but it took me years to learn how to do it properly and safely.'

'Which is exactly why you should be taking the shot tonight.'

'I told you,' she said as she folded her arms across her chest. 'I'm not doing it.'

'Please, babe. I need you.'

'No.'

'Well, then.' He slung the large bag over his shoulder. 'Looks like I've got no choice. I'll have to do it myself.'

'You don't have to *do* anything,' she replied. 'Look, will you *please* just forget about Charlie and all this eco-warrior stuff and walk away *while you still can.*'

He glared back at her. 'You know I can't walk away.'

'Yes, you can. *We* can.' She stepped forward. 'The summer holidays start in a few weeks. I've been thinking, why don't we go away for a while? Head down to Ibiza and chill out for a bit like we've always talked about.'

'And what about Seb?'

She shrugged. 'What about him? We can't do anything to help him.'

'We have to finish what we started,' Tex shot back. 'Otherwise, his sacrifice was for nothing.'

Clem didn't respond.

'So.' He stood to attention now. 'Are you going to help me, or do I have to do this on my own?'

She held his gaze for a long moment, evidently deep in thought, before nodding. 'Okay. I'll help you, but on one condition.'

'Name it.'

'After this we're done.'

He nodded.

'Promise?'

'Yeah. I promise.'

'Okay, then,' she said finally. 'In that case, I'll take the shot.'

———

TEX LED the way from the road, through a gap in the fence that surrounded Ollerton Hall Hotel. Thankfully the complex had been built on thirty acres of tree-filled land, which provided plenty of cover and would allow them to approach the strike zone without being spotted. Ten minutes later he dropped the bag to the ground under the overhanging branches of a large yew tree. 'This is as good a spot as any.'

From where they stood, they had a direct line of sight to the hotel entrance and the ornate fountain located in front of the main steps.

Tex checked his watch once again. 'According to Charlie, Bernstein's itinerary states he'll be arriving at 7 p.m. That gives us exactly thirty minutes to get set up and ready.'

Clem dropped to her knees to unzip the bag, and for the next few minutes carefully removed the contents one piece at a time and began connecting them. 'I still think using a bow and arrow is bloody ridiculous.'

'Considering Bernstein's family history, I think it's a genius idea.' Tex stared down at the competition bow resting on the ground alongside four carbon-tipped arrows, and his pulse quickened. 'Are you sure we're close enough to hit him from here?'

Clem fished her range scope from the bag before placing it to her right eye as she spoke. 'It's a warm day, and there's no wind at all, so we're well within range.'

He smiled as he pulled his phone from his pocket and, a second later, turned the screen to face her. 'This is Bernstein.'

Clem's eyes narrowed as she stared intently at the man.

'He'll be here soon; we'd best get ready.'

For the next ten minutes they kneeled on the grass in silence, their eyes fixed on the hotel entrance ahead of them. Then, bang on 7 p.m., a black Mercedes people-carrier turned off the main road and began making its way up the long drive.

'Is that him?' asked Clem, picking up the bow and standing.

Tex stepped up next to her, pulling the scope to his eye as he did so. 'I can't see. The windows have been blacked out.'

Clem hooked an arrow into position against the bowstring before raising the bow to eye level. Pulling it back to her cheek, she readied herself.

All the time, Tex watched through the scope as the Mercedes slowly circled the fountain, then pulled to a stop in front of the steps to the main entrance.

In one slick movement the driver climbed out of the vehicle and opened the rear door on the right side of the car, where a rotund man slipped out into the sunshine, his face partially covered with sunglasses and shaded by a grey cowboy hat.

'I can't see his face properly,' said Tex, 'but I'm pretty sure it's Bernstein.'

Clem's breathing was now audible as she took long, slow breaths, in through her nose and out through her mouth.

The driver moved to the rear of the Mercedes, where he opened the boot and pulled out a large suitcase, standing it on its end before pulling up the retractable handle.

'Come on, let me see your face,' mumbled Tex.

Clem remained motionless next to him.

A second later the man removed his hat, pulling something from it that he handed to the driver. Through the scope it looked like banknotes, and judging by the driver's reaction, he'd just been handed a sizeable tip.

In that moment, the man turned to face them, and appeared to be taking in the view across the grounds. Even wearing sunglasses, there was no doubting it was their guy.

'Target confirmed,' Tex said flatly. 'Take him out.'

Without flinching, she fired.

Bernstein's agonised scream echoed across those same grounds a split second later, and Tex watched through the scope as the big man lurched back against the Mercedes, instantly grabbing at his left shoulder before sliding down the side of the van onto the ground, the driver rushing to his aid at the same time as shouting for help.

'You missed! cried Tex, dropping the scope and turning to face Clem, who was already dismantling the bow at lightning speed. 'You were supposed to hit the heart, but you shot him in the shoulder.'

'We need to get the hell out of here,' she said without looking at him.

'You *never* miss,' he continued.

'Seriously, it's done. Let's go!' she barked as she zipped up the bag.

'You missed on purpose, didn't you?'

She jumped to her feet now. 'Of course I fucking did.'

'But why?'

'Because this way nobody else has to die. Charlie will believe we did what he asked, and Bernstein will have a very sore shoulder for a while, but gets to go home. I can live with that.'

'You lied to me.'

'I did what I had to do to keep you safe. That's all that matters to me now.' She hurled the bag onto her shoulder. 'Are you coming or not?'

Without answering, he turned and took one last look at the scene unfolding directly opposite them. People had begun looking and pointing in their direction. 'Helter Skelter,' he whispered, gazing back at them from the cover of the trees, then turned and set off at pace after Clem.

36

Phillips was sitting at her desk when Jones appeared at her door carrying a yellow Post-it note, his brow furrowed. 'Guv, I've just had a call from Sergeant Hicks in comms. Looks like there could have been another assassination attempt.'

'Where?'

'A hotel in Bredbury. Ollerton Hall,' he replied. 'Initial reports suggest they used a crossbow this time.'

'Jesus. You've gotta be kidding me?'

Jones shook his head. 'I wish I were. The victim is alive and on his way to hospital.'

'Any idea who he is?'

He glanced at the yellow note. 'One of the guests, a guy called Travis Bernstein. An American, by all accounts; he flew in this afternoon to speak at the Energy Expo tomorrow.'

'I want CSIs and Bov on scene ASAP.' She got up from the chair and moved round the desk.

'I'll speak to him now.'

'Then you and I need to get to the hospital.'

Jones nodded. 'I'll call Sarah and let her know I'm gonna be late.'

'She must hate me sometimes.'

'You? No,' replied Jones. 'The job? That's another story entirely.'

'Sorry, Jonesy.'

He shrugged. 'She'll get over it.'

Half an hour later they made their way into the A&E department and, after sharing their credentials and the reason for their visit, found themselves at the doctor's station, talking to the man in charge, Dr Sharp, who was standing in front of an X-ray light box mounted on the wall behind him.

Sharp cut a striking figure, standing at well over six feet tall with his red surgical scrubs accentuated by his long, ash-white limbs and wispy, thinning hair. 'He's very lucky to be alive,' he said in a soft Irish accent. 'Another inch to the left and he'd have been in real trouble.'

'We understand he was hit by a crossbow bolt,' said Phillips.

'An arrow, actually,' he corrected her.

Phillips felt her face crumple. 'An *arrow*? As in bow and arrow?'

'Yep. The arrowhead is still in his shoulder.' He turned to switch on the light box behind him before tapping the X-ray film with his pen. 'We cut most of it away, but the end is dangerously close to a main artery, so he'll need surgery in the next few hours to remove it.'

Phillips gazed at the long black shadow caused by the arrow. 'Who the hell uses a bow and arrow in this day and age? And why?'

Sharp switched off the light box. 'No idea, Chief Inspector. I just patch them up. The hows and the whys are down to you guys.'

'Can we speak to him?' she asked.

'Yeah, but you should know he's had quite a bit of morphine, so he may not be very responsive.'

'We understand,' said Phillips.

'He's down here.' Sharp gestured with his arm. 'I'll take you to him.'

A minute later, Phillips and Jones stepped through the curtains and into the cubicle to find Bernstein, a round man with a protruding belly, lying on the bed. His plump torso was raised at a forty-five-degree angle, and he appeared to be sleeping. The remains of the arrowhead had been wrapped in surgical dressings but were still visible sticking out from his chest. Around the bed, a host of machines beeped and pinged while a saline drip and morphine PCA pump were connected to the cannula attached to his left wrist.

'Mr Bernstein,' Sharp said loudly.

Bernstein opened his eyes.

The doctor continued, 'These people are from the police. They want to ask you a few questions. Is that okay?'

Bernstein nodded silently.

'I'll leave you to it,' said Sharp before disappearing behind the curtain.

Phillips moved to his bedside. 'Looks like you've been in the wars.'

Bernstein pointed towards his chest and chuckled. 'With a bunch of Red Injuns.' His voice was deep, with a strong American accent, the speech ever so slightly slurred.

Ignoring his inappropriate remark, Phillips pressed on.

'Do you have any idea who might have wanted to do this to you?'

The big man shook his head and closed his eyes again.

'We understand you flew in from the States today.'

'Sure did,' he replied with his eyes still shut.

'Which bit?'

'Texas.'

'And you're here for the Energy Expo. Is that right?' she asked.

Slowly he opened his eyes and turned to face them. 'Yeah. I'm due to speak at the conference tomorrow.' He pointed to his chest once more. 'But I guess I won't be going anywhere for a while.'

Phillips exchanged a glance with Jones, then turned her attention back to Bernstein. 'What exactly is it that you do?'

'I'm senior vice president of Lone Star Oil. We're one of the sponsors for the conference.'

'I see,' said Phillips. 'In that case, I must ask, have you ever been threatened by any environmentalist groups?'

'Only when I come to Europe.' He chortled. 'I'm an oil man, miss, and that makes me a hero back home in Texas.'

'What about an organisation called Terra?' Phillips continued. 'Have they ever contacted you?'

Bernstein slowly moved his head from side to side.

'Who else knew you were going to be at Ollerton Hall tonight?' asked Jones.

Bernstein took a moment before answering, 'My PA, Virginia, and I'm guessing the people who booked it from the conference.'

'Nobody else?' pressed Jones.

Bernstein shook his head before his eyes slowly closed again.

'Mr Bernstein?' Phillips said loudly, but there was no response.

'Looks like the morphine is kicking in again,' said Jones.

'Yeah.'

Just then the curtain opened behind them. Turning, Phillips came face to face with a young short-haired nurse in light blue scrubs.

'I'm afraid we need to prep Mr Bernstein for his surgery,' she said.

'Okay.' Phillips cast her gaze back to Bernstein. 'I think we've got as much as we're going to at the moment, anyway.'

The nurse smiled back sympathetically before Phillips led the way out.

'Wasn't Grayson due to speak at the same energy conference?' asked Jones as they marched along the corridor back towards the car.

'Yeah, I was thinking the same thing,' she replied before stopping in her tracks. Fishing her phone from her pocket, she pulled up the voice-activated search function. 'Energy conference Manchester,' she said aloud, and a second later a host of links appeared on-screen. Clicking on the top one, she was quickly redirected through to the conference's website, where it took a few seconds of scrolling to find what she was looking for. 'Bingo.'

Jones moved to her shoulder. 'What have you got?'

'Not only were Grayson and Bernstein scheduled to speak at the conference, it looks like OPUS Air is also one of the main sponsors for the event, alongside Lone Star Oil.'

'Which is clearly the link.'

'Totally,' replied Phillips. 'And it certainly ties in with Sebastian's comments that the attacks were linked to global warming. Grayson's big in oil and gas, Nixon was high up in the airline business, and Bernstein, by his own admission, is an oil man.'

'So, what are we thinking? That Sebastian could have been telling the truth about this group Terra after all?'

Just then Phillips's phone burst into life in her hand. Bov was calling.

She flicked it to speaker so Jones could hear. 'Bov, what have you got for us?'

'I'm down at the hotel, and I've spoken to a couple of the staff, who say they saw two people running into the trees opposite the hotel entrance shortly after Bernstein was hit.'

'Can they describe them?'

'Not in detail, but they seemed to think we're looking for a white male and a white female.'

Phillips locked eyes with Jones. 'Jonathan and Veronica?'

Jones nodded. 'Could be.'

'Thanks, Bov. Are the CSIs there yet?'

'Yep. Setting up as we speak.'

'Okay. Keep us posted on any updates, won't you?'

'Sure. Will do.'

Phillips ended the call and immediately phoned Entwistle.

As ever, he answered promptly. *'Guv.'*

'I need you to pull up addresses for Jonathan Marsh and Veronica Blake.'

'No problem, just give me a sec,' he replied, the tapping of his fingers on the keyboard audible through the phone.

'Marsh is 58 Whitelaw Road, Prestbury.'

Jones pulled his pad from his pocket and made a note.

Entwistle began typing again for a few seconds. *'And Blake is The Old Rectory, St Stephen's Lane, Alderley Edge.'*

Jones scribbled it down.

'Thanks,' said Phillips.

'How's the American?'

'Doped up the eyeballs, but he'll live. Thanks, Whistler,' she replied, then terminated the call.

Jones glanced down at the addresses on his notepad, then back to Phillips. 'You sure this is a good idea, boss? Given what's just happened with Sebastian.'

'You heard what Bov said. It *has* to be those two.'

'Fox isn't going to like it. Maybe we should wait till the meeting at the school tomorrow morning?'

'Do you really think they're gonna show up after this? Not a chance in hell.' Phillips shook her head. 'We have to find them now, because God only knows what they're planning to do next.'

37

With Jones dispatched in the squad car to Veronica's parents' house, Phillips raced to Prestbury in the Mini Cooper. Traffic was light, and thirty minutes later she pulled up outside the Marsh home, a detached Victorian villa located close to the heart of the village. With the house hiding behind a high wall and impenetrable gates, Phillips took a moment to assess her means of access before she spotted a video buzzer fixed to the side of the gatepost. Pressing it, she waited.

Thirty seconds later the speaker crackled into life. *'Yes? Who is it?'* The voice was sharp and well spoken.

Phillips held her badge in front of the camera. 'Detective Chief Inspector Phillips from the Major Crimes Unit. Who am I speaking to?'

'Warren Marsh. What do you want?'

Phillips put her ID back in her pocket. 'A word with you and your son if possible?'

'Aren't you the person I'm supposed to be meeting at Jonathan's school tomorrow? Can't it wait till then?'

'No. I'm afraid it can't. There's been another incident, and I need to speak to you both as a matter of urgency.'

'Well, you can't because he's not here.'

Phillips felt her jaw clench with frustration. 'I'd really prefer to have this conversation face to face, Mr Marsh.'

'It's late.' Marsh sounded agitated.

'I'm aware of the time, Mr Marsh, but I'd appreciate it if you could let me in so we can speak in person.'

There was a long pause at the other end. *'Very well.'* He sighed. A second later the entrance gates began to open inwards. *'Follow the drive up to the house.'*

Phillips crunched up the long gravel driveway, arriving at the open front door a few moments later.

Marsh was standing on the step in grey suit pants and a white shirt open at the collar, his thick arms folded across his broad chest, a scowl fixed to his heavy brow.

'Good evening, Mr Marsh,' said Phillips as she approached.

'This really isn't on, you know,' he growled. 'We're supposed to be having this conversation in the morning.'

'I know, but like I said at the gate, there's been another incident, and I need to speak to Jonathan urgently.'

'And like *I* said, he's not here.'

Phillips frowned. 'So where is he?'

Marsh shrugged. 'How should I know? I'm not his keeper.'

'But it's almost ten.'

'So?'

'So, as he's a schoolboy, I would have thought he'd be home by now.'

'He's seventeen; he's not a child anymore.'

'I see.'

'Is there anything else, Chief Inspector? I've had a very long day, and I'd like to get back to my supper before it goes cold.'

Phillips bit her lip. She had met a thousand Warren Marshes in her time: pompous, arrogant, privileged arse-holes. She had no idea what he did for a living, but judging by his tone, the size of the house and his total lack of concern for his son's well-being, she guessed he spent the majority of his waking life doing it. 'Did Mrs Freeman explain the reason for tomorrow's meeting?'

He exhaled loudly. 'Something to do with Jonathan getting into a spot of trouble with you lot.'

Phillips flashed a thin smile. 'It's more than a *spot of trouble*, Mr Marsh. We believe he's been involved in a spate of violent crimes, which has left one man dead and another two fighting for life in hospital.'

Marsh recoiled. 'Jonathan has been involved in violent crimes? Freeman never said anything about that. That's absurd.'

'I'm afraid it's not. We have a number of eyewitnesses who claim they saw someone matching his description fleeing the scene of a violent crime just a few hours ago.' She was stretching the truth, but right now she didn't care.

'Nonsense. The boy wouldn't hurt a fly.'

'Really? If that's the case, why has he been in trouble for bullying at school?'

'Pfft,' scoffed Marsh. 'It was high jinks at best.'

'So mentally and physically abusing scholarship kids is high jinks, is it?'

'Look. St Bart's is a fee-paying school. The best in Manchester. Scholarship kids have no place there. It's ridiculous and all because some lefty governors think it's good for the school's image. I for one think it's a terrible idea.'

'It sounds like you're condoning his behaviour, Mr Marsh.'

Marsh shrugged. 'Like I said, scholarship kids don't belong there.'

Phillips nodded slowly, then pulled a business card from her pocket, which she passed across. 'Can you call me as soon as he gets home?'

Marsh's eyes narrowed as he stared at the card. 'What on earth for? Surely this can wait until morning?'

Phillips took a step forward. 'Mr Marsh, your son is now a prime suspect in a murder investigation. Either you call me when he gets home, or I'll come back in a couple of hours with an army of uniformed cops under blue flashing lights and wailing sirens. Which would you prefer?'

Marsh glowered. 'Very well.'

'Thank you,' said Phillips, flashing another thin smile. 'In fact, I have an even better idea. Why don't you give me your number so I can call you.'

A snarl reached the edge of Marsh's mouth. It was slight, but Phillips had seen it.

Pulling her phone from her pocket, she prepared to enter the number. 'Ready when you are.'

Marsh cleared his throat. 'Zero, triple-seven-one, double-six, three-four, one-zero.'

Phillips keyed it in and hit the call icon on-screen.

A split second later, she could hear Marsh's phone ringing in his pocket.

'There you go; we're all connected,' she said with a smile before turning away. 'I'll wait to hear from you,' she added as she set off back down the drive. Soon after, she heard the front door slam behind her.

Back in the car, she called Jones.

'*Hey, guv. How did you get on?*'

'He's not in, apparently,' she replied.

'*Neither's Veronica. I spoke to her mum, Angela, who wasn't sure where she was, but hoped she'd be back soon. She tried calling her, but it kept going straight to voicemail, and she seemed genuinely concerned.*'

'I wish I could say the same for Jonathan's dad. He didn't seem to give a shit where his son was. Said he was old enough to look after himself and seemed more interested in getting back to his dinner.'

'*And they wonder why these rich kids go off the rails,*' added Jones.

'I know, and I'm certainly not condoning what this lot have been up to, but if I had a father like Warren Marsh, I'd want to rage against the machine too.'

'*Speaking of fathers,*' Jones said. '*You'll never guess who Veronica's dad is.*'

'Go on.'

'*Malcolm Blake.*'

'What? As in King's Counsel Malcolm Blake?'

'*Yep. That's him.*'

'Oh shit. That's all we bloody need.'

'*I know. I went up against him when you were on sabbatical, and he was an absolute nightmare. I felt like I was on bloody trial, as opposed to his client.*'

'So how did you leave it with Veronica's mum?' asked Phillips.

'*I told her to call me as soon as she got home.*'

'Me too.'

'*So now what?*'

'Now we wait.'

'*Okay,*' said Jones. '*But I'm going to have to get something to eat. I've not had anything since breakfast.*'

'There's a twenty-four seven McDonald's on the A34. I'll meet you there in ten.'

38

'I'm gonna have to take this.' Tex's adrenaline spiked as he stared down at the unknown caller buzzing on the screen of his latest burner phone.

'Is it Charlie?' asked Clem.

'I'm guessing so; he's the only one who has this number aside from you,' said Tex, stepping away. 'Hello?'

'*What the hell happened?*' a voice growled down the line.

'What do you mean? The mission was a success,' he replied, trying his best to hide the fear in his voice.

'*Was it? Then how come the target is alive and well in hospital?*'

'They can't be. I saw it with my own eyes,' Tex lied. 'It was a direct hit, straight to the heart.'

'*Straight to the shoulder more like. A few stitches and Travis Bernstein will be back in business by the morning.*'

'But I was sure he was dead. Like I say, it looked like a direct hit to the heart.'

'*Well, it wasn't. Bernstein is very much alive.*'

'Says who?'

'*Says all the chatter on the police scanner.*'

'Shit. I'm sorry, Charlie. The target must have moved at the last second or something. I mean, it was never going to be an easy hit with a bow and arrow.'

'*You promised me Clem could make that shot—*'

'And she did,' he said, cutting him off.

'*Then why is the target in a hospital bed and not on the slab?*'

Tex remained silent.

'*Where are you now?*' asked Charlie.

'In the park near my house.'

'*Well, whatever you do, you can't go home. With Sebastian in custody, I'm sure the police will soon start to put two and two together. You guys need to lie low and get ready for the final attack of the campaign.*'

'Look, I've been thinking about that. Maybe we should call it quits now after tonight. Like you say, the cops might be onto us already.'

Silence emanated from the other end of the line.

'Are you still there?' asked Tex.

'*Where is Clem?*' Charlie responded.

'She's here, just a few feet away.'

'*Do you remember what the Manson family did to Sharon Tate?*'

Tex frowned. 'Of course.'

'*Would you like the same fate to befall your precious Clem?*'

Tex turned to face her now, standing under the trees, their eyes fixing on each other.

Charlie continued, '*If I hear any more talk about calling it quits, that's exactly what will happen to her. Do you understand?*'

Clem gazed across at him, eyes wide with anticipation.

'Yes.' Tex turned his back to her. 'I understand.'

'*Good,*' said Charlie. '*I've booked you a room at the Premier*

Inn on the edge of the city centre, next to the Mancunian Way. It's all paid for, and the check-in is automated, so you won't need to speak to anyone. But you must hide your faces from the CCTV in the lobby and along the corridors. And don't use the lift, there'll be cameras in there, too.'

'Okay,' said Tex.

'We move straight to the final phase tomorrow.'

'That soon?'

'Yes. We need to move fast.'

'So, who's the target?'

'I've couriered two different packages with all the details and everything you need to a secure locker near the hotel. I'll email you the address.'

'But won't that leave a paper trail?'

'Yes, it will, and for good reason. If the police find and follow it, they'll be going round in circles for weeks. I've made sure of that. I'm emailing all the details across now.'

'Okay.'

'Remember why you got into this, Tex – the future of our planet depends on soldiers like you and Clem.'

Tex remained silent.

'Helter Skelter, Tex, Helter Skelter.' A second later the line went dead.

Putting the phone back in his pocket, he turned and walked towards Clem.

'What's going on?' she asked.

'Charlie knows you missed.'

'How?'

'It's all over the police scanners, apparently. Come on.' Tex beckoned in the direction of the park gates. 'We need to get out of here.'

'Where are we going?'

'Into the city.'

'Why?' she asked.

'Because Charlie says so. That's why.'

She grabbed his arm and pulled him back. 'But you promised tonight would be the end of all this.'

'I know I did, but things have changed.'

'What things?'

'You don't need to know,' he shot back.

'Yes, I bloody do.'

'No. You *really* don't.'

'What are you not telling me?'

'Look, we haven't got time for this.' Moving directly in front of her, he grabbed both her arms and stared into her eyes. 'Please hear what I'm saying to you. With Seb in custody, Charlie thinks the police will be onto us by now. We can't go home; we need to get off the radar quickly.'

'How?'

'He's booked us a room in a hotel.'

'But I don't want to go to a hotel.' Her lip trembled. 'I want to go home and see my mum.'

'Well, you can't, *Ronnie*. Okay? You just can't.'

39

Phillips found Jones sitting in a booth, devouring a Big Mac like a man enjoying his last meal on this planet. She slid in opposite him. 'You know you're supposed to chew it more than once, don't you?'

He nodded, his jaw noisily fighting against a mouthful of burger.

Turning to face the counter, she studied the menu for a moment. 'When in Rome,' she muttered before sliding back out of the booth and making her way to the nearest self-service terminal. A few minutes later she returned carrying a tray containing a Quarter Pounder, fries and a Coke.

Jones had pretty much finished his food as she took her seat.

'God, I needed that,' he said before sucking on the straw of his drink.

'So I see.' Phillips grinned as she opened her burger box.

For the next ten minutes, as she worked her way through her own meal, Jones briefed her on his conversation with Angela Blake as well as his past experiences of dealing with

Veronica's lawyer father, Malcolm. None of which had been pleasant.

'Do you think either of the parents will actually call us if the kids come back?' Jones said eventually.

Phillips took a drink before answering, 'In all honesty, I seriously doubt it. As much as we want them to, they're not obliged to by law, which is why I made sure I took down Warren Marsh's number.'

Jones pushed his tray to one side. 'I did the same with Angela Blake.'

'Great minds.' Phillips took another bite of her burger.

'So it looks like we can discount Adrian Firth and Kat Holmes,' said Jones.

'Yeah, based on the bow and arrow attack on Bernstein, I think we can. Can't see either of them as budding archers.' She checked her watch. 'Well, it's just after 11 p.m. now. If we haven't heard anything by midnight, then I'm thinking we call both sets of parents for an update. If there's still no sign of the kids, my instinct is to put a force-wide alert out on them. See if that can flush them out.'

'Sounds like a plan.'

Phillips drained her drink, then placed the empty cup on the tray in front of her. 'So how did Sarah take it when you said you'd be working late again?'

Jones pursed his lips. 'Let's just say she wasn't exactly thrilled and leave it at that, shall we?'

'In the doghouse again?'

'Yeah.' Jones sighed. 'I seem to bloody live in it at the moment.'

'Sorry about that.'

'Don't be. It's the job. Deep down she knows that.' Jones

sat back and placed his hands flat on the table. 'How about Adam? Was he okay about you not being home?'

'He's working nights this week, so I didn't even need to call him.'

'Ships in the night, is it?'

'Something like that.' Phillips sighed.

Jones glanced back at the counter behind her, his interest seemingly piqued. 'You fancy a donut while we're waiting?'

She shrugged. 'Why not. In for a penny, in for a pound.'

'Coming right up,' he said with a grin as he slid out of the booth.

Sometime later, with the donuts long gone and the time approaching midnight, Phillips pulled out her phone. 'I guess it's time we called the parents.'

Jones picked up his own handset from the table.

'Probably best we do this outside, away from any prying ears,' said Phillips as she stood.

Jones matched her and followed her out.

As she watched him wander across the all-but-empty car park with his phone to his ear, she pressed redial.

It rang four or five times at the other end before being answered. *'Warren Marsh.'*

'Mr Marsh. DCI Phillips.'

'Really, Inspector. It's almost midnight.' His agitation was evident.

She cut to the chase. 'Is Jonathan home?'

'No. He's not.'

'Have you heard from him at all?'

'I haven't. No.'

'And doesn't that worry you?'

'Not really. He's most likely at Ronnie's house. He's never far away from the place.'

'He's not,' Phillips countered. 'We've checked.'

'In that case, he's probably on his way home as we speak.'

'Look, Mr Marsh, I'm afraid that based on the fact Jonathan is a prime suspect in a murder case and appears to have gone missing, I have no other option than to issue a force-wide alert to try to track him down.'

'And what exactly does that mean?'

'It means that within the next few minutes, every copper in Manchester will be out looking for him.'

'Honestly, I'm sure you must be mistaken in all this. Jonathan comes from good stock. I can't believe he'd do any of the things that you're suggesting.'

'I'm afraid the evidence is leading us to a different conclusion,' Phillips shot back. 'Look. If he *does* come home, then I can't stress enough how important it is that you call me right away, okay? You won't be doing him any favours by hiding him or trying to protect him. And of course, if *we* find him first, I'll be sure to contact you imme-diately. Now I'm very sorry, but I have to go.' With that, she rang off.

'Any joy?' Jones asked as he wandered back towards her.

'No. Still no sign of Jonathan.'

'Nor Ronnie.'

Phillips exhaled as she checked the clock on her phone: 00.05 a.m. 'Right, time to put out the alert.'

'Do we have any recent photos?'

'No, but it should be easy enough to pull some from social media. According to Whistler, they both have active Instagram accounts.'

'Good idea. I'll dig them out now.' Jones began typing into his handset.

Just then Phillips's phone began to ring; it was a number

unknown. 'Hang on a sec, this might be Marsh calling back,' she said as she accepted the call. 'DCI Phillips.'

'Good evening, ma'am, I'm Sergeant Javed.'

'And what can I do for you at this time of night?'

'Yeah. Look, I'm sorry to call you so late, but one of my team, PC Hastings, has been at the MRI with your suspect, Sebastian Heppingstall.'

'Go on.'

'I'm afraid PC Hastings has just called to inform me that the young man died from his injuries fifteen minutes ago.'

In that moment, Phillips's world seemed to grind to a halt, her mouth falling open yet unable to form words.

'I thought you'd want to know right away.'

Phillips nodded but remained silent as Jones looked on, confusion etched on his face.

'Ma'am? Are you still there?' asked Javed.

'Er, yeah. I'm still here,' she managed to mutter.

Jones stepped closer. 'What's going on, guv?' he whispered.

Phillips didn't respond as she attempted to process the maelstrom of thoughts enveloping her brain. 'Have his family been informed?'

'Not yet, but with your approval, Hastings will head to speak to the next of kin now.' Javed paused. *'I have Meredith Heppingstall down on my notes. The address is 37 Hough Road.'*

'His grandmother,' replied Phillips. 'I'm sure he will, but please tell Hastings to be very careful how he breaks the news. Meredith is seventy-five, and a shock like this could kill her.'

'Of course, ma'am. I'll brief him now.'

'We're also going to need to contact his parents,' added

Phillips. 'They live in Dubai. I don't want his grandmother to have to make that call.'

'I'll speak to family liaison, ma'am.'

'Thank you,' said Phillips before hanging up.

'What the hell's happened?' Jones asked with wide, expectant eyes.

'Sebastian's dead.'

'Shit,' replied Jones.

'Died of his injuries fifteen minutes ago.'

Jones ran his hands down his face, causing it to redden.

'This is bad, Jonesy, about as bad as it gets.' Phillips was already back on her phone. 'I need to call Carter so he can get out in front of it.'

'Good idea,' said Jones.

'If Fox gets wind of this before she hears it from one of us, well...' Her words tailed off.

'This wasn't down to us, guv. We didn't leave him alone in custody. You know that, don't you?'

Phillips nodded absentmindedly, but she wasn't really listening as the phone began to ring at the other end.

After what seemed like a lifetime, he answered, sounding half asleep. *'Jane? What is it?'*

Phillips took a deep breath as she walked across the car park towards her car. 'I'm sorry to wake you, sir, but we have a major problem...'

40

After recovering the two packages from the secure twenty-four-hour locker, Tex and Clem made their way to the hotel nearby. Thankfully, as Charlie had suggested, the reception area was fully automated, so, with their heads bowed and faces hidden under the hoods of their sweatshirts, they took the stairs to the second floor and headed for room 222. Once safely inside, Tex dumped the packages on the bed before double-locking the door and fitting the chain for added security. Next, he turned on the TV to avoid being heard by anyone in the adjoining rooms.

'Is there any air-con?' asked Clem. 'It's roasting in here.'

Tex spotted it on the wall next to the bathroom and made the necessary adjustments to reduce the room temperature. Next, he dropped onto the bed and set about opening the packages and pulling out the contents.

Clem took a seat on the small sofa opposite, which doubled up as a bed when required. 'What's all that?'

Tex stared down at the lanyard in his hand, which

contained a staff pass dated for the next day's sessions at the energy conference. 'An access pass for the Energy Expo tomorrow.' He reached in and pulled out another one. 'There's one for you, too.'

Clem shook her head. 'We're not doing this. You promised.'

Tex ignored her as he pulled out a pair of dark blue polo shirts and matching caps, each emblazoned with the expo's logo, and a pair of clear-lens spectacles. After placing them on the bed, he fished out two boxes containing two pay-as-you-go untraceable mobile phones. 'One for you.' He handed over one of the boxes. 'And one for me,' he added before ripping off the packaging from the second box.

'I don't want or need a burner phone. I'm not doing it, and neither are you.'

He stopped and stared back at her. 'Look. You don't have to do this, okay? But I really do.'

'Why?' she asked. 'This afternoon you promised Bernstein would be the last.'

'I know I did, but things have changed.'

'You said that before. What's changed, Jonathan?'

'Hey. Code names only, remember?'

'Oh, shut up!' she growled. 'Enough with this cloak-and-dagger bullshit. I'm not Clem, and you're not Tex. We're *Ronnie* and *Jonathan*, and this war-games crap has gone on long enough. It's time to stop.'

'I can't stop.'

'Why can't you?' she asked. 'What exactly did Charlie say to you on the phone earlier?'

'It's not important.'

She shook her head. 'Whatever it was, it spooked you, I could tell.'

Jonathan remained silent as he held her gaze.

'Did he threaten you? Is that why you think you can't stop?'

'Not me, no.'

'Did Charlie threaten *me*?'

He swallowed hard before answering, 'Yes.'

Ronnie flinched. 'What did he say?'

'I told you, it's not important,' he replied, averting his eyes.

'Tell me what he said.'

Jonathan exhaled sharply before answering, 'He told me he'd do to you what the Manson family did to Sharon Tate.'

There was an audible intake of breath as Ronnie recoiled.

'I can't let that happen, babe,' he said softly. 'And that's why I have to do this last operation.'

She reached out and grabbed his wrists in her hands. 'Let's get out of here. Get a flight somewhere, anywhere away from here, from Charlie.'

'How? We don't even have our passports.'

'We can go home and get them.'

'No, we can't,' he replied. 'The cops will be swarming all over our houses. We'd be arrested on sight.'

Tears welled in her eyes now. 'We should never have gotten involved in all this.'

'I know, but we did and for good reason too.'

'Really? Has any of this made the slightest bit of difference?'

'Not yet, but it will. As soon as this last operation is complete, Charlie will announce Terra to the world, and at last people will sit up and listen. Finally, we can make positive change to ensure our kids have a world worth living in.

Billions of people are relying on us to fight for this planet, Ronnie. *Their* future depends on what *we* do now, today, while we still can.'

'And what about *our* future, Jonathan? In case you've forgotten, we killed a man and seriously injured two others. Where does that leave us?'

He dropped his chin to his chest for a moment before looking up. 'Right now, I honestly don't know, but I'm sure Charlie can figure something out. Maybe he can help us get out of the country?'

'Charlie?' she scoffed. 'A minute ago, you just told me he threatened to butcher me like Sharon Tate if you walked away. Do you really think he's going to help us get out of this mess?'

'He has to,' said Jonathan.

'No, he doesn't, and you can bet he won't. I mean, we haven't actually got the first clue who he really is or what his true motives are. For all we know, he could be some psycho who's been using us to act out his sick fantasies. Have you ever stopped to think about that?'

'He's legit. I know he is.'

'How? You've never even met him.'

'Yes, I have,' he replied flatly. 'I speak to him all the time.'

'You speak to his sodding avatar through an encrypted link. Haven't you ever wondered why that is?'

Jonathan shrugged. 'To protect his identity. Everyone knows that government agencies are watching everything we do. Charlie is playing them at their own game to safeguard the future of Terra.'

'He's playing *you* more like,' she snapped as she sat back on the sofa and folded her arms across her chest.

Jonathan stared back in silence for a while before

turning his attention to the unopened package and, in particular, the yellow and black warning label stuck to its side.

She craned her neck. 'Does that say corrosive?'

He nodded as he carefully removed the seal on the top of the box and pulled out a glass bottle from inside, reading the label aloud as he did. 'Sulphuric acid.'

Ronnie's eyes widened as she stared at it.

'That's why it's called Operation Acid Reign.'

'I don't believe this.' Ronnie dropped her head into her hands, her long red hair falling over her face.

Moving slowly off the bed, he carried the bottle across the room and slipped it carefully into his rucksack.

Ronnie lifted her head again. 'What the hell does he want you to do with that?'

'He didn't say, but I'll know first thing in the morning when he sends through the final orders.'

'Please, Jonathan, I'm begging you,' she pleaded. 'You don't have to do this.'

Walking across the room, he climbed back on the bed. 'I don't have a choice,' he said as he turned off the TV and lay down on the bed. 'Come on, let's try to get some sleep.' With that, he turned out the light, plunging the room into total darkness.

JONATHAN WOKE with a start in the darkened room, his heart pounding in his chest, sweat soaking the back of his neck. Sitting up, it took him a couple of seconds to remember where he was before suddenly realising he was in bed alone. 'Ronnie?' he whispered into the darkness, hoping she was nearby, but there was no reply. Flicking on the main light switch, it was clear he was very much alone.

Reaching for the burner phone on the bedside table, he activated the home screen – it was just after 6 a.m. Jumping out of bed, he moved quickly to the bathroom, hopeful she was sitting on the loo in there – maybe watching her phone out of earshot – but his heart sank when he opened the door and saw it was empty.

His mind raced as he tried to figure out what to do next, his eyes darting around the room, vainly trying to find the answers. It was then he spotted the note resting on the desk in front of him. Picking it up, he scanned the page.

I can't do this anymore. I'm sorry, but I just can't. It's time to try to stop all this. I hope you can forgive me in time.
All my love, always.
R. xxxxx

'Shit!' he said as his mind's eye flooded with images of Sharon Tate lying mutilated in her California home. 'What have you done, Ronnie? He's gonna kill you.'

Staring down at the note, he had an overwhelming urge to follow her, to run away and never come back, but he knew that was the last thing he should do if he wanted to keep her safe. Picking up the burner phone, he keyed in Ronnie's mobile, praying he could talk to her before she did anything stupid.

It rang out, once, twice and then three times over.

'Shit!' he growled as he paced the room, running scenario after scenario round in his mind as he attempted to figure out his next move. Finally with all other options exhausted, he realised there was only one thing left to do. Sitting down on the bed, he opened the web browser on the phone and quickly logged into the shared account he used to communicate with Charlie and, after typing out a short message, pressed send.

'Now we wait,' he muttered to himself.

A few minutes later, an unknown number flashing up on-screen caused his adrenaline to spike. 'Hello?'

'What's so urgent we need to break protocol?' Charlie was clearly pissed off.

'Ronn—' He caught himself. 'I mean, Clem has gone.'

'What do you mean she's gone?'

'She's gone. Left the hotel and gone.'

'Gone where?'

'I honestly don't know, but I really think we should abort Operation Acid Reign. If the police are looking for us both like you say, it's only a matter of time before they pick her up and come after me. At least this way we have plausible deniability.'

'The operation has to go ahead as planned,' said Charlie flatly. *'The success of this entire campaign depends on it.'*

'But if the police are looking for us, then chances are I'll get caught, and if that happens, I could go to prison for the rest of my life.'

'You won't get caught. I'll see to that.'

'How?'

'Trust me, I have my ways,' said Charlie. *'And luckily the final attack is more subtle. You'll be in and out before they know what's hit them.'*

Jonathan rubbed the back of his neck. 'I'm really not sure about this, Charlie.'

'Well, get sure, because if you don't, then you know what I'll do to your precious Clem when I find her, don't you?'

'Yes.' He stared at his reflection in the mirror opposite as dreadful images of Sharon Tate resurfaced in his mind. 'Yes, I do.'

'Do you have the stuff I sent? The passes and the uniform?'

'Yeah.'

'What about the acid?'

'I have that, too.'

'In that case, make your way to the Lowry and wait for my call. While you're doing that, I'll check all the police chatter. Depending on what they know, we may have to make a few adjustments to the plan, but in the meantime, I think it'd be good idea to get yourself some wash-in hair dye. The less you look like you right now, the better.

'Okay,' he said with a heavy heart. 'There's a twenty-four-hour chemist a few streets away. I can get some from there.'

'Just be careful; they may have security cameras.'

'I will.'

'And make sure you walk to the Lowry. If you stick to the back streets, you should be able to avoid any CCTV.'

'Okay.'

'I'll be in touch,' said Charlie finally; then he rang off.

Five minutes later, with his hood pulled up over his head and a backpack slung over his shoulder, Jonathan stepped out into the morning sunshine.

He was setting off on his final mission.

41

A fter very little sleep, Phillips arrived early the next morning for an urgent meeting with Carter and Fox. After hearing of Sebastian's death late last night, the chief constable had insisted the three of them gather in her office at 7 a.m. in order to try to get out in front of, in her words, 'an absolute shit show'. And so, after dumping her bags in her office, Phillips trudged up the back stairs to the fifth floor, fearful of what lay in store. As she turned to make her ascent up the final set of stairs, she found Carter waiting on the top-floor landing.

'Morning, Jane.' His voice lacked its usual levity, and his broad shoulders sagged.

'Morning, sir,' she replied, joining him on the top step. 'You look tired.'

'Yeah.' He ran his fingers through his thick hair. 'I called Fox straight after you told me about Sebastian. You can imagine how that went.'

'I can. I'm dreading this.'

He folded his arms. 'Look. We both know how it'll play

out: she'll make sure someone is to blame for it all, we'll try to counter, argue a few points of our own, which she will of course rebuke, and eventually, when she's given us both barrels, she'll send us on our way to sort it all out as quickly as possible.'

'You know her too well,' said Phillips.

He sighed. 'Sadly, I do.'

'But it shouldn't be like this, should it? I mean, just for once it'd be nice to feel supported by her as opposed to being bollocked for something that, in reality, was out of our control.'

'I know,' he replied. 'But the truth is that, ultimately, Sebastian *was* MCU's responsibility. He was our prisoner, after all.'

'Under the supervision of the *custody team*, sir,' she shot back. 'Look, I'm all for taking responsibility when we mess up, but *we* didn't leave the boy alone so he could hang himself from his cell door, did we?'

Carter nodded. 'You're right, Jane. Of course you are, but we're dealing with Fox here, and the way she was talking on the phone last night, she's holding MCU fully responsible for Sebastian's suicide. So unless she's done a complete U-turn overnight, then all of this is coming our way whether we like it or not.'

Phillips exhaled loudly. 'With respect, this is bullshit, sir.'

'I totally get how you feel, but let's just sit tight, take our medicine and get out of there as quickly as we can, hey?'

'Yeah.' Phillips glanced at her watch. 'Speaking of which, we'd better get moving. It's bang on 7 a.m.'

Carter offered a faint smile, then opened the door and led the way onto the fifth-floor corridor.

Passing quickly through the now empty outer office, they

soon found themselves standing side by side opposite Fox, who was positioned behind an oversized, smoked-glass desk, staring intently at her PC screen.

'Good morning, ma'am,' offered Carter.

Fox remained silent for a second as she turned her gaze towards them. 'Close the door and sit down,' she said sharply.

Phillips obliged before returning to take the seat next to Carter.

Fox got straight to the point. 'A sixteen-year-old boy in *our* custody managed to hang himself right under our noses. Which one of you would like to explain how that happened on MCU's watch?'

'Well...ahem.' Carter attempted to clear his throat. 'It seems Sebastian was being escorted from his cell by PC Ali to make a phone call when there was a situation with another prisoner who assaulted Sergeant Walsh. In the melee that ensued, Ali rushed to defend Walsh, and it appears the boy was left alone with his door open for a couple of minutes. During which time, he managed to use his T-shirt as a makeshift noose.'

Fox sat silently shaking her head. 'Has it seriously come to this? Are we really *this* shambolic as a force?'

Phillips curled her toes tightly in her shoes in an attempt to keep her immense frustration from reaching her face.

'I mean, what the hell was Ali thinking? His first duty in that situation was to ensure the Heppingstall boy was locked back in his cell.'

It was no use; Phillips couldn't stay quiet a moment longer. 'With respect, ma'am, PC Ali followed his instincts – which was to protect Sergeant Walsh.'

'Try telling that to the boy's father,' Fox spat back. 'Have you any idea how much shit this brings to our door, Jane?'

'No, but I'm sure you're about to tell me.' The words came out before she could stop them.

Fox's nostrils flared as she glared at Phillips. 'May I remind you who you're talking to, Chief Inspector?'

Phillips could feel Carter's eyes on her as she held Fox's gaze. 'Apologies, ma'am,' she mumbled without feeling.

Fox continued, 'Jeremy Heppingstall has friends in Whitehall. He went to Cambridge with the newly appointed Home Secretary, for God's sake, and the last thing we need right now is to become the topic of conversation around the dispatches box. The Home Secretary's just itching to make changes to the way the police are funded, and this bloody mess could be all the motivation he needs to get started. It's a total fucking disaster.'

Carter appeared lost for words beside Phillips, while she had come to the conclusion that the best way to get out of this meeting as quickly as possible was to keep her mouth shut from now on.

Fox locked eyes with her. 'Did he show any signs of suicide markers when you interviewed him?'

'No, ma'am.'

'So why did he do it?' Fox asked. 'What made a sixteen-year-old boy think hanging himself was his only option?'

Phillips shifted in her seat. 'Well, ma'am, the evidence we presented against him at interview was pretty damning. Maybe he was worried about spending the rest of his life in prison? He wouldn't be the first suspect to prefer suicide over a life inside.'

Fox's eyes narrowed. 'Did you scare him into doing this, Jane?'

'No, not at all.' Phillips stumbled slightly. 'I mean, naturally I explained what sort of prison time he was facing if he was convicted, but—'

'Which in the eyes of an inquiry could look like intimidation of a minor.'

'But he *killed* a man,' Phillips shot back.

'Maybe so, but his crimes died with him. Now he's just a young lad who felt so scared while he was in our care that he took his own life. I'm sure that's how his father will see it, and most likely the Home Secretary too.' Fox exhaled sharply. 'God, this is all we need right now.'

The room fell silent as each of them processed the reality of the situation.

'Where do we go from here, ma'am?' Carter asked eventually.

Fox sat forward and linked her fingers together on the desk. 'As soon as we're done here, I have a call with the PPC to explain what happened, and no doubt I'll be speaking to the boy's father later this morning. Once all that's done, the comms team will need to send a statement to the press.'

'Very good, ma'am,' said Carter. 'I can liaise with Rupert on that if you'd like?'

Fox nodded. 'And depending on how things go with Jeremy Heppingstall, we may need to do something to camera. A public show of force to demonstrate how seriously we're taking all this.'

'Would you like me to be the one to do that?' Carter asked.

'Well, I'm certainly not doing it. This is your mess, and you can clean it up.'

'Of course, ma'am.'

'That said,' added Fox, 'I'm hoping we can avoid

anything *too* visual. The last thing I want is video all over social media showing us apologising for letting a teenage boy die on our watch. It'll do nothing for the image of the force.'

Her image more like, thought Phillips.

Fox continued, 'And if there is to be an inquiry, which is more than likely, I think it's fair to say PC Ali will be suspended until that has been concluded.'

'Really, ma'am, is that necessary?' Phillips cut in. 'Considering how short-staffed the custody team were when all this kicked off, I don't think anyone can blame Ali for what happened. After all, he was just trying to protect his colleague.'

'That will be for the inquiry to decide. In the meantime, he's gone. It'll look better to the boy's family, and the public as a whole, if we are seen to take definitive action. Plus, I'm sure I don't need to remind you, Jane, that your conduct during Sebastian's questioning will come under intense scrutiny. If there's any evidence of coercive or threatening behaviour, you could be in real trouble.'

'I followed the proper protocols throughout, ma'am,' said Phillips defiantly.

'That's as may be,' Fox replied. 'But Sebastian's father is not likely to take this lying down. Having someone like Ali to shift the blame to may well come in very handy for you further down the line. The reality is that the public can accept mistakes from supposedly overworked cops on the ground, but they automatically hold senior officers to a far higher account. I'd much rather a police constable take the fall than have to explain why one of my chief inspectors messed up.'

Phillips stared back, speechless.

'Right,' said Fox. 'Unless there's anything else, we'd all benefit from getting back to work.'

'Yes, ma'am.' Carter stood.

Phillips bit her bottom lip as she followed him out.

Back on the corridor, once they were out of earshot, they stopped to debrief.

'Are you okay?' asked Carter.

Phillips clenched her fists tightly. 'I don't believe that woman sometimes. Ultimately, this mess is down to her bloody budget cuts, but instead of holding her hands up and taking some responsibility, a young copper who was just trying to protect his oppo is getting hung out to dry.'

'It might not come to that,' Carter countered.

'Pff,' Phillips scoffed. 'Ali is as good as gone. We both know that.'

Carter nodded sagely. 'She is right about one thing though, Jane.'

'Oh? And what's that?'

'If there is an inquiry and they do find evidence we went too hard on him, that could mean serious trouble for MCU.'

Phillips sighed. 'Look, of course I tried to put the wind up him a little. That's standard procedure in these situations, but there was nothing threatening about anything I said or how I behaved. I simply told him the facts about life in prison.'

'I know that, and you know that, but inquiries don't always see things so clearly.'

Phillips ran her hands down her face. 'God, this is a total mess.'

'Can you ask one of the guys to get me video copies of the interviews you did with him?'

She flinched. 'Why? Don't you believe me?'

'Of course I believe you, but I've also been involved in several inquiries in the past. I have a pretty good idea what sort of things they'll be looking for, and if there *is* anything on those tapes that could be used against us, I'd like to be prepared.'

'Sorry, sir,' said Phillips. 'I shouldn't have snapped like that. I'll get Whistler to bring the videos up on a stick for you as soon as he gets in.'

'Thank you.'

'Do you need anything else?'

'No,' replied Carter.

'In that case, I'd better get downstairs. There's still no sign of Sebastian's co-conspirators and, the way things are going, I'm sure it's just a matter of time before they do something else stupid.'

Carter placed his hand heavily on her right shoulder. 'You've got this, Jane. If anyone can find those kids, it's you.'

She flashed a faint smile. 'I really hope you're right, sir, because right now, it feels like we're going backwards.'

42

By the time Phillips walked into MCU, the team were already at their desks.

'How did it go with the Fuhrer?' Bovalino asked.

'Terrible,' replied Phillips as she sank into the chair at the spare desk.

For the next few minutes she brought them up to speed on the meeting with the chief constable, and by the time she was finished, the mood in the room was noticeably darker.

Jones shook his head. 'That woman has a bloody nerve. She's the one asking us all to deliver champagne results on a sodding beer budget.'

'I know, Jonesy,' she replied. 'I feel exactly the same.'

'It's Ali I feel sorry for,' added Bov. 'Poor bugger doesn't stand a chance if this gets in front of an inquiry.'

Phillips nodded. 'And that's another reason why we need to find Marsh and Blake ASAP. If we can prove Sebastian was part of the attack on Grayson as well as Nixon, it'll go some way to reducing the impact of his death in custody and maybe mitigate some of the damage to Ali's career.'

'I checked the update on the alert, guv,' said Entwistle, 'but so far there's been no sign of either of the kids.'

Phillips exhaled loudly as she sat back in the chair.

Entwistle continued, 'I also checked out their social media accounts. Looks like Ronnie Marsh is big into archery.'

'And why wouldn't she be?' Phillips shot back sardonically.

'Which would suggest she was the one who fired the arrow at Bernstein,' Jones said.

'I always said Manchester was like the Wild West,' quipped Bovalino.

The team chuckled in unison.

'Anyway, on the subject of Bernstein,' said Jones, 'I spoke to one of the nurses at the MRI earlier, and it looks like Bernstein will make a full recovery.'

'Well, that's something at least,' replied Phillips before turning her attention back to Entwistle. 'What about Jonathan Marsh. Anything of interest on his social media?'

'Not really. In fact, there was surprisingly little posted on his various profiles of late. He had been pretty active on Instagram and TikTok, but it all seems to have dried up about three months ago.'

Phillips frowned. 'I wonder why?'

'No idea, boss, but there's certainly nothing on there to suggest why there's been a sudden lack of activity.'

Just then the door to MCU opened behind her.

'Aye, aye,' said Bov. 'Who's this?'

Phillips turned to see a uniformed officer making his way towards them. The name badge on his chest announced him as PC Henning.

'Ma'am, I'm sorry to interrupt, but someone just gave me

this at the front door and asked me to pass it on to the person in charge of the Nixon murder.' He handed across an A4 padded brown envelope.

Phillips felt her eyes narrow as she took it. She reached inside and pulled out a staff lanyard for the Energy Expo, which she placed on the table along with a folded piece of paper.

The team watched on as she checked the envelope for anything else.

Satisfied it was empty, she opened the folded paper and read the handwritten note aloud. 'Operation Acid Reign, spelled R-E-I-G-N.' She turned it around so the guys could see it.

'What the hell does that mean?' asked Jones.

Phillips wasn't listening; all her attention was focused on PC Henning. 'Who gave this to you?'

'A young girl, ma'am. She seemed pretty upset about something.'

Phillips sat to attention. 'How young?'

'I don't know for sure, but she looked about the same age as my sister, who's sixteen.'

'What colour hair did she have?'

'Red, you know, like ginger,' said Henning.

'And how long ago was this?'

'About five minutes, ma'am. I came straight up here with it.'

Phillips bolted from the chair and raced out of the office. A minute later she burst through the main door to Ashton House and out into the car park, but there was no sign of the girl. 'Damn it,' she muttered as she raced off towards the Mini.

Speeding out of the car park a minute later, she had a

choice to make: left or right? Her instincts suggested right, and a second later she was racing up Oldham Road towards the M60. 'Where are you?' she muttered as she scanned left and right, looking for the red-headed girl. And then, a moment later, there she was – walking briskly along the pavement up ahead – Ronnie Blake.

Screeching to a halt at the side of the road, Phillips killed the engine and jumped out. 'Ronnie!' she shouted.

The girl turned, her eyes instantly widening before she set off running.

'Shit,' said Phillips, giving immediate chase.

Ronnie already had a head start and was clearly no stranger to running as she raced away up the street.

Phillips did her best to match her step for step, but remained at a distance, her legs and lungs soon burning as she attempted to keep up the pace.

As Ronnie moved further away, Phillips contemplated heading back to fetch the car, but dismissed the idea out of hand. In the time it would take to do that, Ronnie would be out of sight and likely gone for good.

Rounding the bend, Phillips spotted the junction to the M60 up ahead, a hellishly busy feeder road for the motorway that would take time for Ronnie to cross – and maybe even just enough time for Phillips to catch up. With renewed vigour, she gritted her teeth and picked up the pace.

Soon after, and as expected, Ronnie came to a halt up ahead as she reached the M60 feeder road, which teeming with cars moving left and right onto the motorway.

'Ronnie, I just want to talk!' Phillips shouted above the noise of the traffic.

Ronnie's head darted back and forth as she searched desperately for a place to cross.

Phillips was almost upon her.

Suddenly the traffic began to slow to a stop, and as the lights turned red, Ronnie bolted across the road.

'Come here!' shouted Phillips, reaching for the hood of Ronnie's top, which was hanging over her back, missing by a fraction.

As Ronnie continued to run, she glanced over her shoulder before turning back. But in that moment, she caught her foot on a bump in the pavement and fell, stumbling forward.

That was all the help Phillips needed, and with Ronnie now off balance, she tackled her to the ground, landing on her with a thud.

'Let me go!' screamed Ronnie as they both fought for control of the clinch.

Phillips, who had been in this exact same position many times in her career, knew exactly what to do, instantly wrapping both arms and legs tightly around Ronnie, using every ounce of strength to force her into submission.

Finally, Ronnie stopped moving.

'In a second, I'm going to let go of you,' Phillips said breathlessly directly into Ronnie's ear. 'And I want you to stay exactly where you are, okay?'

The girl remained silent.

'It's time to stop running. We know all about you and Jonathan; we know what you did.'

The silence continued.

'Remember, stay exactly where you are,' said Phillips, her voice returning to normal now, before releasing her grip and rolling to the side.

As quick as a flash, Ronnie was up on her feet and running once more.

'Shit,' growled Phillips as she jumped up to give chase again, before realising there was a better way to stop the girl. Cupping her hands around her mouth, she bellowed after her, 'Sebastian's dead!'

Ronnie immediately stopped in her tracks, turning a second later.

Phillips took a step forward. 'He tried to hang himself in the cells yesterday.'

'You're lying,' Ronnie shot back.

'I really wish I were, but I'm not,' replied Phillips. 'He died last night from his injuries.'

Ronnie's face crumpled as she began to cry.

Phillips edged closer. 'It's time to stop this. No more running, okay?'

Ronnie dropped her head into her hands. 'I never meant for any of this to happen,' she said, her shoulders shaking as she broke down in tears. 'Nobody was meant to die.'

Phillips moved in and wrapped a comforting arm around her shoulder. 'It's okay, Ronnie,' she said softly. 'It's okay.'

43

Two hours later, Phillips and Jones took their seats in Interview Room Four opposite Ronnie and her father, Malcolm Blake, who was now acting as her legal counsel. Blake was a tall, angular man, likely in his mid-forties, thought Phillips. He had thick red hair that matched his daughter's, and his navy blue pinstripe suit was offset with a crisp white shirt and maroon tie. Everything about him screamed confidence.

By contrast, Ronnie, sitting to his right, looked small and frightened, her cheeks flushed from crying, her head bowed slightly as she stared at a plastic cup of water on the table between them.

As expected, Blake attempted to take control of proceedings from the outset. His voice deep and booming, he said, 'After speaking to Veronica, she has agreed to tell you as much as she can about the events of the last week. I would naturally have preferred she invoke her right to make no comment at this stage, but against my wishes, she feels compelled to speak to you. She believes enough people have been hurt and wants to help you stop Jonathan Marsh before he harms anybody else.'

Phillips moved her gaze to Ronnie in the hope she would acknowledge her father's comments, but instead she continued staring at the table.

Jones opened his notepad and placed his pen on the page in readiness.

'Before we go any further,' said Blake, 'I would like Ronnie's willingness to speak in order to help the investigation be noted and passed on to the CPS. As you'll soon hear for yourselves, it is my firm belief that my daughter has been manipulated by Marsh, as well as several others; that, ultimately, she had no intention of causing serious harm to anyone.'

'Noted,' said Phillips before activating the DIR. When the long tone had passed, she turned her focus back to the girl. 'So, Ronnie, let's start at the beginning, shall we? Can you confirm that on the third of June, you, Jonathan Marsh and Sebastian Heppingstall were responsible for the car-bomb attack outside the David Lloyd health club in Cheadle?'

Ronnie glanced at her father, who offered the faintest of nods.

'Yes,' she said, her voice almost a whisper.

Phillips continued, 'And were the three of you also responsible for the knife attack in St John's Gardens that killed Robert Nixon on Friday the ninth of June?'

Ronnie nodded silently.

'For the tape, Veronica Blake nodded her agreement,' said Phillips. 'Furthermore, were you and Jonathan Marsh responsible for the assault with a deadly weapon on Travis Bernstein last night at the Ollerton Hall Hotel?'

'Yes,' she whispered.

Phillips nodded. 'Can you tell us *why* you committed these crimes?'

Ronnie paused before answering, 'To make a statement to the world, to try to stop global warming.'

'I see.' Phillips cleared her throat. 'And were you acting alone, or were these actions carried out as part of a wider group?'

'A wider group.'

'And what was the name of that group?'

'Terra,' replied Ronnie.

'And is that Terra as in T-E-R-R-A?'

'Yes.'

Jones scribbled in his pad now.

'So who is behind Terra?' asked Phillips.

'Charlie.'

'Charlie? I see, and does Charlie have a last name?'

Ronnie shook her head. 'Not that I know of, but then I've never dealt with him.'

'So how did you know he was behind the group?'

'Jonathan said so. Everything went through him, you see.'

'And how did they communicate? Jonathan and Charlie?'

'Encrypted video calls mainly, but the instructions for the operations would come via secure email.'

Jones scribbled again as Phillips continued, 'Are you saying that, of the three of you, only Jonathan knows what Charlie looks like?'

'Yeah, well, no, not really. You see, Charlie always uses a digital avatar on-screen for extra security.'

'So Jonathan has never actually *seen* this Charlie character in the flesh?'

'No.'

Phillips shifted in her seat. 'Am I right in thinking that *none* of you knows who Charlie *really* is or where he comes from?'

'Yes.'

Phillips frowned. 'But you were willing to kill for him?'

'That's just it, *I* wasn't,' Ronnie retorted. 'I never intended to hurt anyone. It all just got out of hand.'

Phillips tilted her head at a slight angle. 'And you expect us to believe that – with two victims in hospital and another man *dead*?'

'It's true, Chief Inspector,' Blake cut in. 'Tell them what you told me, Veronica.'

Phillips held Ronnie's gaze.

'When we set the device off at David Lloyd, I thought it was just the car we were going after, because it was a gas guzzler. I had no idea Grayson wouldn't be able to get out after the engine exploded.'

'Really?'

'It's true, I swear it is,' she pleaded.

'Okay, if that *is* actually the case, then what about the knife attack on Robert Nixon?'

Ronnie closed her eyes for a moment.

'If you didn't want to hurt anybody, what made you stab him?'

'I didn't.' A tear streaked down her cheek. 'I went along with Jonathan and Seb, but I didn't stab him. I just pretended to.'

'But why?' asked Phillips. 'Why pretend? Why not just walk away after the car attack?'

'Because Charlie told Jonathan he'd kill me if I did.'

Phillips stared at her in silence.

Ronnie continued, 'He said that Charlie would not accept failure or treachery. That if any of us tried to walk away, then another cell within Terra would be sent to take us out.'

'My daughter feared for her life, Chief Inspector,' Blake chimed in. 'That's why she continued with the attacks, under severe duress.'

Phillips ignored him. 'Terra is made up of different cells. Is that what you're saying?'

'I think so, yes.'

'But you don't know for sure?'

'Like I said, Jonathan was the only one who spoke to Charlie, so all I know is what came from him.'

'And where is Jonathan now?'

Ronnie glanced sideways at her father once more.

He nodded.

'I left him in the Premier Inn at the end of the Princess Parkway in the city.'

'When was that?'

'About four a.m.'

'Did he see you leave?'

'No,' said Ronnie. 'He was asleep.'

'What room is he in?'

'Two-two-two.'

Phillips turned her attention to the DIR machine now as she checked her watch. 'DCI Phillips suspending the interview at 10.31 a.m.'

'What's going on?' demanded Blake.

Phillips jumped up from the chair. 'We just need to take a short break,' she said before rushing out of the room.

A couple of minutes later she and Jones made their way

into the observation suite, where Bovalino and Whistler were watching proceedings on the screen.

'We need to get to that hotel right now.'

'I can go,' said Bovalino, standing.

'Great,' Phillips replied. 'You should go too, Jonesy. It's clear Jonathan isn't afraid to use deadly force, so there's safety in numbers.'

'But what about the interview with the girl?' asked Jones.

'I can handle that.' Phillips glanced at the screen showing the camera feed from Interview Room Four. 'And besides, after what happened to Sebastian, as soon as she started crying in there, it got me thinking it might be better for me to do the whole thing alone. That way no one can accuse us of being mob handed with a minor for a second time.'

'If you're sure?'

Phillips nodded.

'I'll drive,' said Bovalino.

'And be careful, guys, okay? Age-wise, Jonathan may be just a kid, but he's also a killer.'

Both men nodded.

Phillips flashed a quick smile, then set off back to Interview Room Four.

Soon after, she retook her seat and restarted the DIR before turning to Ronnie. 'DCI Phillips resuming the interview at 10.37 a.m. Before the break, you mentioned that you'd never met Charlie.'

'That's right.'

'Help me out here, will you?' said Phillips. 'Because I'm struggling to understand how an intelligent young woman like you would want to get involved in a group like Terra – I mean, based solely on the word of your mate. To risk every-thing for someone you've never met.'

'I did it for Jonathan.'

'Why?'

Ronnie bit her bottom lip as she shot an anxious look at her father.

'Why, Ronnie? Why did you do it for Jonathan?'

'Because we wanted to get married after university, and he was desperate to do everything he could to make sure our kids had a world worth growing up in, a planet that could offer them a half-decent future.'

'She's young and impressionable,' Blake cut in. 'Marsh manipulated her, pure and simple.'

'No, he didn't, Dad,' Ronnie protested. 'Jonathan's fighting for our future, and I *love* him.'

'Nonsense, Veronica,' spat Blake. 'You're just a child.'

Phillips – keen to avoid this turning into a domestic between father and daughter – pressed on. 'But how does hurting someone like Ross Grayson help you save the planet?'

Ronnie straightened, her eyes exuding defiance. 'Because GBOG is one of the world's biggest energy companies and directly responsible for heating up the Earth's atmosphere. Jonathan said somebody had to make a stand and take affirma-tive action to stop them killing the planet, before it's too late.'

Phillips recoiled. 'By *blowing up* their finance director?'

'I told you. I didn't know we were going to do that,' Ronnie shot back.

'And is that why you went after Nixon? Because he works for Opus Air? Because they're a big polluter, too?'

'Yeah.'

'And let me guess,' said Phillips. 'Bernstein was targeted because he's in the oil business?'

'Yes.'

Phillips felt her eyes narrow. 'So why the bow and arrow? Seems an odd choice of weapon.'

Once more, Ronnie turned to her dad for approval.

'Go ahead,' he said.

'Charlie wanted each operation to have as much impact as possible, to increase our media exposure. He also wanted to scare the bosses at the other big polluters into making changes.'

'I get that,' said, Phillips, 'but a bow and arrow? Really?'

'Charlie called it Operation Navaho because Lone Star Oil was founded on sacred grounds that belonged to the Navaho people.'

'So, what? Last night's attack was about getting revenge for the Navaho people?'

Ronnie hooked a thick strand of hair behind her right ear. 'Yes.'

'I see.' Phillips handed across a picture of Ronnie taken from her Instagram profile. 'For the tape, I'm showing Veronica Blake a picture of her holding a bow and arrow at a recent archery competition.'

Ronnie glared at the image as Phillips continued, 'According to this post taken from Instagram a couple of months ago, you took first place in the English schools Target Championships last August. Is that correct?'

'Yes.'

'So, were you the one who took the shot at Travis Bernstein last night?'

Ronnie remained silent.

'Ronnie,' Phillips pushed, 'did you take the shot at Bernstein last night?'

'Yes,' she whispered finally.

'Can you repeat that? I didn't quite catch it.'

'Yes,' she said louder.

Phillips sat forward. 'A minute ago, you told us you had no intention of hurting anyone, and that things had gotten out of hand.'

'That's right.'

'Yet Travis Bernstein is lying in a hospital bed as we speak with a large hole in his shoulder. An injury he sustained when you fired an arrow at him.'

'Yeah, but he's alive, isn't he?' Ronnie countered, her eyes defiant.

'And what do you mean by that?'

Ronnie continued to glare back. 'I mean I shot him in the shoulder on purpose.'

'As opposed to what?'

'Shooting him in the heart like Charlie wanted. That would have killed him, and I couldn't have that.'

'But why shoot him at all?' Phillips frowned. 'Why not just walk away?'

'Because if I had, Jonathan would have taken the shot himself, and God only knows where that arrow would've ended up. At least this way I had some kind of control over what happened.'

'Okay,' said Phillips. 'If you're that good, then why not miss completely and just blame it on the wind or something?'

'It had to look real. If Charlie worked out I'd done it on purpose, I'd have been next on his hit list.'

Phillips pursed her lips for a moment before changing tack. 'When did Jonathan first talk to you about Charlie?'

Ronnie shrugged. 'A few months ago.'

'Can you be more specific?'

'Erm, Easter time, I think.'

'And how did they first connect?'

'Online,' said Ronnie. 'Jonathan had become obsessed with the Manson family.'

'As in Charles Manson?' Phillips flinched. 'The cult leader?'

'Yeah. We studied the whole family in history, and it was all Jonathan ever wanted to talk about. He must have binge-watched every TV show on Netflix and YouTube about them. He even set up his own social media accounts under the name Helter Skelter. That's where he and Charlie first connected.'

'Are you telling me you studied a bunch of mass murderers at school?'

'Yes. Dr Bell, our history teacher, did his doctorate thesis on the destructive power of iconic figures throughout history. He knows everything about the family and how Manson's incredible charisma and communication skills led him to become one of the most feared men in US history. He and Jonathan would talk after school – for hours at a time – about the Manson legacy.'

'I'd hardly call murdering a pregnant woman in cold blood a legacy,' said Phillips, her voice icy. 'So Jonathan and Charlie had a shared fascination with Manson?'

'Yeah, like I say, not long after Jonathan set up his Helter Skelter page, Charlie reached out to him. He told Jonathan that he'd spent his whole life studying the "great master's work", as he called it, and was preparing to finish what he started. Said he was Charlie Manson three-point-oh – and he was planning to use same the scare tactics from the sixties: fear and intimidation – to bring about a new world order and save the planet. Said he was looking for a new family, soldiers to bring the fight to the masses, and he wanted Jonathan to join him.'

'And that's all it took, was it?' said Phillips. 'For Jonathan to start a killing spree?'

'No, of course not,' Ronnie shot back. 'That was just the beginning. Over the next month or so they talked every day, and Charlie began to teach Jonathan about the horrifying effects global warming is having on the planet, and the catastrophic consequences and existential crisis waiting for us all if nothing changes. He was very persuasive.'

'How do you know?' asked Phillips. 'I mean, you've never even met the guy.'

Ronnie folded her arms across her chest. 'I didn't need to. Jonathan told me everything they talked about each time: the reality of what's facing us if we don't stop the big polluters is truly terrifying. Based on that, I totally under-stood why Jonathan wanted to be part of Terra, because I did too, back then.'

Phillips took a moment to process what she was hearing before continuing, 'Have you ever considered the possibility that Charlie and Jonathan might actually be the same person?'

Ronnie frowned. 'What do you mean?'

'Well, have you ever stopped to ask why only Jonathan ever got to speak with Charlie?'

'That was just the way Charlie wanted it.'

'But how do you know that?' asked Phillips.

'Because Jonathan said so.'

'And did Jonathan ever tell you *why* Charlie wanted it that way?'

'For security reasons. The less we saw or knew, the less we could share with people like you.'

'I see,' said Phillips.

Ronnie continued, 'Charlie was really big on security. We even had code names to help protect our identities when communicating.'

'Code names?' Phillips raised her eyebrows. 'Such as?'

'Jonathan's is Tex, mine is Clem, and Sebastian is—' She caught herself. 'Sorry, *was* Squeaky.'

Phillips remained silent.

'Like the Manson guys. Tex, Clem and Squeaky were the names of three of the Manson family: Tex Watson, Clem Grogan and Squeaky Fromme. Charlie wanted to honour their work by using their names, and Jonathan was really strict with it too – he made sure we only ever called each other by our code names when talking in public.'

'I see.' Phillips glanced down at her notes for a moment before looking up again. 'You mentioned earlier that each of the attacks had an operational name; Navaho, in the case of the bow and arrow. What about the first two operations? What were they called?'

Ronnie took a sip of water from the plastic cup. 'The car attack was Operation Wild Fire, and the second was Operation Slice and Dice.'

Phillips jotted down the names in her pad, then pushed across the handwritten note and lanyard Ronnie had handed to PC Henning earlier that morning. '"Operation Acid Reign". Tell me about this stuff?'

'I only saw those things for the first time last night. I have no idea what the operation name means or what the pass is for.'

'Really? So where did you get them?'

'Charlie told Jonathan to head to a secure locker to pick up a package before we went to the hotel. That stuff was inside.'

'Whose handwriting is it?' asked Phillips.

'Charlie's, I guess.'

'Not Jonathan's?'

Ronnie glanced down at it again. 'Definitely not.'

Phillips used her pen to point to the last word written on the note. 'I'm wondering if that is deliberate or a spelling mistake: R-E-I-G-N as opposed to R-A-I-N.'

Ronnie shrugged. 'Beats me.'

'Either way, I'm guessing Operation Acid Reign refers to the next attack?'

'I guess so.'

'Oh come on, Ronnie,' urged Phillips. 'Surely you *must* know.'

'*I don't.* Not for sure, anyway. Like I keep telling you, everything went through Jonathan. Charlie was mega paranoid about security and would only ever send the final instructions a few hours before the attack was due to take place. I left the hotel before anything came through.'

Phillips held the lanyard up in front of Ronnie's face. 'Based on Charlie's desire to bring down the big polluters, I'm guessing this is the location for the next attack. The Energy Expo at the Lowry theatre?'

'Your guess is as good as mine,' said Ronnie.

'Do you have any idea what they might be planning? What Operation Acid Reign is all about?'

Ronnie opened her mouth to speak, but seemed to think

better of it as she turned to her father, drawing him in so she could whisper in his ear.

His brow furrowed as he listened intently before turning his head to whisper his response, then straightened a few seconds later – his face giving nothing away.

'What is it?' asked Phillips.

'There were two packages in that locker. One containing the note along with the lanyards, as well as a couple of logo'ed baseball caps and T-shirts for the Energy Expo.'

'Okay,' said Phillips. 'So what was in the other package?'

Ronnie shot a nervous glance at her dad before focusing back on Phillips. 'Sulphuric acid.'

'You what? And you only thought to tell me this now?' Phillips growled as she turned to the DIR machine. 'DCI Phillips terminating the interview at 11.11 a.m.'

A few seconds later, as she stepped outside, she pulled her phone from her pocket and called Jones. Her relief was palpable when he answered after just a couple of rings.

'*Guv, we're a couple of minutes out,*' he said, the squad car siren audible in the background.

'Stand down, Jonesy. Until we can get a firearms unit to you, I don't want you going anywhere near that hotel.'

'*Why? What's going on?*'

'Ronnie just told me that Jonathan picked up a package last night that contained a bottle of sulphuric acid.'

'*Holy shit. You're kidding?*'

'He must be going to use it for Operation Acid Reign. Based on what he's done before, there's no way we can risk going in after him without backup.'

'*I'll call the firearms unit now, guv.*'

'Okay. Ronnie also said there was another package that

contained a couple of logo'ed baseball caps and Energy Expo T-shirts as well as a second staff pass.'

'*That must be the location of the next attack, then?*'

'Yeah, and I'm guessing he's going in disguised as a staff member. These conferences use casual agency workers all the time, so if he's dressed the part, no one will give him a second look.'

'*If that's the case, then we need to speak to the security team at the Lowry ASAP.*'

'Yeah. I'll do that now.'

'*Okay, boss. A soon as I have an ETA on the firearms guys, I'll let you know.*'

'Thanks, Jonesy,' she replied, then hung up.

A minute later Phillips re-entered the observation suite to find Entwistle on the phone.

'I'm emailing over a picture of the suspect now,' he said, typing into his laptop.

Phillips moved to his shoulder. 'Are you on to the Lowry?' she asked in a low voice.

He nodded before talking into the phone once more. 'He'll likely be wearing a staff uniform and lanyard, although we don't know for sure, so make sure you check everyone coming into the building whether they're working *or* members of the public.'

'Make sure they confiscate all liquids, too,' added Phillips.

He gave her a thumbs-up. 'And ensure no liquids get past the bag searches.' There was a pause while he waited for the response. 'Great, thanks,' he said before ending the call.

Phillips's phone beeped, indicating she'd got a message; glancing down, she could see it was from Jones. 'Looks like the firearms unit will be at the hotel in two minutes.'

'Let's hope Jonathan's still there.'

'Yeah. Let's.'

'While you were talking to Ronnie, I took the liberty of checking any social media accounts using the search words "Helter Skelter".' Entwistle opened the browser on his laptop. 'There's quite a few on there, given Manson's notoriety, but after a bit of digging, I found this Twitter account.'

She stepped in to get a closer look.

He tapped the screen with his pen. 'This was posted a couple of hours ago.'

Phillips read aloud. *"The Acid Reign is coming to an end, and the red wall will fall, burning from the inside out.'*

'Has to be Jonathan, right?'

'Or this Charlie character,' she replied. 'Pull up the Expo homepage, will you?'

Entwistle obliged.

'Scroll down.'

Again, he followed the instruction.

'What are those red blocks?' she asked, pointing to the screen.

'It looks like a logo of some kind,' he said. 'The Chinese Mining Corporation.'

Phillips's eyes narrowed as she inspected the photo of the man pictured next to the red blocks. She read his name aloud – 'Gui Yìchén' – in a flawless Cantonese accent.

Entwistle raised his eyebrows. 'I'm impressed, guv.'

'Fifteen years growing up in Hong Kong. Comes in handy every now and again.'

'Looks like he's speaking today, just after 2 p.m.' Entwistle began typing. 'Let's see what Google has to say about him.'

After a few more clicks, he pulled up a *Guardian* article posted just a few days earlier. 'Says here that the Chinese

Mining Corporation was founded just after the fall of Communism in China.' He read a little further, 'And owing to its exponential growth in the early days of free trade, it was given the nickname *hóngqiáng juéqǐ* or—'

'Red wall rising,' she cut in.

'He *has* to be the target.'

Just then, Jones called back.

'Have you got him?' she asked.

'*No, guv. Looks like he's long gone.*'

'Shit! Any sign of the acid?'

'*No. And the room's already been cleaned by housekeeping, so there's literally no trace of him anywhere.*'

'Right, well, we're pretty sure we know who the next target is. A guy called Gui Yìchén who works for the Chinese Mining Corporation. He's onstage at the Expo at two o'clock.'

'*What makes you think it's him?*'

'I'll explain when I see you,' she replied. 'I'll meet you and Bov outside the Lowry in half an hour.'

'*Sure thing.*'

'And make sure you bring the firearms unit with you, because I have a horrible feeling we're going to need them.'

44

As he entered the rear of the building just after 11 a.m., Jonathan had been surprised to find almost zero security at the staff entrance; he passed through without so much as a cursory look from the two men on the gate. Once inside, as per Charlie's instructions, he'd made his way up to the top floor of the building and taken refuge in a disabled toilet positioned out of sight of the main stairs. Thankfully, this part of the theatre was closed off to the general public today, which meant he was unlikely to be discovered and could remain hidden until the time came to activate the final part of the plan. Since his arrival, he'd set about dyeing his hair black using the cheap, wash-in-wash-out formula he'd bought from the chemist's on his way over here. He marvelled at how different he looked, his blond hair now jet black, protruding from under the Expo baseball cap. He slipped on the metal-framed, clear-glass spectacles, and the transformation was complete. Staring at his reflection in the mirror, the reality of what he'd done over the last few weeks crashed over him like a tidal wave.

What at first had seemed like a noble idea had now turned into a nightmare he was desperate to wake up from. Once again, every fibre of his being urged him to run, but the truth was he had no choice but to action the plan. It was the only way to guarantee Ronnie's safety, because the reality of Charlie's threats about what he'd do to her didn't bear thinking about. Exhaling sharply, he dropped to one knee and carefully slipped the bottle of acid into the Energy Expo tote bag he'd found lying on a table when he'd first arrived. Standing again, he slipped the bag over his shoulder before checking his watch. It was almost time.

ON HER RAPID twenty-minute drive to Salford Quays, she and Jones had conferred on how best to tackle the impending threat. As she saw it, they had two options: shut the conference down and hope they could find Jonathan in the subsequent exodus of guests and staff – or let it play out and hope they could catch him as he approached his target. Phillips had opted for the latter, reasoning that shutting the whole thing down would alert Jonathan to their presence, and the last thing she wanted was him going to ground. Plus with the eyes of the world on Manchester right now, the political fallout of shutting down such a high-profile event would be far reaching. No, if Gui Yìchén was the target, then all they had to do was keep him safe and wait for Jonathan to make his move. It was a risky strategy, but she felt it was the quickest way to flush him out and stop this madness once and for all.

As she arrived, she pulled the Mini up next to the squad car and the Tactical Firearms Unit's BMW X5, which were both parked up at the front of the Lowry. Jumping out, she spotted Jones and Bovalino, along with the head of the TFU, Sergeant Rhodes, standing to the side of the main entrance. They appeared to be in conference with a muscular man sporting a buzz cut – and with the word SECURITY emblazoned on the back of his tight-fitting black polo shirt.

Jones looked over as she approached, and moved towards her. 'Just briefing the head of security, guv. The guy's name is Geoff Hooper. Ex-2Para, so he knows what he's doing.'

'Is he aware of the full threat?' she asked.

'Yeah, but he understands that the information is need-to-know, so only the security team will be privy to it. If word gets around, it could spook Jonathan before we get a chance to grab him.'

'Makes sense,' said Phillips.

'Are you sure we shouldn't just shut the whole thing down, boss?' he asked. 'It's a big risk letting it play out like this.'

'I know, but like I said in the car, we need to catch him, not scare him off.'

'Okay,' said Jones.

'Are they confiscating all liquids going into the building?'

'Yeah, but only from the people who came in in the last forty minutes since Whistler briefed them. If Jonathan got into the building before then, his bag won't have been searched.'

'Well, in that case, based on the fact he left the hotel early this morning, I think we have to assume he's already inside and has the acid with him.'

'That's what we've briefed security. Hooper's guys will act as eyes and ears on the ground, but they know they're not to approach Jonathan. If they see him, they're to switch to radio channel B and alert the TFU. They'll take it from there.' He handed over a radio. 'You'll need this. We've each got one.'

'Thanks,' she said before checking her watch. 'Gui Yìchén's session is starting in ten minutes. I need to speak to Rhodes before we head in.'

'Of course.'

Sergeant Rhodes had remained in conference with Hooper, standing with his back to Phillips as she approached.

'Dusty,' she said, using his nickname as she patted him on the back.

As he turned to face her, his freckled face was partially hidden under his black sniper's hat, the skin wrinkled around the eyes – a legacy of three tours of Afghanistan during his previous career as a Royal Marine. Standing at around six two, he was a big man who loomed large in his dark combat gear, the ubiquitous Heckler & Koch G36 assault rifle slung across his chest. 'We're ready when you are, ma'am.'

'We need to keep this as low-key as possible, okay?' said Phillips. 'I don't want to spook the kid and risk him going to ground.'

'Understood,' said Rhodes. 'I'll go in with Keano, while Bennett and Taf secure the main exits front and back.'

'Good,' she said before pointing to the door. 'We'd better go in.'

'OI! Mate. Finish up the cleaning and get offstage,' the man shouted from the wings. 'It's about to start.'

Jonathan half turned to acknowledge the stage manager, careful not to show his full face as he straightened up the small table and chairs positioned in the middle of the platform. Reaching down, he picked up the tote bag, then made his way to the side of the stage where a number of people wearing headsets and mouthpieces were moving around at a frenetic pace.

As he moved into the wings, his head slightly bowed, he glanced left to see two men in suits standing to the side of the stage. It appeared they were in the process of being mic'ed up by a couple of sound engineers who were carefully feeding thin wires from belt-pack transmitters through to the tiny lapel mics fixed to their ties.

'How does that feel? Comfortable?' asked one of the engineers.

'Yeah, fine,' one of the suited men replied.

Just then the PA system boomed into life.

'Ladies and gentlemen, the final session of the day will commence in two minutes. Anyone wishing to be part of it, please take your seats in the Quays Theatre immediately.'

The stage manager moved next to the two men, who were now fully mic'ed up. 'So, John, just as we did it in rehearsal, you'll go on first and do the introduction.' He turned to the second man now. 'And Mr Gui, all you have to do is wait for the cue, then head on and take your seat.'

Gui nodded.

'Right,' the stage manager shouted. 'Everybody get ready.'

PHILLIPS MADE her way into the Quays Theatre. Once inside, she took up position standing halfway down the aisle running from the right of the stage to the back of the auditorium. Bovalino had chosen the same spot on the opposite side of the theatre, with Jones covering the exits to the rear.

A second later the house lights dimmed, and a voice boomed out through the PA.

'*Ladies and gentlemen, please welcome onstage your host for the final session of the Energy Expo, host of* Northwest News Tonight, *Mr John Packham.*'

Suddenly the stage was drenched in bright light, revealing two leather armchairs angled opposite each other, with a small glass table sitting between them. In that moment a short man, whom Phillips placed in his early sixties, sauntered out from the wings, waving to the audience as he did so.

'Good afternoon, ladies and gentlemen,' Packham said through a wide grin as he came to a stop at the front of the stage. 'I'm delighted to be here with you today at the Energy Expo to facilitate our final session of the week. It truly has been a remarkable few days, and I think it's fair to say that the future of energy in our world is not as cut and dried as many would have you believe. Despite the continued messages of doom and gloom championed by environmentalist groups around the world – not to mention journalists like me – warning of rapidly rising temperatures, I have to admit that I personally have been buoyed tremendously hearing all about the growing number of opportunities for renewable energy sources that could mean our world becomes carbon neutral – one day at least.'

A wave of applause broke out.

Packham remained silent and lifted his hand to acknowl-

edge the support, clearly enjoying the moment. He continued, 'Which is what makes this final session *so* interesting.
Because the man you're about to hear from has no business
in renewables and, as it stands, no interest either. No. He
believes the future of energy is fossil-fuel based, and that
there are enough resources still sitting under the ground to
power our world at the current rate of consumption for
another *two* centuries.' He paused again. 'Just let that sink in,
will you. Enough energy for *two hundred years.*'

'Get ready,' Phillips whispered into the radio.

'Ladies and gentlemen.' Packham turned sideways and
raised his left arm. 'Will you please give a big Manchester-
style welcome to the CEO of the Chinese Mining Corporation, Gui Yìchén!'

Phillips's adrenaline spiked as the crowd erupted into
applause, and the man she recognised from the Expo
website walked out onstage, offering a polite wave as he
smiled and made his way towards Packham. After shaking
hands like they were the best of friends, they both took seats
on the armchairs.

All the time, Phillips's eyes darted around the auditorium, looking for any sign of Jonathan, but so far, he
remained hidden.

'Gui Yìchén, welcome and thank you for coming to talk
to us today,' said Packham.

'Thank you for having me,' Gui replied, the American
undertone to his unmistakably Chinese accent suggesting he
might have been educated in the US.

Packham was talking again, but Phillips had no interest
in what was being said as she looked at Bov and Jones in
turn. Each of them responded with a shake of the head.

Meanwhile, on the screen hanging above and behind

Packham and Gui, a video began to play loudly as the stage lights dimmed.

'Where the hell is he?' Phillips growled into the radio.

'No sign of him from here,' replied Bovalino.

'All quiet at the back,' added Jones.

'This doesn't make sense,' said Phillips. 'Unless he's waiting till the end of the session.'

'Maybe,' Jones replied. 'The ultimate grand finale.'

'I'm gonna get closer to the action,' said Phillips. 'See if he's anywhere near the front.'

'I'll head backstage,' Jones added. 'See if he's hiding out there.'

'Good idea,' said Phillips, moving quietly down the aisle, scanning the faces of the audience members as she did. A minute later and with no sign of Jonathan anywhere, a sudden wave of doubt flooded her mind. What if this was all a set-up? Ronnie coming to the police station and handing over the envelope, the handwritten note, Operation Acid Reign, the Energy Expo staff pass. What if she and Jonathan had planned the whole thing to lure them here while the real attack happened somewhere else?' Her head was spinning as she fought hard to bring her focus back to the facts. Surely that couldn't be the case. Why would they do that? What would be the point of deliberately involving the police and making them aware of everything that had gone on? And why would Ronnie be party to something like that if it meant she would spend a large chunk of her adult life in prison? No. That didn't make sense at all.

At that moment, the second video came to an end, and once again the stage lights illuminated Packham and Gui, who remained seated in the armchairs as their conversation continued.

Once more, Phillips blocked their voices out as she carried on moving, casting her mind back to the Helter Skelter Facebook post. '*The Acid Reign will end, and the red wall will fall, burning inside out,*' she muttered as she continued to scan the faces around her. '*The Acid Reign will end, and the red wall will fall, burning inside out,*' she repeated again. 'What the hell did he mean? How could someone burn from the inside out?'

Packham was laughing loudly now, which drew Phillips's attention towards the stage.

It appeared Gui was suffering a coughing fit.

Phillips locked eyes on him as Packham poured him a glass of water from a small pitcher resting on the glass table between them. And then it hit her: *Burn from the inside out.* 'Stop!' she yelled as she lurched forward and began running towards the stage.

'Seems we have a heckler,' Packham joked, his voice in sharp focus now.

Gui smiled as he lifted the glass to his lips.

'Stop!' Phillips bounded up the steps to the side of the stage. 'Don't drink the water!'

Gui appeared confused, turning to face her as he lifted the glass to his lips.

Phillips was upon him, swatting the glass out of his hand, which smashed to the ground, the contents smoking as the liquid burned into the stage.

'How dare you!' raged Gui as he jumped from his chair. 'This is an outrage.'

'Security!' Packham shouted to no one in particular.

Bovalino arrived onstage a moment later. 'We're police,' he said, flashing his ID.

Phillips turned to the wings, stopping dead in her tracks

as she spotted a face staring back at her with wide eyes. The hair and glasses were different, but there was no mistaking it was him: *Jonathan.*

'I have eyes on the target,' Phillips announced into the radio. 'Backstage.'

Jonathan turned on his heel and bolted.

'Stay and look after Gui, Bov,' Phillips shouted over her shoulder as she gave chase.

The backstage area remained cloaked in darkness, but Jonathan was visible up ahead.

'Jonesy, what's your location?' gasped Phillips as she continued running.

'I'm coming up the back corridor towards the stage.'

'He's heading your way,' Phillips barked.

A second later, Jonathan burst through a set of the double fire doors and out onto the corridor.

Phillips reached the same doors just in time to see Jones attempt to tackle him, but Jonathan pivoted and sidestepped out of reach as Jones's momentum forced him off balance, and he tumbled forward, his left shoulder landing heavily against the breeze-block wall before slumping to the ground.

Jonathan was still running.

Resisting the urge to stop and check on Jones – she was sure he'd be okay – Phillips gave chase down the long corridor. It was then she noticed the glass bottle Jonathan was holding in his right hand like a relay baton.

'Clear the area!' she shouted to several backstage staff up ahead who were evidently unaware of the danger in their midst.

Jonathan glanced back over his shoulder.

'TFU. Target is heading for Exit D to the rear of the building,' said Phillips, trying hard to keep up.

Out of nowhere, a burly member of the security team, built like an Olympic shot-putter, stepped out into the corridor ahead of Jonathan.

'Police!' Phillips bellowed. 'Clear the area!'

The man ignored the instruction as he attempted to block the exit.

Jonathan skidded to a stop in front of him. 'Get out of my way,' he screamed as he began yanking at the lid on the bottle.

'Step back,' Phillips shouted down the corridor.

The big man lurched forward as Jonathan thrust his hand upwards.

An agonised scream filled the air as the security guard grabbed his head and stumbled backwards.

Jonathan was on the move again and a second later burst through the exit doors and out into the sunshine.

A couple of steps behind, Phillips shot out after him, stopping in her tracks a second later.

Standing just a few feet in front of her, Jonathan was pointing the bottle of acid towards Sergeant Rhodes and Keano, who in turn had their Tasers trained on him.

'Armed police. Put the bottle down now!' Rhodes demanded.

Phillips attempted to regulate her rapid pulse. 'Do what he says, Jonathan. It's finished.'

Jonathan remained motionless, the bottle of acid locked in his grip.

Jones appeared through the exit doors and moved quickly to Phillips's shoulder.

'Put the bottle down,' Rhodes repeated. 'Now!'

'Do it,' said Phillips. 'Enough is enough.'

Jonathan turned a fraction to look at her before spinning

back towards Rhodes, his right hand containing the acid rising rapidly.

A loud crack burst through the air as Rhodes deployed his Taser.

In that instant Jonathan's body became rigid, and he dropped to the ground like a falling tree, landing with a thud as the bottle of acid smashed down onto the concrete, its contents spilling out.

Rhodes maintained his position as Keano moved swiftly forward and dragged Jonathan out of the acid's reach before turning him onto his front and cuffing him.

'Jonathan Marsh,' said Phillips, 'I am arresting you for the murder of Robert Nixon. You do not have to say anything, but it may harm your defence if you do not mention when questioned something which you later rely on in court...'

45

A few hours later, back at Ashton House, the team – sitting around the bank of desks in the main office – debriefed.

As usual, Entwistle passed round hot drinks and sandwiches he'd picked up from the canteen in readiness for their return. 'That looks sore, Jonesy,' he said, placing a cup of peppermint tea down in front of him.

Jones grimaced as he adjusted the icepack he was holding with his right hand against his heavily swollen left collarbone. 'I've had worse.'

'Haven't we all,' chirped Bovalino, already chewing on a mouthful of sandwich. 'We should get danger money doing this job.'

'Yeah, we should.' Phillips took a tentative sip of her coffee. 'Any news on the security guard?'

'He suffered severe burns to his left ear,' said Entwistle. 'Sounds like he'll need plastic surgery at some point in the future.'

'I told him not to try to stop Jonathan.' Phillips shook her head. 'But *he* had to play the hero, didn't he?'

'You can kinda understand why he did though, guv,' replied Bov. 'I mean, he was twice the size of the kid.'

'Yeah, but size means bugger all against sulphuric acid,' she fired back. 'He'll be scarred for life now, the bloody fool.'

The room fell silent, and for the next few minutes, the team worked their way through their food without speaking. When everyone was finished and all evidence of their lunch-slash-dinner had been tidied away, Phillips decided it was time to plan the interview with Jonathan. She was acutely aware that his expensive lawyer – despatched by his father – would be with them within the hour. 'So, if we're to believe what Sebastian and Ronnie told us, then it seems the elusive Charlie is the brains behind the attacks, and the gang was a single cell, or unit if you like, acting on behalf of this group Terra.'

Each of the team nodded in unison.

'Ronnie also suggested there could be other cells waiting in the wings. So finding Charlie is our number one priority.'

'I've arranged for a courier to express Jonathan's and Ronnie's phones over to digital forensics,' said Entwistle. 'If they made any type of contact with Charlie, they'll hopefully be able to find a trace.'

'Yeah. Let's hope so.' Jones grimaced as he adjusted the icepack.

Phillips focused on Entwistle. 'Ronnie mentioned some-thing else in her interview this morning that I keep coming back to.'

'Really? What's that?'

'That Jonathan was obsessed with Charles Manson and the rest of the family.'

'Yeah, I remember her saying that.'

'Well, one of the people who shared his passion was his history teacher, Dr Bell. Check him out; see what you can find on him.'

'What you thinking?' Jones cut in. 'Bell could be involved in all this?'

Phillips exhaled loudly through her nose. 'I'm not sure, but my gut's telling me there's something quite odd about a schoolteacher talking to a student – out of hours – about a murderous cult.'

'Could *he* be Charlie?' asked Bovalino.

'I can't see it,' Jones cut in. 'I mean, what possible reason would a history teacher from a posh private school have to wage war on the world?'

'I honestly don't know,' replied Phillips, 'but I think we should check him out.'

As Entwistle made a note in his pad, Phillips's phone began to ring on the desk in front of her. Glancing down at it, she groaned. 'What the bloody hell does *he* want?'

Jones frowned. 'Who is it?'

'Don bloody Townsend.' She stepped up from the chair and headed for her office. 'What is it, Don? I'm kinda busy right now.'

Townsend got straight to the point. *'A little birdie tells me a sixth-form student from St Bart's died in custody on Monday night?'*

Phillips closed her eyes as she attempted to suppress the rage spreading through her body.

'Any truth in that?'

'Who the hell is giving you this shit? Have you any idea how sensitive this stuff is for the family? Or have you forgotten how it felt when you lost Vicky?'

'*Vicky's death has nothing to do with this, Jane.*'

'It has everything to do with this, Don. *Everything.* You know better than anyone how hard it is to lose someone without any warning. I saw firsthand how devastated you were when she was killed.'

'*Maybe so, but murder is very different to suicide in custody.*'

'Who told you it was suicide?'

'*So the boy is dead, then?*' he said flatly.

'Go to hell, Don!' she spat back before slamming the phone down on her desk.

Jones appeared at the door a second later. 'What's he done now, boss?'

She turned to face him. 'He knows about Sebastian's death in custody.'

Jones recoiled. '*How?*'

Phillips exhaled. 'I don't know, but it's about bloody time we found out,' she said as she picked up her phone and began scrolling through the contact list.

CARTER WAS SITTING at his desk reading a report when she tapped on the open door.

'Have you got a minute, sir?'

He looked up from his file. 'Sorry, Jane. I didn't hear you come in.'

'Diane's not at her desk, so I thought I'd come through on the off chance you had a few minutes.'

'Of course.' He removed his glasses as she took a seat.

'So how are you getting on with the Marsh boy?'

'Still waiting for his lawyer to show, but he should be arriving any time now.'

'Okay. Well, I don't need to tell you that after what happened to the Heppingstall boy, we need to tread carefully around him.'

'Absolutely, sir. In fact, it's one of the reasons I'm here.'

'Really? How so?'

'I need your authorisation to open an internal investigation so I can run financial checks on the five people I suspect may be feeding confidential information to Don Townsend.'

He flinched. 'I didn't think we had enough evidence to do that?'

'We do now.'

'Really? What's changed?'

'About half an hour ago, I took a call from Townsend asking me to confirm whether a sixth-former from St Bart's had died in our custody yesterday.'

Carter's mouth fell open. 'How the hell does he know about that? That's not public knowledge.'

'Far from it,' replied Phillips. 'Aside from you, me, Fox and my team, only a handful of people on the entire force who knew about Sebastian's death *also* knew that he was a pupil at that particular school. And *each* of those individuals was on the original list I showed you last week pertaining to the other leaks. So it has to be one of them.'

'Remind me who they are again.'

'Sergeant Walsh and PC Ali in custody—'

'Walsh?' Carter cut in. 'The more I think about him, the less I believe he could be involved.'

'I'm the same, sir, but we have to check to be certain.'

'And I have to say,' added Carter. 'Ali seems very unlikely. I'm mean, given the trouble he's in for leaving Sebastian alone in the first place, surely he'd be the last person to leak anything about the boy's death.'

'I'm sure you're right, but we still need to check him out.'

'And the other three?'

'Andy, Clara, and Frankie Aziz from forensics,' Phillips replied.

'I remember them now, but I have to say, Jane, I'm still struggling to believe any of them could be Townsend's mole.'

'I know, sir, but just before I came here, I put a call into Evans. He thought it was a routine follow-up on Sebastian's case, but what I was really trying to find out was who in his team had full access to Sebastian's file. Turns out all three of them did.'

Carter blew out a long breath. 'Authorising an investigation like this is not easy, Jane. We'll need to pull together a robust enough case for a magistrate to sign off on the financial checks.'

'All I need is the green light from you, sir, and my guys will do the rest.'

Carter took a moment, deep in thought. 'Normally I'd need to see your proposal before sanctioning the investigation, but because I know you're up against it at the moment, you can have your green light – on a provisional basis, of course.'

'Thank you, sir.'

Carter continued, 'But I will need to sign off on it officially before you take anything to the magistrates.'

'Of course, sir. I'll get everything to you ASAP.'

'Was there anything else?'

'No, sir.'

'In that case.' Carter smiled. 'I'd better let you get back to your interview with Jonathan Marsh, then.'

'Very good, sir,' she replied, then took her leave.

———

46

Having had his baseball cap and spectacles taken away, Jonathan looked more like his normal self – aside from his hair, which remained jet black. His Energy Expo T-shirt had also been replaced by the standard-issue grey tracksuit given to prisoners when their clothing was submitted into evidence. Now sitting opposite Phillips and Jones in Interview Room Three, he stared back defiantly, his lawyer, Vincent Noble, next to him.

As expected, Jonathan's father had hired one of Manchester's finest – not to mention most expensive – legal minds to defend his son. Standing at just five feet five with a round face, thick glasses and lank hair, Noble cut an unremarkable figure, but Phillips knew better than to underestimate him. Having been up against him on a number of high-profile cases, she was acutely aware of just how good a defence lawyer he was.

With the formalities taken care of, she activated the DIR and began the interrogation. 'Tell us about Charlie, will you, Jonathan?'

A slight snarl formed on the young man's lips.

'That's right. Ronnie and Sebastian told us all about him,' she added.

Jonathan remained silent, taking a sip of water from the plastic cup on the table between them.

Noble made a note in his pad.

'Why did you do it?' asked Phillips. 'Why throw your life away for a total stranger?'

'No comment,' Jonathan finally said.

'I see.' Phillips nodded. 'And you think that's the best course of action here, do you?'

Noble looked up from his pad. 'My client has invoked his right to silence, Chief Inspector.'

Phillips ignored the remark. She was well aware of Jonathan's rights. 'Ronnie has admitted that she took part in the car-bomb attack at the David Lloyd leisure club that seriously injured Ross Grayson, the fatal stabbing of Robert Nixon in St John's Gardens, as well as the attempted assassination of Travis Bernstein outside Ollerton Hall Hotel...'

Jonathan glared back.

'She also told us that *you* were the ringleader of the gang that committed these offences. A gang that also included Sebastian Heppingstall. What do you have to say to that?'

'No comment,' he replied, his voice cracking slightly.

Phillips glanced at Jones. Having carefully planned the interview, he was aware of what was coming next and offered the faintest of nods. She turned her focus back to Jonathan. 'You may not be aware of this – and I'm sorry to be the one to tell you if you're not – but Sebastian passed away on Monday evening.'

The boy's eyes widened as his mouth opened.

'Tragically, he took his own life while in police custody.'

'You're lying,' Jonathan spat back.

Noble placed a calming hand on the boy's wrist.

'I wish I were, Jonathan,' replied Phillips softly. 'I really wish I were.'

All of his defiance seemed to melt away in that instant.

Phillips continued, 'We're not entirely sure why he did it, but we have to consider that the thought of spending the rest of his life in a maximum-security prison was too much for him to bear.'

'The actions and state of mind of another prisoner while in your custody has nothing to do with my client,' Noble said curtly.

'Really?' Phillips replied. 'His co-conspirator took his own life because of the crimes *they* committed together – I'd say it has everything to do with him.'

'*Alleged* crimes,' Noble corrected.

Phillips flashed a thin smile, then returned her gaze to the boy. 'Is that what *you* want, Jonathan? To spend the rest of your life a prisoner in Hawk Green?'

He swallowed hard as he stared back.

Phillips continued, 'A rich kid like you, watching your back, day after day. I wouldn't fancy his chances, would you, DI Jones?'

'No, I wouldn't.' Jones folded his arms across his chest. 'It's like the Wild West in that place. Overcrowded, noisy, violent and filled to the brim with the dregs of society.'

'I really must protest; this is tantamount to intimidation. May I remind you both that my client is still only seventeen, meaning he cannot be tried as an adult and therefore would not be sent to Hawk Green.'

'Not straight away, no,' Jones shot back. 'But once he

turns eighteen, that'll be his home for the rest of his sentence.'

'Which for one murder and three attempted murders,' Phillips cut in, 'means he's looking at at least twelve years before he's eligible for parole.'

The colour seemed to drain from Jonathan's face now as the stark reality of his situation finally dawned on him.

Phillips was keen to use this to her advantage, so she pressed on. 'Enough is enough, Jonathan. Sebastian is dead, and Ronnie has confessed to everything in exchange for leniency from the Crown Prosecutor. Now is the time for you to stop this nonsense once and for all and tell us where we can find Charlie. It's the only way you're getting out of this with anything but a life sentence.'

'You'll never find him,' he sneered.

Once again, Noble placed his hand on his client's wrist in an attempt to silence him.

But Phillips was determined to keep him talking. 'What makes you so sure? Thanks to digital forensics, we can find anybody these days.'

'Pah,' scoffed Jonathan. 'Charlie's too clever to leave a trail.'

'That's quite enough,' Noble said firmly.

'But it's true,' he protested. 'Charlie is too smart to get caught out by this lot.'

Noble glared at Jonathan for a moment before fixing his eyes on Phillips. 'My client is not in his right mind. No doubt due to the aftereffects of the Taser. I really think we should take a break so he can be checked over by a health care professional.'

'He was thoroughly examined by the paramedics at the scene of his arrest,' Phillips volleyed back. 'I see no significant change to his health that would warrant a second assessment.'

Noble's round face wrinkled as a faint snarl reached the corner of his mouth.

Phillips moved her attention back to Jonathan. 'Come on. Where is he? How can we contact him?'

Jonathan straightened, his defiance slowly returning.

Phillips changed tack. 'Ronnie tells us that you guys classed yourselves as soldiers in the war to save the planet. Is that true?'

'No comment.'

'She also said that *you* in particular believed the ends justified the means. That killing Robert Nixon was an act of war as opposed to a cold-blooded murder. What do you say to that?'

Jonathan took another mouthful of water. 'No comment.'

'How do you think this all ends?' she asked.

Jonathan would not be drawn.

But Phillips was not letting up. 'We have testimony from Sebastian and Ronnie that you all waged this ridiculous eco-war together—'

'It's not ridiculous,' he cut her off. 'It's a just cause and the only way we can save the planet.'

'Jonathan, please!' spat Noble. 'Enough.'

'What?' He turned to his lawyer. 'They need to know the truth.'

'What truth?' Phillips prodded.

Jonathan fixed his gaze on her. 'That the world we live in will literally burn up if we don't find a way to stop climate change immediately.'

Noble cleared his throat. 'Jonathan, I really must caution against revoking your right to silence.'

'Why?' he replied. 'So I get a lesser sentence? If people knowing the truth about why I did what I did helps bring about change, then that's a sacrifice I'm willing to make.'

Noble leaned in and drew Jonathan into a whispered, yet heated exchange. A few moments later he nodded and sat upright again. 'Despite my best advice, Jonathan is revoking his right to silence. As his counsel, I feel this is the wrong course of action to take, and I request the opportunity to pause the interview so I can consult with his father.'

'Is that what you want, Jonathan? To pause while Mr Noble speaks to your dad?'

'No, I don't.' The boy shook his head. 'He doesn't give a shit about me anyway. All he cares about is his precious business.'

Phillips turned to Noble. 'He's seventeen, so it's his choice.'

Noble folded his arms. 'I'd like it noted on the record that I am against this course of action.'

'Duly noted,' said Phillips, feeling suddenly buoyed, before continuing, 'Jonathan, have you ever considered the fact that Charlie might not actually be who he claims to be?'

Jonathan frowned. 'What are you talking about?'

'Well, as Ronnie told us, Charlie used an avatar whenever you spoke.'

'So?'

'*So* if you've never met him or even seen his face for that matter, how do you know for sure he's who he says he is – and the leader of this group, Terra. I mean, for all we know, he could be a complete fake. A fantasist messing with you and getting you to do all this stuff just for the hell of it.'

'He's real, don't you worry about that,' Jonathan sneered. 'And so is Terra.'

'Really? So why haven't they taken credit for the attacks? I mean, what's the point of activism if no one knows about it?'

'Charlie will make sure everyone knows what this is all about. When he thinks the time is right.'

'Are you sure about that?'

Jonathan's jaw clenched as he glared back in silence.

Phillips changed tack again. 'Is it true you studied Charles Manson at school earlier this year?' She looked down at her notes for effect. 'In, er, Dr Bell's class?'

'Yeah. So what?'

'How long after that did Charlie approach you?'

He shrugged. 'I don't remember.'

Phillips passed across a selection of computer printouts. 'For the tape I'm showing Jonathan several screenshots taken from various social media accounts registered under the name "Helter Skelter".'

Jonathan stared down at the images in silence.

'Helter Skelter is *you*, isn't it? On TikTok, Instagram and Twitter.'

He looked up and sniffed defiantly. 'So?'

'So, based on these posts, it's fair to say you're pretty into Charles Manson,' she replied. '*Obsessed* was the word Ronnie used, if I remember rightly.'

'And?'

'*And*, just that if you're all over the web telling the world you're into Manson, then you're an easy target, aren't you? For all the weirdos and freaks out there looking to live out their own twisted Manson fantasies. That's why I'm not convinced *your* Charlie is actually who he says he is.'

Jonathan's nostrils flared. 'He's real. How else would he know where the targets would be, and when they'd be at their most vulnerable? And what about the staff passes and uniform for the expo? He's *real* all right.'

Phillips nodded slowly.

Just then there was a knock at the door, and Entwistle appeared in the doorway. 'Sorry to interrupt, but there's something you need to see.'

She turned to the DIR, then checked her watch. 'DCI Phillips suspending the interview at 3.20 p.m.,' she said, then followed him out.

He handed her an email printout.

'What's this?'

'Digital forensics managed to trace an active email account on Jonathan's phone that's been logged on continuously for the last couple of weeks.'

She began reading.

'These were saved in the drafts folder.'

'Instructions for each of the attacks.'

'Yes, guv. It's an old Taliban trick, apparently. Each person connected to individual terror cells would access the same email account and communicate by writing a message in draft form, but without ever sending it, meaning whatever was being said could never be traced or picked up by the security agencies monitoring online chatter.'

'Bloody hell, that's smart,' said Phillips. 'Totally untraceable.'

'Kind of.'

'How do you mean?'

'Well, back in the early 2000s it was untraceable, but these days, with more sophisticated kit, the tech boys have been able to isolate certain details of the secondary user through a TOR.'

Phillips frowned. 'What's a TOR?'

'Sorry,' replied Entwistle. 'It stands for The Onion Router. It's basically a bespoke network that bounces the connection from a designated device across multiple points to hide the IP address. It's a pretty robust way of hiding a trail, but it's not entirely secure, and based on that, the tech guys are suggesting that whoever sent it is not what they'd class as a top-level professional. More likely someone with a high degree of computer knowledge compared to your average Joe, but not what they'd identify as a serious player.'

'So what does all this mean? Can we track the secondary user?'

'Yes.' He passed over another printout. 'Thanks to a new piece of kit that landed three months ago, the tech guys have been able to tap into the network and retrace the origins of their IP address to this location.'

Phillips stared down at the paper.

'You gotta be shitting me,' she muttered as she looked up. 'And is this new kit reliable? I mean, has it been sufficiently tested?'

'Ninety percent accurate, so far.'

'Ninety percent will do for me,' she replied before opening the door to Interview Room Three and heading back inside.

Jones raised a quizzical eyebrow as she moved back to stand in front of Jonathan, holding the printed email up for dramatic effect. 'I'm sure you'll be delighted to know that we've managed to track Charlie's IP address.'

Jonathan's face fell. 'You're lying.'

She shook her head. 'Thanks to your shared email account, our tech guys have narrowed down the location to somewhere you know very well.' She placed the printout on the table in front of him.

Jonathan recoiled as he read it. 'That's not possible. There must be some mistake.'

'No mistake.'

'But Charlie's based in America.'

'No, Jonathan.' Phillips took back the email. 'Charlie's at St Bart's.'

47

With Bovalino at the wheel and Jones in the rear, Phillips and the team raced to St Bartholomew's in Wilmslow. Ordinarily, at this time of day with the traffic building, the journey time from Ashton House would be well over an hour, but under blues and twos and with the big man driving, they would likely be there in half the time.

'I think you were right about this Dr Bell fella,' Jones chimed through from the back seat.

'Yeah, he certainly looks the most likely,' replied Phillips as they zoomed through traffic.

'But why?' Bovalino asked. 'What would drive a history teacher to turn a bunch of his students into terrorists?'

'Who knows what goes on behind closed doors in these places,' said Phillips. 'And let's face it, *we* know better than anyone that killers come in all shapes and sizes.'

'Very true,' said Jones. 'So how far out are we, Bov?'

He glanced at the speedometer. 'Five minutes, max.'

'Are the uniform on their way?'

'Yes, guv,' replied Jones. 'They'll be ready with the custody van.'

Three minutes later the car raced down the long school drive past a bunch of students being put through their paces on the athletics track to the right of the building. Screeching to a halt outside the front entrance, the team wasted no time in exiting the vehicle before setting off towards the main office block.

Luckily, Freeman happened to be standing in the administration office, giving some form of instruction to her assistant, Mrs Drabble, as they walked in. 'You again?' she said, her face oozing disdain. 'And three of you this time.'

Phillips wasted no time on pleasantries. 'We need to know the location of every computer on this campus.'

'What on earth for?'

'We have reason to believe that someone has been using a PC or laptop within the confines of the school to orchestrate serious criminal activity that has led to the death of one man and caused serious injury to three more.'

'I beg your pardon!' Freeman was incredulous. 'Whatever will you accuse us of next?'

Phillips pulled the email printout from her pocket and passed it across. 'This is the IP address we need to trace as a matter of urgency.'

Freeman examined the contents for a few seconds, and her eyes widened. 'Are you absolutely sure?'

'Our digital forensic teams don't make mistakes,' Phillips replied coolly.

Freeman's posture visibly softened as she turned to Mrs Drabble. 'Call Glen. Tell him to get over here as quickly as he can.'

Drabble nodded.

'We can wait in my office.' Freeman gestured towards her open door.

A few minutes later, a dark-haired man appeared at the door, carrying a large iPad in one hand. He was wearing a shirt at least a couple of sizes too big for him, paired with a Homer Simpson tie, jeans and Doc Martens boots. When he spoke, his accent was unmistakably West Midlands. 'You wanted to see me, Mrs Freeman?'

'These people are from the police, Glen. They need to know the location of all our computers and laptops on campus.'

Glen's brow furrowed. '*Our* computers?'

'That's correct,' replied Freeman.

'That could take some time.' He sucked his teeth. 'I mean, we've got over a hundred machines scattered all over the school.'

Phillips stepped in now. In an attempt to expedite the process, she presented her ID. 'Glen, we're from the Major Crimes Unit.'

Glen gazed at the badge in her hand.

'It's imperative that we locate this laptop and its user as quickly as possible, as we believe it could be being used to help perpetrate terrorist attacks.'

Glen nodded before taking a seat at the conference table in the corner of the office.

For the next few minutes, the room fell silent aside from the sound of his fingers tapping away at the iPad screen. Finally, Glen nodded. 'Looks like that particular machine is one of our laptops that we class as spare stock.' He turned the iPad so it was visible to the room.

Phillips stepped forward to get a closer look.

'A-Level students can borrow them if they don't have one

of their own, but to be honest, that's rare. In this place, pretty much every kid has a brand-new machine and will upgrade them as soon as the latest piece of kit comes out. So the spare stock is mainly used when a student is doing a big project that requires a specialist piece of software, like CAD or something similar.'

'Does anyone else use the spare stock, aside from the kids?' asked Jones.

Glen shrugged. 'The staff book them out from time to time, but again, only if they need a specialist programme or extra machines for a specific lesson or project.'

'So where is that machine now?' Phillips cut back in.

Glen began tapping at the iPad screen once more before looking up again. 'According to the logs, it's been booked out.'

'Who to?'

'Er...' Glen scrolled down the screen. 'Dr Bell.'

Phillips turned to Freeman. 'Where is he now?'

'You can't seriously think David has anything to do with all this?'

'All that matters now is finding that laptop,' Phillips replied. 'Is it the same classroom where we picked up Sebastian?'

'Yes,' replied Freeman.

'Thank you for your help, Glen,' said Phillips as she led Jones and Bovalino out of the room.

Five minutes later their footsteps echoed around them as they walked briskly down the long, darkened corridor to Bell's classroom.

Freeman remained a few steps behind. 'I'd really prefer it if I can speak to David first.' 'No doubt,' said Phillips as she reached the door and looked back. 'But I'm afraid that's not possible,' she added before stepping inside.

Bell, who was sitting at his small desk at the far end of the classroom, looked up, a puzzled expression on his face. 'Can I help you?'

'We need to know where the laptop is,' replied Phillips, striding towards him.

'What laptop?' he asked, frowning.

'The one you used to communicate with Jonathan Marsh in order to orchestrate a series of violent attacks.'

Bell recoiled. 'I did what?'

'Where is it?' Phillips demanded as she stood in front of him.

Bell looked to Freeman. 'Do you have any idea what on earth they're talking about, Claire?'

Freeman opened her mouth to respond, but Phillips cut across her. 'We have reason to believe that someone using a fake online persona and a laptop registered to this school has been manipulating a group of students into committing violent crimes, one of which resulted in a man's death last week. The last person to book that laptop out was you, Dr Bell. So I'll ask you again, where is it?'

Bell blinked furiously. 'But I've not booked out any laptops this term; I've no need to. The kids all have their own; plus this is history; we don't need any specialist programmes.'

'Well, if that's the case,' replied Phillips, 'I'm sure you won't mind coming back to the station with us to answer a few questions, will you?'

'Well, I would, actually,' Bell retorted. 'Firstly, these accusations are absolutely preposterous, and secondly, I'm in the middle of marking exams for my first-year A-Level students, which need to be completed for the lesson tomorrow.'

Phillips smiled thinly. 'I don't think you're hearing me, Dr Bell, so let me spell it out for you. Either you come with us now, or Detective Constable Bovalino here' – she nodded in the big man's direction – 'will arrest you, place you in cuffs and walk you out to the car in full view of all the students and staff out on the front field.'

'But I haven't done anything!'

'Have it your way,' said Phillips flatly. 'Bov.'

Bovalino took a step closer as he reached for his cuffs.

Bell's eyes widened as he stared up at the man mountain. 'All right, all right. There's no need for that. I'll come, I'll come.'

'Thank you,' said Phillips. 'DC Bovalino will escort you to the car.'

'After you, sir.' Bov gestured towards the door with his arm.

Bell looked him up and down one more time before finally acquiescing.

Phillips watched them exit the classroom, then turned back to Jones. 'We need to check every cupboard and drawer in this room. Hopefully that laptop is in here somewhere.'

Jones nodded, and they both got to work.

'Erm, what do you think you're doing?' asked Freeman.

'I would have thought my instructions just now to DI Jones were clear enough to understand,' Phillips volleyed back.

'Don't you need a search warrant for something like that?'

'Not if we have your permission.' Phillips opened the top drawer of Bell's desk as she fixed her with a hard stare. 'We do have your permission to perform a search in order to avert a potential terror attack, don't we, Mrs Freeman?'

'Er, well...' She appeared lost for words.

Phillips straightened. 'If this is a problem, I can always get a warrant and come back with a full search team?'

Freeman offered a weak smile. 'No, not at all. Please do what you need to do.'

Phillips held her gaze. 'Thank you,' she said before continuing the search.

For the next ten minutes they checked every possible space that would be big enough to conceal even the smallest of laptops, but to no avail.

'It's not here, guv,' Jones said eventually.

Phillips turned to Freeman standing just a few feet away. 'Is there anywhere else he could've hidden the laptop within the school?'

Freeman shrugged. 'This is an enormous building, Chief Inspector. Full of all kinds of nooks and crannies. It could be anywhere.'

'In that case, it's time for Plan B.' Phillips pulled her phone from her pocket and headed for the door.

Jones joined her outside a moment later, and they set off down the corridor. 'Who are you calling, boss?'

'Whistler to get a search warrant for Bell's house.'

'On what grounds, guv?'

'Imminent threat to life.'

'Based on what?' asked Jones. 'The suspects are all off the streets.'

'Charlie's not.'

'True, but as we have no concrete proof Bell *is* actually Charlie, *or* that he even sent those messages to Jonathan – there's no way we'll get a warrant.'

Phillips knew he was right, but it didn't make it any less frustrating.

'Why don't we go back to Ashton House, sweat him under interview conditions and see what we can get out of him? Maybe he'll give it up.'

Phillips shook her head. 'If he *is* Charlie, then based on the way he's manipulated the kids so far, he's way too smart to incriminate himself. By the time we gather enough evidence for a warrant, the laptop will be long gone.'

'So what else do you suggest?'

Phillips paused before answering, 'We kick his door down while he's not there.'

'What?' Jones stopped in his tracks as they reached the top of the stairs. 'And how is that ever going to stand up in court?'

She flashed a knowing grin. 'I'll tell you when we get there.'

Jones frowned. 'Why not tell me now?'

'Because I'm giving you plausible deniability,' she declared before setting off down the stairs.

48

While Bov escorted Bell to Ashton House alongside the uniformed team, Phillips and Jones headed to the nearby suburb of Cheadle Hulme. Having sourced Bell's address through Entwistle, they made the short journey in less than fifteen minutes and arrived at his house just after 5 p.m. – a stone, semi-detached cottage set back from the road, complete with a small garden to the front.

'Number twenty-two,' said Phillips as she stepped out of the car.

'So what's the plan?' Jones asked.

'I'll tell you in a sec,' she replied, walking down the path towards the house.

Arriving at the front door, Phillips stopped for a moment, then turned to her second in command. 'Did you hear that?'

His brow furrowed. 'Hear what?'

'Sounded like it was coming from the back. Come on.'

A moment later, Phillips surveyed the area to the rear of the house, which comprised a second garden – deeper than the front and protected on all sides by a mature privet hedge standing at around ten feet high along its length.

'Nice and private,' said Jones.

'Yeah,' Phillips replied as she stepped forward to get a closer look at the glass-panelled back door.

'Seriously, guv. What's the plan?'

Suddenly her eyes narrowed. 'What was that?'

'What was what?'

'That noise.' She paused.

'I didn't hear anything.'

'There it is again,' she shot back. 'Sounds like someone shouting inside.'

Jones did a double take. 'You what?'

Bending down, she picked up a small terracotta plant pot – which was surprisingly heavy – then slammed it against the glass panel just above the door handle, shattering it on impact.

'What the hell are you doing, guv?'

'Dealing with the imminent threat to life,' she said as she returned the plant pot to its original position before turning to face him. 'Under article 2 of the Human Rights Act 1998, as members of a law enforcement agency, we are obligated to take reasonable steps to protect a person whose life is in "Real and Immediate Danger". I thought I heard someone shouting for help inside the house and acted accordingly, making this a legal search.'

'Jesus, guv.' Jones shook his head. 'This is thin, even by your standards.'

Pulling a couple of pairs of latex gloves from her pocket, she handed one to Jones. 'Thin's good enough for me,' she replied before reaching inside and releasing the latch. 'Come on, we need to find that laptop.'

Over the next hour and a half, they carefully searched the house, checking every cupboard, drawer and wardrobe they could find, but to no avail.

'Could it be in the loft?' Phillips asked as they stood on the small landing between the two bedrooms of the first floor.

Jones craned his neck to the ceiling. 'Looks like it doesn't have one.'

'Damn it,' she muttered in frustration.

'So what now, guv?'

Phillips exhaled heavily as she took a moment to think, then fished out her phone. 'I've had another idea,' she said, pressing redial.

Entwistle answered promptly. *'Hi, guv.'*

She got straight to the point. 'Is it possible to trace the location of a laptop in the same way you can a phone?'

'Possibly, I guess, but I'm not sure. I can check with the tech guys if you'd like?'

She looked at her watch. It was almost 7 p.m. 'How long will that take?'

'There's usually somebody in the office till about 8 p.m., so hopefully we can get an answer straight away.'

'Okay. See what they say and call me straight back.'

'Will do.'

Phillips ended the call.

A couple of minutes passed before her phone vibrated. She pressed the speaker function so Jones could hear. 'Any joy?'

'Yes and no.'

'Which means what?'

'Sam in tech reckons it is possible, but only if you have access

to some heavy-duty kit, and sadly the GMP budget wouldn't stretch to something like that.'

'Of course it wouldn't.'

'But he did say that that kind of hardware is available to the national security agencies.'

'Such as the counter terrorism squad,' Phillips cut in.

'Exactly.'

'I'll call Flannery.'

'By the way, where are you? Bov says Bell is getting restless. Seems he's threatening to leave unless he speaks to someone in authority within the hour. Says he's come in of his own free will and can walk out anytime he chooses.'

'Well, if he tries anything like that, tell Bov to arrest him for conspiracy to murder Robert Nixon.'

'Will that stick based on what we have so far?'

'It'll do for the time being.'

'Okay, I'll speak to Bov now.'

'Thanks.' Phillips hung up, then scanned through her contacts for Flannery's mobile. A few seconds later, it connected.

'This is Flannery.'

'Danny. Jane Phillips.'

'Hi, Jane. I heard on the wires you've had your hands full since we last spoke.'

'Yeah, I have. And that's why I'm calling. I need your help.'

'What can I do?'

'I'm led to believe that the national security agency teams have access to hardware that can trace the location of a laptop in pretty much the same way you'd track a phone. Is that true?'

'It is, yeah. As long as you have the IP address.'

'Which I do.'

'In that case, we should be able to get you within fifty metres of the machine's last known location.'

'Even if it's switched off?'

'Yep.'

She pulled the printed email from her pocket. 'How long does it take?'

'Not long. A few minutes, in fact. I'm on the road at the moment, but I can pass it to my tech team if you'd like. Just text through the IP details, and I'll do the rest.'

'Brilliant. Sending it now.'

'No worries, I'll keep an eye out for it,' Flannery assured her.

The next twenty minutes passed cripplingly slowly as they waited for an update. The small house appeared poorly insulated, the air inside hot and muggy, so Phillips decided they should head back out into the garden.

Standing on the patio, she glanced back at the broken door and wondered what the fallout might be if they failed to locate the laptop. An illegal search was a very serious matter.

'I'll back you up,' said Jones, standing at her shoulder, evidently reading her mind. 'I definitely thought I heard someone shouting earlier.'

She produced a half-smile. 'Thanks, Jonesy.'

Just then, her phone vibrated as Flannery called back. She switched it to speaker. 'How'd you get on?'

'Have you got a pen?'

'Yeah, just give us a second.'

Jones opened his notepad in readiness.

'Go ahead,' said Phillips.

'We use What3words as a locator, and you're looking for moon-learns-fixed.'

Jones scribbled it down.

Flannery continued, *'It targets up to ten feet square, so it's very accurate.'*

'Thanks, Danny,' said Phillips. 'I owe you one.'

'Any time. Let me know how you get on, won't you?'

'Yeah, sure.'

'Good luck,' he said before ending the call.

Phillips quickly pulled up the What3words app on her phone and typed in the location. A second later, as the address appeared, she felt her eyebrows rise.

'What is it?' Jones asked.

'Not quite the address I was expecting for Charlie: Cymbal Gardens.'

'The place just off the M60, near the Pyramid? Bit rough round there, isn't it?'

'Yeah.'

'So how on earth did a laptop from St Bart's end up there?'

Phillips put her phone back in her pocket. 'I guess we're about to find out.'

49

The drive from Cheadle to Cymbal Gardens in Stockport took just over ten minutes, and it was approaching 7 p.m. when they pulled into the car park that serviced the six-storey block of council flats known as Stonemasons Terrace. The block itself, along with the adjacent Hanfield Tower, had become unofficial landmarks along the M60 – Manchester's outer ring road – their distinctive white and green facades standing proud on the side of the hill that overlooked the industrial valley below.

As they stepped out of the squad car, the warm early evening air was filled with the sound of traffic from the motorway, along with kids playing in a nearby park.

'What number are we looking for?' asked Jones.

Phillips checked the phone screen. 'Doesn't say, but as Flannery said, the locator is accurate within ten feet square.'

Jones moved to her shoulder to see the screen. 'Moon-learns-fixed,' he repeated as he gestured to the six-storey block. 'So if that's the location reference point there, on the ground, does that mean the laptop could be in any one of the flats above it?'

'I'm guessing so, yeah.'

'Well, this should be a piece of piss.' Jones's tone was laced with sarcasm.

'You never know, we might just get lucky, for once.'

Jones sighed. 'So how are we going to do this? I mean, we don't have a warrant for *one* flat, never mind *six*.'

Phillips closed the app before hitting redial.

Entwistle answered within a couple of rings. *'Guv, any luck with the counter terrorism boys?'*

'Yeah. We've tracked the laptop's last location to Cymbal Gardens in Stockport.'

'Bloody hell, that's amazing.'

'Problem is, there are six flats on the same location, from the ground floor up to the fifth floor.' Phillips stared up at the massive structure. 'So we need to try to narrow it down to a single address.'

'How can I help?'

'We need to figure out who lives in each apartment. That's as good a place to start as any.'

'I'll check the council tax database. Should only take a few minutes.'

'As quick as you can, yeah?'

'On it.'

Phillips hung up.

For the next quarter of an hour, Phillips kept her eyes fixed on the front doors to the six different flats as Jones paced up and down in front of her, nibbling the end of his fingers as he did so.

'You'll have no nails left at this rate,' she ventured.

'I know.' He stopped pacing and looked down at his fingers. 'Sarah's always telling me off for doing it.'

It was then that Entwistle called back.

Phillips switched the phone to speaker. 'What have you got?'

'A mixed bag, really. Starting at the top, the tenant in flat five-seven is a guy called Derek Adebayo. He's fifty-six and lives alone.'

'What about the next floor down?'

'Four-seven is rented to a family of four: a woman called Chelsea Barratt and her three kids, all under the age of sixteen.'

'Right.'

'Flat three-seven is empty currently, as is two-seven.'

'Either of those could be an option,' she replied. 'Quiet spaces away from prying eyes.'

'Yeah, that's what I was thinking.'

'And what about the ground floor?'

'A woman called Gill Worthington,' said Entwistle. *'According to the council's records, she has one dependent living with her, and – this is the interesting bit – six months ago, a guy called Darren Cowley was added as a resident at the same address.'*

'And why is that significant?' Phillips asked.

'I cross-referenced all the names against the PNC, and it turns out Cowley has got form.'

'Do we know what for?'

'Fraud mainly, including a bunch of different online and mobile scams. Got out on licence six months ago after serving half of a six-year sentence.'

'Sounds like a prime ratbag,' said Jones.

'Yeah,' replied Phillips, 'and definitely someone who would know his way round encrypted emails.'

'Do you want me to organise a warrant, guv?'

'No, we don't have enough just yet for a full search. We'll have to do this the old-fashioned way: knock on the door and ask him what the hell he's been up to. As he's out on licence, he's obliged to talk to us.'

Jones nodded his agreement.

Phillips continued, 'While we're doing that, see how we get access to those empty flats tonight, and get a couple of uniform teams down here to make sure no one goes in or out without our knowledge.

'*No problem, guv.*'

She rang off. 'Right, let's see what Mr Cowley has to say for himself, shall we?' she said as they headed for the door.

Soon after, Jones rapped his knuckles on the door to flat G-seven.

A dog immediately started barking inside, followed shortly after by a man shouting at it to be quiet.

A moment later, they could hear the chain being released on the other side, along with a couple of locks, before the door opened a fraction.

'Yeah?' A man with a shaven head, likely in his thirties, peered out through the gap. 'What do you want?'

'Are you Darren Cowley?' asked Phillips.

'Who wants to know?'

She flashed her ID. 'DCI Phillips and DI Jones. We need to ask you a few questions.'

The man remained half hidden behind the door.

'We can either do it here, or we can take you back to the nick,' said Jones. 'It's your call, mate.'

'Shit,' muttered Cowley before opening the door wide to reveal his enormous frame. Standing at around six feet three in a white singlet and black tracksuit bottoms, he had the look of a heavyweight boxer.

'Whatever it is you lot think I did, I didn't,' he said flatly. 'You can ask my probation officer; she'll tell you.'

'We understand you're a bit of a computer whizz, Darren,' ventured Phillips.

He shook his head. 'Not anymore. Never touch the things these days. Not allowed to.'

'Really? So if we search this flat, we won't find any PCs, tablets or, say, *laptops*?'

'Well, yeah.' He shrugged. 'But they're nothing to do with me.'

'So who do they belong to?' said Jones.

'My girlfriend, Gill, and her daughter, Izzie.'

Phillips felt her brow furrow. 'Izzie?'

'Yeah. She's never off the bloody thing.'

'And where is Izzie now?'

He thumbed over his right shoulder. 'In her room, as always. Hardly ever comes out.'

Phillips glanced at Jones, whose expression suggested they had come to the same conclusion. 'Can we speak to her?'

Cowley shrugged. 'Be my guest,' he said as he swivelled and suddenly bellowed, 'Izzie! Get out here!' before turning back, his large frame once more filling the doorway.

Behind him a moment later, Phillips heard a door open and loud rock music bleeding out as someone moved down the corridor towards the door.

Cowley glanced over his shoulder. 'Here she is,' he said, stepping to the side so they could see through into the hallway.

There, staring back at them was a face filled with dark makeup and piercings that Phillips recognised only too well

– the girl they'd met at St Bart's while waiting outside Freeman's office: Isabelle Worthington.

'Hello, Izzie,' said Phillips. 'Or would you prefer I call you *Charlie*?'

50

ASHTON HOUSE – THREE DAYS LATER

'There you go,' said Carter as he passed across a mug of hot coffee.

'Thank you, sir,' replied Phillips before taking a sip. 'You must be quite a rarity in the world of chief supers.'

'And why is that?'

'Making a drink for your staff.'

'My mother taught me well,' he said with a smile. 'And besides, you're not my staff. We're all one team. I just happen to be in charge of the paperclips.'

She returned his smile. 'Well, it doesn't go unnoticed, sir.'

He took a tentative sip from his own cup. 'So, I understand the CPS have authorised charges against Isabelle Worthington.'

'Yes. Three charges of conspiracy to murder, and one charge of conspiracy to commit aggravated assault.'

Carter blew out a long breath. 'It's hard to believe one teenager was behind the whole thing. I mean, what on earth motivated her to create such an elaborate scheme in the first place? And why drag the other kids into it all?'

'Sadly, it was down to bullying.'

'Seriously?'

'Yeah,' replied Phillips. 'She was a poor kid in a rich kids' school, and Marsh, Blake and Heppingstall took exception to her. She's gone on record saying the reason she did it was to get back at them; it was revenge for making her life hell at school, as well as on social media. Sounds like they really took a dislike to her and resented sharing their precious school with kids living in social housing.'

'Spoilt brats. Don't know they're born. If it weren't for mummy and daddy's money, they wouldn't be at that school at all. At least the Worthington girl earned her place there.'

'Very true,' replied Phillips. 'I read her psych report this morning, and her IQ is off the charts: genius level.'

'Which may account for the elaborate plan to turn the kids into eco-warriors?' Carter took another mouthful of coffee.

'In part yes, but having spoken to her at length, it's clear Izzie *genuinely* believes in the cause the kids were fighting for. I guess that's why she was able to convince them of its importance to the future of the planet. Plus, they were easy prey for her. Having spoken to Ronnie and Jonathan, it's clear that while the kids may have enjoyed the external trappings of having wealthy parents, it seems none of them really felt loved or even noticed at home. Charlie and Terra's plan to save the planet filled that void, just like the real Manson did. And it was double bubble for Izzie, really: she wreaked havoc on the people she felt were profiting from polluting the world, and in the process put her three tormentors in the frame.'

Carter sighed. 'The thing I don't get is that these were intelligent kids. What did they think was going to happen when they started committing murder? They must have known they were never going to get away with it.'

'Maybe, maybe not. I remember seeing a lecture by Dr Simon Peterson, a renowned psychiatrist who's studied the human brain his entire career. During the lecture, he shared the fact that our brains aren't fully formed until we reach twenty-five. In fact, he made the joke that all the parents in the room could never really bollock their kids for making stupid decisions until they reached their twenty-sixth birthday.'

'So what you're saying is kids can be easily manipulated.'

'*Exactly,* and especially nowadays. It was hard enough trying to figure out who we were growing up in the seventies and eighties. I can't imagine how hard it must be these days when every single thing that kids do is broadcast to the world through social media – and there's literally *nowhere* to hide. Can you imagine? All that teenage, hormone-fuelled insecurity being exacerbated by the need for approval via Facebook, Instagram and TikTok?'

Carter shuddered. 'If half the daft stuff I did as a teenager had been posted online, I can tell you now, I wouldn't be sitting in this chair.'

'No.' Phillips chuckled. 'Me neither.'

The room fell silent for a moment as they both took sips from their drinks.

'So,' said Carter, placing his cup on the desk. 'Before you came in, I took a call from the IPCC regarding your unauthorised search of Dr Bell's house.'

'Ah, right.'

'I'm pretty sure I managed to sell them on the fact that

the imminent threat to life superseded the need for a warrant, and was necessary given the severity of the previous attacks. So there'll be no further action regarding that.'

Phillips exhaled loudly. 'Thank you, sir.'

'*But* they have upheld Bell's official complaint regarding the damage to his back door.'

She nodded.

'Thankfully, it appears he's quite happy to settle the complaint as long as we buy him a new door.'

'That's a relief, sir.'

'Yes, it is, but to be fair, as I understand it, the head-mistress is less than happy that his interest in all things Charles Manson has had such a negative effect on three of his students. Based on that, I think she's quite keen to move on from the whole thing as quickly as possible, *including* his complaint.'

'I can understand why. St Bart's kids committing violent crimes; it's not a great look for the school, is it?'

'No. It's really not.' Carter sat forward and linked his fingers together on the desk. 'Look, Jane. You're a first-rate copper, and MCU is in the best possible hands with you at the helm...'

'I can feel a "but" coming.'

He nodded. 'But you can only bend the rules so many times before they catch up with you.'

'I know, sir. Honestly, I do.'

'I couldn't wish for a better DCI, I really couldn't, but please, do me a favour, will you? Keep it by the book from now on.'

'Of course,' she replied. 'Everything to the letter of the law, I promise.'

He stared back across the desk in silence for a moment. 'I'll believe it when I see it,' he said with a wry grin.

She chuckled. 'I'll try, sir. Honestly, I will.'

'Was there anything else you needed? Only I've got a meeting at the town hall in an hour, and with all the road-works in the city, I really should be making a move.'

'There was just one more thing,' she said as she picked up the manila folder she'd left sitting on the empty chair next to her, and passed it across. 'I think I've found our mole.'

'Bloody hell.' Carter raised his eyebrows as he took it from her. 'That was fast.'

'As I suspected, we found what we were looking for in the financials.'

Carter's eyes scanned the documents.

'Regular payments of fifteen hundred pounds landed in that account each time confidential information was passed to Townsend.'

'And whose account is this?'

'It's on the last page, sir.'

Pulling out the final sheet, he stared down at the sheet. 'Oh no,' he said softly as he closed his eyes.

'I didn't want to believe it either.'

He opened his eyes again. 'But why?'

'I have no idea, sir, but it's time I found out.'

51

A n hour later, and with a heavy heart, Phillips opened the door to the forensic unit and made her way towards the main lab, clutching the manila folder in her hand. As she stepped through the double doors, she spotted Evans with his back to her on the other side of the room. Wearing a lab coat, he was hunched over and taking photographs of something laid out on the table in front of him.

She coughed to get his attention.

He spun round, a wide grin spreading across his face instantly. 'Jane, I wasn't expecting to see you today. I haven't forgotten to put a meeting in the diary, have I?'

'No, not at all.' Her stomach was churning as she scanned the space. Through a window on the far wall, she could see Aziz working in an adjacent lab. He hadn't noticed her come in. 'Where's Clara?'

'Off sick,' he replied. 'She came down with shingles, poor thing, so she'll not be in for a few weeks. I kept telling her she's been working too hard and something like this would happen if she didn't slow down, but she wouldn't listen.'

Phillips nodded absentmindedly.

'Is everything all right? You don't seem yourself.'

'I think it might be better to talk in your office,' she replied.

Evans's face straightened as he placed the camera down on the side. 'Why do I get the feeling you're about to give me bad news.'

'Let's go to your office, Andy,' she said flatly.

A minute later he led the way into his shoebox of an office at the rear of the building and took a seat at his desk.

Closing the door behind her, she moved to sit down opposite him, placing the file on the desk between them.

His eyes fixed on it. 'What's that?'

She took a deep, silent breath before replying, 'For the last eighteen months, we've suspected someone working within the force has been passing sensitive information regarding ongoing investigations to the journalist Don Townsend. A mole, for want of a better word.'

She watched as he swallowed a lump in his throat. 'And what does this have to do with me?'

'We've been trying to track down the mole for well over a year now, and we've narrowed down the suspects to five people – all of whom knew the details of the information passed to Townsend regarding each case.' She paused. 'We're now certain the leaks have been coming from within your team.'

He shook his head vigorously. 'No, no, that can't be. There must be some mistake.'

She passed across the folder. 'Take a look at that.'

Tentatively he opened the file and stared down at the document.

'That's a list of transactions made over the last eighteen months. You'll note the payments of fifteen hundred pounds made at irregular intervals.'

He continued to stare down in silence.

'Each of those payment dates coincides with the leaking of sensitive information to Townsend. The bank account responsible for those payments belongs to the *Manchester Evening News*.'

He didn't respond.

'Why did you do it, Andy?'

Evans closed his eyes and dropped his chin to his chest.

'*Why*, Andy?'

He exhaled loudly before lifting his head. 'Bridge.'

Phillips recoiled slightly. 'Bridge, as in your *wife*, Bridgette?'

He nodded. 'She has PNH, or paroxysmal nocturnal haemoglobinuria to give its official name. It's a stem cell disorder and incredibly rare. Basically, the red blood cells break apart prematurely, and if not treated, it's fatal.' A tear streaked down his cheek.

'Oh, God, Andy. I had no idea.'

'No. That's how she wanted it. You know Bridge, she's incredibly private.'

'So what does this have to do with the payments from Townsend?'

'The drugs that she needs to treat it aren't available on the NHS.' He swatted away another tear. 'Her only hope was to go private, and each treatment costs thousands of pounds. We don't have that kind of money sitting around. When we first found out, we borrowed some from her parents, then when that ran out, my parents helped out, and finally we remortgaged the house.'

Phillips's heart went out to him.

'But that still wasn't enough, and that's when I finally gave in and agreed to help Townsend.'

'Finally? Had he approached you before that?'

'Yeah,' said Evans. 'About two years ago.'

'Where?'

'Remember the double murder in Ashton where that guy from Burnage killed his ex-girlfriend and her new lover in his car?'

'Yeah.' She nodded, willing him to go on.

'Well, we'd just finished the job, and as I was packing up the car, he asked if he could talk to me about forensics. Said he was doing a piece on crime scene investigations and wanted to pick my brain as an expert in the field. I was flattered and had no idea he was a hack, so I agreed to meet for a coffee and share what I could for his article.'

'And was that when he made the offer to pay you for inside info?'

His shoulders sagged. 'I was totally shocked and refused point blank. Told him he was barking up the wrong tree and left. Anyway, he'd insisted on giving me his card, and for some reason, I really don't know why, I'd kept it. When we finally ran out of money for Bridge's treatment, I didn't know what else to do, so I called him. It felt like the only way I could keep her alive.'

Phillips nodded, understanding his terrible predicament.

'I never intended for it to escalate the way it did, and I tried to get out of it a couple of times, honestly I did, but he said I was in too deep, and if I tried to walk away, he'd reveal his source...to you.' He broke down now, his shoulders shaking as he began to cry. 'I'm so sorry, Jane. I never wanted to do it, but I had no choice.'

'I understand how hard it must have been for you and Bridgette, Andy,' she said. 'I really do, but nothing makes it right.'

He lifted his head as tears rolled down his cheeks. 'What are you going to do?'

Phillips stared back in silence for a long moment, then sighed. 'Passing over sensitive police intel is a crime, Andy. You know that as well as I do.'

He wiped his nose with the back of his hand.

'But, given the nature of your circumstances, I have to say I have no interest in bringing any charges against you.'

He let out a huge sigh of relief. 'Thank you, Jane.'

'But, ultimately, it's not my call. Chief Superintendent Carter is aware of what's been going on, and it'll be his decision to make.'

'I understand.'

'That said, I'm more than happy to go to bat for you...*if*, that is, you offer your resignation with immediate effect. Given Bridgette's condition, you can cite personal reasons, and no one will look any deeper into your departure.'

'I'll do it today.'

'Thank you.'

Evans opened his mouth to speak but seemed to think better of it.

'Was there something else?'

'What about Townsend? What if he goes public?'

'He won't,' she said, standing. 'I'll see to that.'

Tears welled in his eyes again. 'I really am sorry, Jane.'

'I know,' she replied, then turned and headed for the

door, turning back as she opened it. 'By the way, I'm sorry I never asked. How is Bridgette doing?'

'She's a fighter, and the doctors aren't giving up hope.' He offered a weak smile. 'Ironically, they've just approved the drug on the NHS, so she's got a fighting chance now.'

Phillips returned his smile. 'I really hope she pulls through, Andy.'

'Thank you, Jane. That means a lot.'

With that, she turned on her heel and set off back to the car.

The thirty-minute drive home seemed to pass by in a blur as Phillips's mind swarmed full with mixed emotions: sadness that Evans had been so desperate to save his beloved wife he had betrayed not only his colleagues, but every value he had ever held dear. Anger that Townsend had taken advantage of someone so vulnerable in the first place – just to get ahead with an exclusive, and genuine concern at the state of the world she was now expected to police. It was terrifying to think how easy it had been for Isabelle masquerading as Charlie to manipulate three intelligent kids into committing heinous acts of violence – all in the name of the so-called greater good. Was this the way society was heading? Murderers prowling on social media in search of their next victims? She shuddered at the thought as she pulled the Mini onto the drive and parked up next to Adam's Jag. Switching off the engine, she sat in silence for a time as she attempted to process how she was feeling. The truth was she didn't really know, but she was sure of one thing – whatever the future looked like and no matter how frightening a prospect it might be – while there was breath in her body, she would never stop fighting for justice.

ACKNOWLEDGMENTS

This story is dedicated to the loving memory of my mum, Catherine Ryan, who died while I was writing this book, and it was fitting that I completed it on what would have been her eighty-sixth birthday.

Sadly in the last five years I've witnessed the passing of far too many people I loved.

Those experiences have made me want to live every single day to the full, and I hope you can do the same.

Squeeze the important people just that little bit harder tonight, and never forget to tell them what they mean to you.

God bless, Mum. I hope you and Dad are dancing together again.

I'll love and miss you always. Xxx.

And finally, thank you to my readers for reading *Deadly Veil*. If you could spend a moment to write an honest review, no matter how short, I would be extremely grateful. They really do help readers discover my books.

www.omjryan.com

ALSO BY OMJ RYAN

The DCI Jane Phillips Crime Thriller Series

(Books listed in order)

DEADLY SECRETS (a series prequel)

DEADLY SILENCE

DEADLY WATERS

DEADLY VENGEANCE

DEADLY BETRAYAL

DEADLY OBSESSION

DEADLY CALLER

DEADLY NIGHT

DEADLY CRAVING

DEADLY JUSTICE

DEADLY VEIL

DEADLY INFERNO

―――――――――

DCI JANE PHILLIPS BOX SET

(Books 1-4 in the series)

Printed in Great Britain
by Amazon

44292239R10199